THE LONG STAIR

The Long Stair

AN ALBANY MYSTERY

Kirby White

Fox Creek Press   Albany, New York

ISBN 0-9773501-0-X

Published by Fox Creek Press,
an underground nonprofit publisher

Printed by Newkirk Products, Albany, New York

Designed and typeset in ITC Stone Serif by Becky Fischbach

Photo credits:

FRONT COVER TOP: View of the New York State Capitol
Building from Albany's Empire State Plaza Mall.
Photograph by Ann Sullivan.

FRONT COVER BOTTOM: Sheridan Avenue viewed from the
corner of Swan Street, Albany. Photograph by El-Wise Noisette.

BACK COVER: The long staircase that connects Sheridan Hollow
to Capitol Hill. Photograph by El-Wise Noisette.

For

United Tenants of Albany
Capital District Community Loan Fund
Albany Community Land Trust
Affordable Housing Partnership
and for
the many dedicated people who have built and
sustained these organizations over the years

Acknowledgements

I am grateful in a very immediate sense to the people who volunteered time, energy and talent to transform a languishing manuscript into this book. My old friends Bob Radliff and Louise McNeilly of the Capital District Community Loan Fund were the first to suggest local nonprofit publication of *The Long Stair* and have provided enthusiastic support and practical assistance that have been crucial to the effort. Louise's friend Becky Fischbach, a loan fund supporter and professional book designer, spent many hours not only as a designer but as a knowledgeable, meticulous copy editor/proofreader, cleaning up the various glitches that an author who thought himself a competent editor had missed. Newkirk Products printed the book on the remarkably generous terms with which they have supported the work of a number of community-based organizations in the Capital District for many years.

On another level I am grateful to those through whom and with whom I became involved in affordable housing and community development work in Albany's north-side neighborhoods, where this novel is set. I would not have been a part of that work at all — and *The Long Stair* could never have been written — had it not been for United Tenants of Albany and Roger and Maria Markovics, who founded that organization thirty years ago and continue today as its co-directors. And of course there are many other people, too numerous to name, from whom I have learned so many things in the course of working — and for a time living — in these neighborhoods. This book owes much to them.

Among those who read an early draft of *The Long Stair* and offered useful criticism and encouragement, I would particularly like to thank my old friend and co-worker John Davis and my daughters Nancy and Bonny White, all of whom are discriminating readers of mystery novels as well as much else.

Finally, I am deeply grateful to my wife Nola, not only for her encouragement and many helpful suggestions concerning *The Long Stair* but for her longstanding tolerance of my addiction to the lonesome pastime of fiction writing.

Fox Creek Press

Fox Creek Press, Inc., is a not-for-profit corporation organized to publish books and other materials relating to the fields of affordable housing, community development and environmental conservation and to dedicate all net proceeds derived from these publications to the support of nonprofit organizations working in these fields.

Fox Creek Press shares office space with other nonprofit organizations on Orange Street in Albany's Sheridan Hollow neighborhood. It is named in memory of the creek that once flowed as a natural stream through Sheridan Hollow but has now been forced underground.

All net proceeds from the sale of *The Long Stair* are dedicated to Albany Community Land Trust. Thanks to the generosity of others, Fox Creek Press has incurred only minimal out-of-pocket expenses in publishing this book, so purchasers can be confident that most of the book's price will go to support ACLT's longstanding efforts to provide permanently affordable homeownership opportunities in Albany's north-side neighborhoods.

For information, contact:
Fox Creek Press
255 Orange Street, #103
Albany, NY 12210

I

The drive back to Albany was always an odd in-between time. I'd been on Bog River and the Oswagatchie, paddling, fishing a little, letting the sounds of wind and water slow my rhythms. It was June. Along the shorelines, Labrador tea was blooming. On the upper Oswagatchie, the brook trout were numerous and lively, as were the black flies, and, because of the flies, people were scarce. I hadn't heard another human voice in four days.

Now I was back on the Northway in the Mazda pickup, rattling south at what felt like a dangerous speed. It was all I could do to force the speedometer needle up to sixty. Never mind that the rest of the traffic roared past at seventy plus miles per hour.

Southbound, the traffic gradually thickened and pressed more urgently out of the mountains. Streams of SUVs, vans, pickups with boat trailers charged past in the left lane, rushing back to suburban homes in Clifton Park, Colonie, Niskayuna, as though there was some Saturday night curfew they all had to meet.

I was glad that it was just Saturday, the weekend not yet ending. Even though there was a lot of work waiting for me and no reason to let it wait until Monday, I could allow myself to feel I had a cushion of time — that all I had to do was complete the transition back to the city, then relax for a while.

So maybe I was not that different from all the others rushing down the Northway to get home and relax. By the time I crossed the Mohawk River into Albany County, the speedometer needle had crept past seventy.

Leaving the Northway at the sprawling Exit 2 interchange, I headed east on I-90 along the northern edge of Albany, until finally the highway dipped toward the Hudson River, lifting the Rensselaer hills across the valley into view against the evening sky, just as the Arbor Hill exit came into view on my right. The exit ramp swung me high over the railroad tracks at the bottom of the ravine, and soon I was stopped in the traffic backed up from the light at Henry Johnson Boulevard and Livingston Avenue. Here, as I waited for the light, the people in the cars around me, making their way toward downtown, were white. The people on the street were black.

Two blocks later as I crossed Second Street on Henry Johnson, the edge of my vision was snagged by a ragged swarm of flashing blue lights. A block up Second, three police cruisers, all their lights flashing, had jammed the one-way street. It was a sight that always made my stomach sink because of what it said about the need of the police to answer every call in the neighborhood with a show of force. But I didn't want to think about it. I was ready to get home.

A block after crossing Clinton Avenue, I made the right turn onto Orange Street, and a few minutes later, after crossing Lexington, I entered Orange Street's final block, where the pavement changed from asphalt to red brick and the sound of my tires on the pavement changed to the comfortable rumpling sound that meant I was home. The house was on the left, halfway up the block, across from the back of the Salvation Army warehouse.

I parked in front of the house on the left side of the one-way street. I stored the boat overhead in the garage next door, where I pay ten dollars a month to keep my two canoes above my neighbor's ten-year-old Buick. Then I hauled my pack out of the back of the pickup, carried it up my front steps and let myself in. I turned on a few lights against the gathering dusk, got a can of beer from the refrigerator, and went back out to sit on the front steps and breathe the June evening. As always, I enjoyed being home much more than I enjoyed the transition. This little house is, after all, the only home I've ever had that is entirely my own — not my parents', not a landlord's and not the domain of a wife.

Almost immediately my eleven-year-old neighbor Jesse appeared on the sidewalk in front of me, straddling his bicycle. He had a half-eaten slice of pizza in one hand and a pale strand of mozzarella looped across his dark chin. He wanted to know if I had another beer. "Go good with this pizza," he said.

I told him he was too young.

"What they always say. Where you been anyway?"

"Up north taking some time off."

"What you do up there?"

"Camp out. Poke around. Take it easy."

"Sound boring to me."

"But you like fishing," I said. "I did some fishing."

"So what'd you catch?"

"Lots of trout." I knew I would have to be more specific before he was through interrogating me.

"How big?"

I spread thumb and fingers to show the length of a six- or seven-inch brook trout.

"Minnow," Jesse said scornfully.

Behind me in the house, the phone began to ring. Getting up to open the screen door, I told Jesse I'd rather eat those little trout than almost anything.

"You can have'm," he said. "I'll take this here pizza."

The phone was on the wall in the kitchen, behind the little front room that was my living room. I took my time, half inclined to let the machine take it. But I thought it might be Lisa, so I answered it.

The voice I heard was not Lisa's. It was a man's voice hoarse with urgency. "Warren? Is this Warren Crow?"

I knew I should recognize the voice but it didn't register until he introduced himself. "This is Harry Cooper. I'm really sorry to be bothering you but something terrible has happened. To Jonah. I'm here at the office — the NHA office, here on Second." He took a quick breath. "Jonah's been killed. Someone killed him. Here in the office."

The blue lights flashed again in my head. That was where it had been. The police cruisers on Second Street had been in front of the building where the Neighborhood Housing Association — the NHA — has its little basement office. Jonah Lee was the organization's extraordinary Executive Director and only employee. Harry Cooper was the NHA's board president, a solid citizen with a decent state office job who could probably afford to move out of the neighborhood but stayed by choice. A year earlier I had done some work for the organization, volunteering to do the kind of work I otherwise do for pay, helping to put a project back on track. I ended up doing a lot more than I planned. But it was all right — I got to know a lot of neighbors I wouldn't otherwise know.

Now Harry Cooper was looking for help again. "I hate to call you this way, but I don't know what to do."

"The police are there, right?"

"Yes, they're dealing with...with their part. But there's also, you know...I'm telling myself the NHA is not shot dead, but it feels that way right now. I hate to call you this way."

I told him I'd be right over. I didn't know how I could help, but I would go over.

The office on Second Street was only a five-minute walk from the house. I went back out the front door and headed across the street, angling toward the corner. Jesse, on his bicycle, appeared at my side. "Where you going?"

"There's been some trouble over on Second Street. Guy asked me to come over."

"What kind of trouble?"

"They said someone was killed."

"Oh man," Jesse said.

It was about all anyone could say. Both of us were silent as we crossed Clinton and headed north on Judson. Daylight was almost completely gone. People sat in quiet groups on their porches, so you noticed their shadowed faces only when they moved. Voices murmured in what might have seemed a peaceful way, but they were people who had heard gunfire a block or two from their homes within the hour. And not for the first time. There had been two drive-by shootings in the neighborhood since winter, both reportedly drug-related. The teen-age victims were people whose families I knew, but I hadn't known the victims themselves. This time the victim was someone I did know and had worked with, and someone who was certainly not dealing drugs.

At the corner of Second, kids were clustered, gazing toward where two police cruisers remained outside the NHA building. A knot of men, one of them in uniform, stood where the steps went down to the building's basement level. Jesse nosed his bicycle in amongst the kids on the corner. I joined the small group by the steps. Most of them, including the uniformed cop, were familiar African-American faces that I saw occasionally in the neighborhood but didn't know by name.

I told the cop that Harry Cooper had called and asked me to come over.

"Okay, I'll tell them," he said and moved down the steps and into the building.

"You know Jonah?" one of the remaining men asked.

I said, yes, I knew him.

"Last dude we needed to get shot around here."

One of his companions said, "Crazy bastard, but he done some good."

"Place is fucked up worse'n ever," the first said.

"Neighborhood's got some problems," was the mild response from the second.

"Neighborhood, shit. Whole fucking city, man. We just get

more'n our share of the shit in this neighborhood."

The cop appeared in the doorway below and beckoned. "Harry's in the back room," he said as I came down the steps.

Moving down the narrow hallway, I had a quick glimpse through the door of the NHA office. There were several men in there, one of them with a camera aimed toward the floor. Looking where he was aiming I was jolted by the fleeting sight of Jonah's body sprawled among open file folders and blood-streaked paper.

At the end of the narrow hallway there was a small conference room, where I found Harry and another man sitting in folding chairs on either side of the plywood conference table. Harry introduced the other man as Detective Reilly. He was a balding middle-aged white man, hunched over the table writing in a small notebook. He continued writing and didn't acknowledge the introduction — until finally he closed the notebook and looked up. "Sorry," he said. "Thanks for coming over. Harry says you're the only person might be able to figure out where some stuff is at with this organization — now with Jonah gone."

"I don't know about that," I said. I didn't think I wanted the responsibility that was being nudged toward me.

"Well, anyway," Reilly said, "we'd like your help. There's a lot of paper on the floor in there. Right now we don't know anything. Could be someone was looking for something in those files. Or more likely that had nothing to do with it. But, when we're through in there, maybe Harry and you could help us look at what's on the floor — the paper — and help us put the files back together and identify what's there."

"It could take a while," I said. I was thinking of the mess I had just seen on the office floor. I was also thinking about the work I needed to get done in the coming week.

"Has to be done though. Soon as possible. Hate to ask for your time on a Sunday, but how about tomorrow? Meet you here in the morning at, say, ten? Both of you?"

Harry nodded. I stood up. "Sure, do what I can."

"Much obliged." Reilly said. "And just one question before you go. Harry was saying he thought some of the tenants here pay their rent in cash. That true as far as you know?"

"As far as I know. It would be safer to only accept checks or money orders, but for some of the residents it would mean an extra trip downtown for a money order, and Jonah didn't want to make them do that."

"So when he had cash," Reilly asked, "what'd he do with it? If he didn't go straight to the bank, where'd he keep it? Maybe in one of those file drawers that was dumped in there?"

"I'm afraid so," I said.

"And the rent's due now?"

"It was due the first of the month. People generally pay during the first week of the month — so, yeah, this past week money would have been coming in."

"How much in cash could he have had at any one time?"

I looked at Harry, who said, "I never dealt with that."

"He really shouldn't have had any cash over night," I said. "Much less over a weekend."

"But if he didn't get to the bank Friday, he could've had how many people's rent — and how much would that be?"

"In cash, two or three households at the most. So possibly something between four and twelve hundred cash." I looked again at Harry, who responded by nodding and shrugging at the same time.

Reilly opened his notebook. "Thanks, see you tomorrow," he said.

*   *   *

Back at the house, I got another beer from the refrigerator and took it upstairs to the one-time bedroom that is my office. I sat down in front of my computer and rummaged through the pile of papers beside the keyboard until I found my pocket calendar. I wanted to look at my schedule for the rest of the month of June.

There was work that had to be done right away for an organization in Rochester. There were also commitments to clients in Syracuse and Trenton that might soak up a lot of time, as well as some ongoing work here in the Capital District. Now, in addition, there was what had happened at the NHA and whatever it was going to mean. And everything had to be done before I went north.

In the calendar space for June 28, I had written in large letters, "TO LABRADOR." Then the whole month of July was blank. It was a lot easier to think about that large empty space than about what had to be done to get there. A large empty space of time in a large empty country — the country north of Shefferville, beyond the railroad, beyond civilization. A month of traveling northward by canoe to Ungava Bay. I wanted to turn my mind loose in that huge empty country, but right now I couldn't. My thoughts were pulled back to the blood-splattered papers that I was going to have to deal with tomorrow. I still hoped that it wouldn't take long, that I could do whatever was in my power to do, fulfill whatever was my duty in this matter, and move on. Go to Jonah's funeral, pay my respects to a man who took on too much, tried too hard to fix a fucked up world. Do my duty and pay my respects without getting drawn too deep into Jonah's unfinished business.

It was time for bed. I was glad I had spent the first part of the day paddling into the wind. I would sleep deeply.

2

Lisa called as I was eating breakfast — to see if I was home and confirm our plans for dinner. I asked if she had heard about Jonah, but she had not seen the article in the *Times Union*. "Sunday is the *New York Times*," she said. "Every other day is local, but Sunday I'm surrounded by the *Times*." So I told her, and she was silent for a long moment before asking, "Do you know what happened?" I said I didn't but might know more by evening.

Harry and Reilly were talking on the steps in front of the office on Second Street when I got there. After finishing his cigarette, Reilly plucked the yellow crime scene tape from the entrance and unlocked the door. In the office, the body was gone, but where it had been the quantity of blood was appalling. I hadn't thought of myself as being much bothered by blood. I had killed and bled large animals from time to time — both on the farm and in the woods — but I had never before seen this much human blood. Or smelled it. And in all my paperwork I had certainly never had to deal with blood-soaked paper. I was relieved when Reilly produced a pair of rubber gloves for each of us.

"They already lifted prints," Reilly said, "but in case we find anything interesting we'll use the gloves."

"So what's the story?" I asked. I didn't know how much he'd be willing to say, but thought I might as well ask. "I mean I read the story in the *Times Union*, but it didn't say much."

Reilly shrugged and sat back against one of the two cluttered desks. "Yeah, well, okay, a little background. But we don't have much more than was in the *T-U*. Two possible stories. Story A: Jonah comes in late on Saturday to do some work. Harry says he was in and out of the office pretty much any time, any day. So he was in here working, left the door unlocked and some guy just walks in on him with a gun, demands cash. Jonah resists, or at least manages to panic the guy. Gets shot. Story B: the guy is already in here. Jonah comes in, surprises him going through the desk or files or whatever. Guy shoots him."

"How do you figure the Story B guy might have got in — if Jonah hadn't unlocked the door?"

"No sign of forcible entry. One possibility of course is that Jonah did unlock it — that he was in for a while, went out for a while and left the door unlocked, and when he came back the guy was there. Otherwise we have to figure either the lock was picked, which makes the guy more of a pro than seems likely, or it was someone who had a key."

"Like I said," Harry offered, "I think there were just those three women he gave keys to. The three women who volunteered in the office, who did a lot of work and he trusted them to be in and out."

"Three is a lot," Reilly said, "especially when they all have kids and God knows who else in the household. Three is a lot of keys to put in circulation in the community. Anyway, I'll be talking to those women."

"No one saw anyone leaving?" I asked.

"Looks like the guy didn't leave by the front. There were people on the street who heard the shots — no one who'd been hanging out for long, but people coming and going. One of them, across the street here, ran into her house and called 911, keeping an eye out the window. She didn't see anyone come out. No one saw anyone."

"Easy to go out the back door," Harry said. "Just flick the lock release from the inside, you know, and you're out in the vacant lot that goes through to Third."

"And the back door was unlocked when we got here," Reilly said. "What's weird though is that there were no prints on the lock release, no prints on the knob. Not even the man's own, Jonah Lee's. Wiped clean. Doesn't really fit. It's easy to see some punk kid with a gun looking for cash, blasting away when they're confronted, and then running. Not so easy to see the asshole stopping and getting out his hanky to open the back door."

"What about prints in here?" I thought I might be asking too many questions, but Reilly didn't seem to mind. It was easier to go on talking than to begin work with the bloody papers.

"You bet. All kinds of prints," he said. "Front door, inside door, desk, filing cabinets, everything with prints like you'd expect —

but the only match we've come up with so far is Jonah's own. And we haven't learned too much else in here either. Nothing obvious taken. Computer hasn't been messed with, which fits if we're talking about a kid who's just looking for cash, with no idea where to fence a computer. Desk drawers shut like you see them now. Contents messy, but no indication anyone went through them for anything except maybe looking for a pencil — and no reason to think someone *didn't* go through them either. Just the top two file drawers in that cabinet pulled out and most of the contents dumped. Bottom two drawers still closed. Files were dumped before Jonah went down. Obvious from what you can see there, he was on top of some of the paper."

The three of us stared at the bloody papers in the middle of the floor. "Let's get it over with," Harry said.

I reached down and tugged at one of the lower drawers that had remained closed. There was resistance, but then it rolled open. So it wasn't locked. I tried the other one, the bottom drawer. It wasn't locked either, and as I pulled it open, I had a clear memory of Jonah keeping his rent roll and receipt book in the back of that bottom drawer, and sometimes rent money itself. I decided there was no need to look at it now, and closed the drawer again.

"You got some kind of idea there?" Reilly asked.

"Just trying to remember how things were organized here," I said. "Not that Jonah was all that systematic. He mostly knew where things were, but he didn't exactly keep them in alphabetical order."

"So if something's missing it would be hard to say," Reilly suggested.

"It would be very hard to say."

The process of sorting and reassembling files was laborious. Ninety percent of the paper either remained within a folder or could be easily identified with a nearby folder, but the plan was not to move a folder from where it lay until we were fairly sure there were no more stray pages that belonged in it. And there were enough strays to make the work painfully slow. I consoled myself with the idea that, although the work probably wouldn't contribute much to solving the murder, it was at least useful to put these things back together for the organization.

It wasn't hard to separate the contents of the two different drawers. The contents of the top drawer had been mostly archival — old board meeting notices and minutes, old newsletters, grant proposals, old financials, old IRS Form 990s, assorted old correspondence. The next-to-the-top drawer had held mostly property-by-property files, with multiple files for some properties, covering both original acquisition and rehab of the buildings and later maintenance and repairs, as well as a certain amount of corre-spondence with residents, copies of property tax bills, and other odds and ends that hadn't found a more appropriate place in some other part of the filing system.

Harry and I worked at putting files back together and identifying the appropriate drawer for each as best we could, then passed them on to Reilly, who wrote down the file names, making separate lists of files for each drawer before returning the folders to the drawers.

We were less than halfway through when there was a startled grunt from Harry. "Look at this." Stuck to the corner of the folder in his hand was a battered hundred-dollar bill, torn and mended with scotch tape. The tape had stuck to the folder.

"So..." Reilly said. "We've got rent money. People don't pay their rent with a bunch of little bills, right? When they cash their check they get a few big ones to pay the rent. Twenties for food, hundreds for rent."

Neither Harry nor I disagreed, but I was puzzled. The file draw-er that should have held rent cash, if there was any, was closed, but two other drawers had been pulled and dumped. It was hard to make sense of it. But Reilly was happy. He slipped the bill into a plastic evidence bag like someone slipping a very nice trout into his creel.

By early afternoon, we had disposed of most of the paper and most of the folders. The bloodiest sheets of paper were identified as board meeting minutes from 1997 — summarizing, for a period of time, the month-by-month efforts of this odd little organization, now stained with the blood of its founding executive director. Once the dates were identified and recorded, Reilly slipped these blood-stained sheets into an evidence bag. What then remained was a stack of several dozen sheets of paper that we hadn't been able to connect with particular files — most of them being odds and ends of correspondence that had no apparent relevance, which Harry and I agreed to look through later.

Also remaining on the floor was one file folder, crisper and cleaner than most of the other folders. The label on the tab was a lightly penciled "XXX." It was empty and there was no way to know what papers might belong in it. Reilly studied it. "Triple X — porno stash or what? But there's some numbers and stuff on the inside of it here." He handed the folder to Harry, who glanced at it and passed it on to me.

There was a short column of four-digit numbers jotted in pencil. Each number was followed by either a check mark or a set of two or three capital letters. I was curious but could make nothing of it. "Who knows? Could be anything."

"Maybe Helen Hamilton will know something about it," Harry said. "I'm hoping she can come in tomorrow." He looked at Reilly. "Can we open the office? It would be good if people could see we're still here. Having Helen here would mean a lot. People trust her."

"It might not work for you to open up first thing," Reilly said, "but we should be able to clear it by mid-morning. And this Hamilton woman is one of the three with keys, right? So we need to talk with her anyway. No reason not to do it here in the office."

"She's the one who puts in the most time here," Harry said. "She's on the board, but then she also volunteers in the office so much it's like having a part-time staff person. We can call her now if you want."

Harry made the call and arranged for her to come in at ten o'clock to talk with Reilly, and then to keep the office open at least for a few hours.

No one was asking me to contribute any more of my time at this point, but I was beginning to think I really didn't want to be left out. There were too many unanswered questions — and not just the questions Reilly was interested in. There were the questions the organization needed to deal with in order to carry on — which were my kind of questions, whether I had time for them or not. "Suppose I come in later in the morning," I said, "and maybe Helen and I can start pulling together some information for the board. Someone needs to pull together the rent payment records, checkbooks, look at possible payables, see if checks need to be written, that sort of thing." I looked at Harry. "Unless you think the board should get into that stuff itself before anyone else does."

"No," Harry said, raising both hands quickly. "No, no, if you have the time it would be great. I don't know who else we could get to do it who knows about our financial stuff."

Reilly cleared his throat. "If it looks like there's rent payments unaccounted for..."

"I'll let you know," I said.

3

"So tell me about this Neighborhood Housing Association and this Jonah person," Lisa said.

We were eating at Lombardo's. It was not a place where I often ate, but I liked coming here with Lisa because the place amused her and, as she said, satisfied her Italian side. Her other two sides were Irish and Jewish, and all three sides had been in Albany for generations. She had just consumed a large plate of sausage and peppers and was now finishing off the side-dish of pasta, still eating with obvious pleasure. Her trim body seemed to be capable of converting unlimited quantities of food into unlimited quantities of purposeful energy. Her appetite was one of the things that attracted me to her, and not only her appetite for food. She approached all the things that interested her in the same way — food, conversation, business. I imagined she also approached sex with the same healthy appetite, but we hadn't got to that yet. I had known her only slightly for some years. She was a real estate broker, a very successful one, and business had sometimes brought us together, occasionally for lunch, a few times for dinner. Recently we'd decided we enjoyed eating and talking together enough to make a habit of it.

She was looking at me over her wine glass. "I used to assume it was another one of these NHS things — Neighborhood Housing Services, with a loan fund and all that. But it's not one of those, is it?"

"No, it's its own kind of neighborhood housing organization. Or Jonah's kind of neighborhood housing organization."

"Who *was* he? I used to hear his name here and there, and people always said it as though there was something, I don't know, *unusual* about him."

"He was unusual for sure. A different mix of things. African American or African Caribbean. One side of his family was Jamaican. And Native American. I don't know that he was Mohawk but I've heard he spent some time with the Mohawks who occupied that state land in the Adirondacks and held out for some time against the state. But he actually grew up on a farm in Washington County."

"Like you."

"In my case it was Rensselaer county, but yeah, one of us farm boys. Apparently we were also at Cornell at more or less the same time, though I don't remember him. I guess we traveled in different circles — because if you met Jonah you remembered him. Big and handsome and vital, a head taller than most people, with a smile that could stop people in their tracks half a block away."

"Oh!" Lisa said.

"You're remembering?"

"I'm remembering someone I used to see on Central Avenue once in a while. Who would stop me in my tracks half a block away. Taller than everyone, and gorgeous. Could that have been him?"

"It sounds like."

"Good Lord, I used to fantasize about him." She stared at me, her brown eyes intense, Jonah's murder having become the murder of someone she actually knew in a certain way. Finally she shook her head. "So...this organization...he started it?"

"He started it seven, eight years ago. He'd worked in housing for a while in Albany — different kinds of jobs. With South End Improvement, with the Urban League, with Capitol Hill Improvement for a while. People liked him but I think no one thought he had much of a future in the nonprofit housing world because he had a radical streak that he didn't bother to keep under wraps. Then next thing anyone knew here's this new little organization in Arbor Hill and West Hill, with a little neighborhood board and with Jonah as director. And of course everyone thought, well, the last thing this town needs is one more neighborhood-based housing organization, one more little undernourished organization competing with all the others for a little piece of the city's housing and community development money. People wished Jonah well, but they also had a certain interest in seeing him fail and close up shop sooner rather than later."

"And how come he didn't fail? He certainly didn't have much going for him starting out."

"Well, the competition wasn't exactly a bunch of Goliaths, and, you know, it's the old story — most of them were turning into little extensions of the bureaucratic programs that funded them. They were pretty good at doing the kinds of projects those programs supported, but those programs and the opportunities for those kinds of projects were starting to dry up, and these groups were not adjusting to the situation. Meanwhile Jonah's out hustling."

"But where did he find the wherewithal?" She rubbed her fingers together briskly. "You don't do housing without capital — or had you noticed?"

"Oh, I've heard anyone with pocket change can make a million dollars in real estate in their spare time. You just borrow the capital."

She made a face at me. "I'm serious."

"Well, the community loan fund financed the first projects. Other than that I'm not sure. He had his own set of connections and I think there were some individual donors, maybe some fairly big ones. He knew some professional athletes who had some money. But the organization got no public money in its first years. A lot was done with sweat, his own and other people's. Sweat and charisma and opportunism and frugality. He worked out of his apartment, paid himself a pittance, walked the streets looking for bargain properties. He didn't go to quite the extreme of your colleague Eddie McFadden — studying the obituaries and calling up surviving family members and making low-ball offers..."

"I beg your pardon." She sat up straight. "Eddie McFadden may have slithered into a certain niche in the local real estate business, but it is not *my* niche, and he is not *my* colleague."

"Sorry, dumb joke."

"McFadden is not a joke."

"Okay. Anyway, Jonah was a very serious shopper, and he managed to find buildings that didn't need too much work, projects that weren't too complicated. At a time when the other organizations were doing expensive projects with big bucks from the Housing Trust Fund, and having to bid everything out and deal with the city's regs and DHCR regs — and maybe do one building a year — Jonah started right out doing three a year. And managing to match the buildings with solid families who became members of his organization, so he was building the organization in the process."

"All of them rental properties?"

"Rentals, but the tenants actually have 99-year leases. They don't use the term, but it's sort of a mutual housing association. A scattered-site, neighborhood-based mutual housing association."

"I don't believe that one's in the glossary of my handy-dandy Real Estate Practices Handbook. A w h a t? Mutual housing association?"

"The term gets used to mean different things, but in this case it's sort of a hybrid non-equity housing co-op."

She shook her head. "Thank you for clarifying."

"Residents have these very long-term leases, so as long as they make their payments and don't trash their homes, they can stay forever. Then a little more than half the board of directors is made up of residents and prospective residents, so, ultimately, they control the program."

"Isn't that some kind of conflict of interest — at least if they're now using public money?"

"You mean people owning their own homes is a conflict of interest?"

"Most people don't own their own homes as tax-exempt entities."

"Well, no, most people own their own homes as tax-*advantaged* entities. They're entitled to homeowner tax deductions, which tenants aren't."

She started to respond, but stopped and gazed at me. "There's a lot I'd like to talk with you about — and probably argue about. But not now. I want to hear about the work you did for them last year. What was going on? They were in trouble, weren't they? With that big old building on Clinton Avenue?"

One of the things I liked was the way she could seem to be interested in everything that came up and yet steer the conversation to what she most wanted to know. "They'd called me about a problem project," I said. "They'd taken on that building. They knew it was a more complicated project than they'd done before, and they'd pretty much covered the more obvious complications. It would have worked out okay but there were some structural problems that were worse than expected, and, on top of that, they discovered chemical contamination in the cellar, and the two things together of course added up to a lot more cost than Jonah had planned on. I helped him redo the numbers, and we went back to the city and to the state and squeezed out a little more subsidy, and reworked the numbers some more, and it still looked pretty tough. But in the meantime I was learning some surprising things about the organization — both good and bad. The scary thing was, here they had come to own almost twenty properties, with almost forty resident households, more than could be managed with the seat-of-the-pants approach that Jonah had started out with. For a while I thought it was going to be one of those situations where there was just barely enough structure in the operation — and just enough cash flow — to keep things afloat as long as they didn't hit a snag, but not enough to survive a problem project like this one.

"I got involved in trying to help upgrade the financial management systems, and lined up a new auditor who wasn't as half-assed as the guy they'd been using. This new guy reviewed all their properties with the idea that he should adjust book values to reflect the grim realities of the market in the neighborhood. But the balance sheet he finally came up with wasn't as bad as I expected. In fact it was actually quite a happy surp rise — showing a net worth for the organization well beyond what I'd imagined. Because th e re were all these bargain properties, and th e re was enough donated sweat, donated materials, donated dribs and drabs of money in them, so the mortgage debt was modest and the organization had substa n-tial equity in quite a few properties. So Jonah was able to borrow enough money, secured by second mort gages on some of those properties, to finish the Clinton Avenue project."

"But then he sold it."

"Yeah, to Arnold Duber."

"Which doesn't make any sense. All that effort and he sells it to a *slumlord*? And how could the city let him do it? There was public money in it. Back in Albany's bad old days it might not h ave been any surprise to have the city of Albany subsidizing a slumlord like that — but today, I don't know. What went on?"

"I'm still puzzled by it too. It was after I'd pretty much finished my wo rk with them. I did ask Bock Calloway at the Community Development Agency if the city had taken its money back out of the project, and he fell all over himself to assure me th ey had — which means Jonah must have sold it for enough to pay back not only the bank debt but the city's money too. Which is very hard to figure."

"On that part of Clinton bet ween Dove and Swan? Yo u're damn right. Impossible to believe Arnold Duber would pay that kind of price for that building, unless he knew something I don't kn ow — or else th e re was something on the side, some kind of quid pro quo."

"More likely the latter, but I don't know what the quo was."

"And now Jonah Lee is dead, and yo u're going to be digging in to the organization's finances. Who knows, maybe you'll find something." She had pushed her plates to the side and was lean-ing forward, elbows on the table, eyes bright.

I was stirred, as well as amused, by her intensity. "Do you want some dessert?" I asked.

She looked at her watch. "What I would really like would be to take you back to my place, have a little brandy, maybe more than a little, maybe get drunk with you the way I've been wanting to — but there is this client I'm supposed to meet for an early breakfast, and it's a flat-out day from then on. But I really *do* want to get drunk with you some evening soon."

"Sounds good to me," I said, truthfully. I was more than ready to have this relationship move beyond the let's-get-together-for-dinner stage.

4

Monday morning I got up at five and made myself sit down at my desk and do several hours of billable work before I headed off for the NHA office.

On the way, walking north on Judson, I caught sight of Jesse on his bicycle at the far end of the street by the entrance to Tivoli Lakes Park — the bicycle making leisurely circles and figure-eights around the sign where the trail goes down to the so-called park in the overgrown land by the railroad tracks. He was on his way, more or less, to Phillip Livingston Middle School, or so I hoped.

It had rained hard for a time during the night. Now the day was heating up and only a few puddles remained in the street, but there was still a smell of damp earth, and the vegetation in the vacant lots looked refreshed. It was one of those times when it made me happy to be walking in this neighborhood. One of those times when I felt connected to the neighborhood and what was going on in it, even though some of what was going on was pretty bad. I had never felt this way about the suburban neighborhood in Colonie where I had shared a home for almost three years with Martha. That in-between, disconnected part of my life that didn't seem real any more — that, in fact, hadn't seemed entirely real when I was in it.

The office smelled of air freshener, lilac scented, recently sprayed. Helen Hamilton was sitting at one of the two desks talking on the phone. She gave me a quick smile and raised an index finger without interrupting the solemn mixture of condolence and reassurance she was delivering to someone. "One of those terrible terrible things. We're going to be okay, but we're going to miss him terrible. I know, it's not going to be the same. Terrible. We're just going to have to pray extra-hard and work extra-hard."

When she hung up, she rose from the desk and faced me, short, trim, composed. I had never been sure how old she was. Somewhere between forty-five and sixty-five — probably closer to the latter, though she didn't look it. "Good morning, Mr. Crow," she said.

"Good morning, Mrs. Hamilton. I'm sorry. You know how sorry I am about Jonah." We were not strangers. The previous year we had spent a lot of time working together in this small office, and it had seemed to me that we ought to be on a first name basis, but she had persisted in addressing me formally. I didn't think there was anything subservient about it, but there was this certain space formally defined between us, and I wasn't sure if I should be the one to step across it.

"Yes," she said. "Thank you for coming in. Thank you for helping us again." She turned toward the desk. "I knew you would want the checkbooks, so I've got all three of them here, that's including the one for the operating fund, which I had at home, doing the, you know, balancing."

"I suppose Detective Reilly wanted to know if it looked like anyone had messed with things like that in the office."

"He did ask, but I really didn't see anything out of the ordinary that way. The other two checkbooks were in the cupboard in the corner there, and it didn't look like they'd been touched. He also said to tell you to call him if you found anything that looked like there was rent money that someone might have taken."

"What about you? Do you know if there was cash here?"

"I wasn't aware of any. The only people who paid when I was in the office last week had checks or money orders. And I think he went to the bank Friday anyway. There's no checks or cash in the folder with the rent roll."

I went to the file cabinet, pulled open the bottom drawer, and found the file with the rent roll and receipt book. I took these and the checkbooks to the vacant desk and sat down. At the other desk, Helen Hamilton picked up the phone. "If you'll excuse me.... Some of the residents I still haven't reached. I'm trying to talk to everyone."

It didn't take long to confirm that a bank deposit had been made at the end of the previous week and that it included rent from five residents, whose names Jonah had noted on the deposit slip along with the amounts each had paid. In the receipt book there were carbon copies of receipts given to each of those five, and no evidence of more recent receipts.

When Helen put down her phone, I picked up the phone in front of me and called Reilly. I told him that if there had been any cash in the office, there was no evidence of where it might have come from.

After a brief silence Reilly said, "Except the hundred. Anyway it doesn't tell us much about the motive. If the shooter was looking for cash, he'd be just as likely to pull the trigger because there wasn't any."

"I suppose," I said.

"Okay, let me know if you do find anything useful." He hung up abruptly.

He still seemed awfully eager to find evidence that the murder had been committed in the course of a robbery or attempted robbery — which would reduce the crime, at least in the eyes of many, to the level of every-day street violence — still a murder but not especially newsworthy. But I wasn't sure I wanted to think of Jonah's life snuffed out simply because he was in the way of some fifteen-year-old off the street who was looking for cash to buy crack. I wanted to think Jonah's life had been more important than that.

I spent another hour methodically reviewing rent-collection information from the beginning of the year forward. Household by household, I compared the rent receipt book with the bank deposit slips and then with rent roll information. I found just one thing that puzzled me. There was one resident, named Zera Kay, for whom there were no rent receipts and no evidence on the deposit slips that her rent was ever deposited. And yet the rent roll showed her rent as having been paid for every month, including June. I didn't know Zera Kay, but I recognized the name as belonging to one of the women who was said to have a key to the office.

I went back and double checked the deposit slips and receipts before finally asking Helen. "There's something here I don't understand. This Zera Kay — I can't figure out her rent records."

She dropped her eyes for a moment, then raised them and looked steadily at me. "No reason you would know. She hasn't been there that long, just since last summer, but he was living with her. Jonah and her — they shared that apartment. I think he paid the rent himself even though it was in her name."

"Okay, I guess that would explain it," I said. It did not explain the whole thing, but I decided to say nothing now about the fact that there was no record of rent being deposited for that apartment from anyone at all. Instead, I asked, "She's one of the women who's been working here in the office, isn't she? Reilly was going to talk to her."

"He did — last night I think."

"It's got to be an awfully hard time for her. How is she doing?"

"Lord knows it's hit her hard. But she's got all those babies to keep her mind off it, and Zera's not one to take hard times lying down."

"All those babies? How many babies does she have?"

"Oh — one's hers, one's her daughter's, the rest she takes in daytimes. It's not a regular daycare business like some have. She just helps them out — the mothers — and they help her out."

I thought I would like to talk to this person — who might know things about what Jonah was doing that no one else knew — but not today.

As Helen resumed her telephone duties, I penciled a list of documents I wanted to copy and take with me, including quarterly financial reports and board meeting minutes for the year since I'd been involved in the organization's business. I then pulled all the necessary files and began the annoying photocopying chore — several times having to ask for Helen's help in finding and clearing jams in the old third-hand machine, contributed by a church that had itself received it as a donation from a parishioner. When I was finished I bundled the paper into my daypack, said goodbye to Helen and escaped back out into the sunshine.

Outdoors the day had lost none of its seductiveness. I thought I would take just a short walk — westward on Second Street for a few blocks — before heading back toward home and my desk. But turning back wasn't easy. I walked all the way to Manning Boulevard, then looped southward and back to the east through Washington Park. By the time I got home, I was feeling I'd wasted too much of the day. I made a sandwich and got to work, and stayed at work until six o'clock.

* * *

After supper, I called Harry Cooper and filled him in on my review of rent receipts and my brief conversation with Reilly.

Harry said, "I would just as soon it *wasn't* some messed up kid that shot him. I don't know why it matters. He'd still be just as dead. But if it's just some poor messed up kid who never had a chance and is going to get his own self killed before he's twenty, or else spend the rest of his life in jail...well..."

"I know," I said. "I don't want it to be that way either."

"I guess I don't want the bad guy to be just another one of the people who's got trapped in what's happening to the neighborhood — what Jonah was trying to change."

"What all of you have been trying to change."

Harry sighed. "Carry on as best we can, I guess."

"I want to do what I can to help," I said. "And as long as I'm involved I would really like to figure out what was going on that might've got Jonah killed. Because there are still a lot of problems with Reilly's robbery scenario. Even Reilly admitted some things don't fit. So, if I seem to be prying into things you don't want a consultant to pry into...."

"Don't worry about that. We don't think of you as a consultant anyway." There was a short laugh like a half-smothered cough. "Maybe you noticed, we don't *pay* you. Consultants get *paid*, is what I hear."

"Okay, here is something I did want to ask about." I outlined the puzzling rent-payment record for the apartment that Jonah and Zera Kay had shared. "So I just wanted to get clear what the deal was. Helen thought Jonah paid the money himself, but I couldn't find any record of the money actually coming in and being deposited, except that the rent roll did show it as paid. Not that there would be anything wrong if he wasn't paying a cent of rent. If you added free rent to the salary he was getting he still would've been a bargain for the organization. So I wondered if that was actually the kind of deal you had with him — free rent? It would have made sense."

"That's what I *wanted* him to do," Harry said. "But, no, he said it was Zera's apartment; he moved in with her and part of his contribution to the household was to pay the rent. I told him he already was paying the rent by working the way he did for what we paid him. But you know how he was — if there was another dollar he could scrape up for NHA he would do it, even if it had to come out of his own pocket."

It didn't surprise me that Jonah would refuse an offer of free rent if it meant cutting into his organization's cash flow. He was no different from certain other managers of nonprofit — and even for-profit — organizations, whose egos wind up more deeply invested in the success of their organizations than in their personal wealth. But I still didn't know what he had been doing with the money. "Did he ever say anything about setting that rent money aside for some special purpose?" I asked.

"Not to me," Harry said. "I thought he was treating it like any other rent."

"He was *recording* it like any other rent and I don't know why he would do that if he wasn't actually paying it, but he wasn't putting it into the bank, at least not into any bank account I'm aware of. So $420 a month, probably in cash, was going somewhere else. He wouldn't have been using it to pay regular bills, would he? I know he used to buy a lot of odds and ends of building materials with cash, back before the organization had credit at the building supply places, but he didn't have to do that anymore, and I don't know why he would if he didn't have to."

"I can't help you there," Harry said. "You know more about

that stuff than I do. But if this means there could have been a big wad of hundred dollar bills floating around somewhere...and someone with a gun knew about it..."

"Yeah, we should try to find out. I gathered from Helen that Charlotte Wolf is still doing the bookkeeping — coming in once a week to do the posting. I want to talk with her and see what she can tell us. Then I guess the other person I'd like to talk with is Zera Kay. I have no idea what information Jonah did or didn't share with her, but I'd like to try to find out, and I'm wondering if it's too soon to be bothering her. I'd really rather not wait until after the memorial service."

"Give her a call," Harry said. "She might rather talk sooner. She's not one to keep things bottled up."

So I did call Zera Kay. I expected to hear an African American voice, but the voice that answered the phone was different, somewhat formal — maybe originally from some English-speaking part of the Caribbean — but eager. She seemed so eager to accommodate my awkward request that I almost told her that there was no rush, that the whole thing could wait until next week. But next week was already the middle of June, and I hardly dared think about how I was going to finish all the things that had to be finished before I left for the north at the end of the month. So I asked if I could stop by her apartment the next morning. She not only agreed but thanked me, as though I was doing her a favor. Confused, I thanked her in return.

I hung up the phone, went downstairs to the kitchen, peered into the refrigerator. But I had finished eating only a little while ago and was not really hungry. I went into the living room and stood at the front window looking out through my own reflection at the darkening evening street. There was plenty to think about. Tomorrow I had to finish a piece of work for the people in Rochester and e-mail it to them in time for their evening meeting. It was the better part of a day's work. Now there was also my morning appointment with Zera, and in the evening I was going to Lisa's for dinner, and maybe more than dinner. I wasn't sure. I was certainly looking forward to finding out, but it wasn't one of the things I needed to think about now.

The batch of photocopies I'd made in the NHA office was still in my daypack unread. I went back upstairs, got the daypack from my office, took it back downstairs and laid out the photocopies on the kitchen table. From the cabinet under the sink I got a bottle of Jack Daniel's and poured myself a drink before sitting down at the table. I had spent enough time for one day looking at numbers, but I could at least read through the board minutes.

The first six months' worth of minutes told me only that the board had voted to make an offer on — and had subsequently approved financing for — a single-family home on Third Street. It was a typical NHA acquisition, the sort of project the organization should be getting back to after the problem project on Clinton Avenue. It was what I expected to see. The March minutes, however, were startling. In the March meeting, the board had approved a recommendation from Jonah that the organization enter into a purchase agreement for two properties — a three-family building and a four-family building — on lower Sheridan Avenue. The purchase agreement was with Arnold Duber. The price for the two struck me as being on the high side of what would be reasonable in that neighborhood. Skimming through the minutes for the next two meetings, I found that the purchase of the properties had in fact been completed, with mortgage financing from a bank.

I freshened my drink and carried it into the living room, which was lit only dimly by light from the front windows. I sat in the beat-up over-stuffed chair that I had retrieved from my parents' barn when I bought this place after Martha and I separated. I sat looking out onto Orange Street, where the glow from the streetlight two doors down had replaced the last of the twilight.

Sheridan Avenue ran parallel to Orange Street one block south. To the east, both streets ran down through Sheridan Hollow, one of the several ravines eroded into the east face of the city where it sloped down to the Hudson. It was one of the most badly run-down parts of the city, a mix of decaying rental properties, low-end commercial uses and vacant lots — not an area where I would have expected NHA to be acquiring property, especially three- and four-family rental properties at a price that was no bargain. It looked like I might have found the other half of the deal between NHA and Arnold Duber that included Duber's purchase of the Clinton Avenue property. It was a deal that might conceivably have worked for Duber, but I couldn't understand what advantage Jonah could have found in it. It seemed to leave NHA with a problem worse than the Clinton Avenue problem had been. I decided that tomorrow on my way to Lisa's I would walk down Sheridan and look at the properties.

5

The apartment that Jonah had shared with Zera Kay occupied the second floor of a two-family building on Third Street, a block and a half from the office. On the porch, I pushed a buzzer that was still labeled "Lee/Kay." After a minute's wait, the door was opened by a tall, golden-skinned woman clasping a baby against each shoulder, one arm supporting both diapered bottoms as she held the door with her free hand.

"Good morning, you must be Mr. Crow," she said with the same surprising eagerness that I had heard on the phone. She turned and headed up the stairs and I followed. The denim-sheathed legs above me on the stairs were long and attractive.

Following her through a doorway at the top of the stairs, I had to swallow an exclamation. The room was a nursery that looked as though it had been imported whole from a toy store. Two walls were painted cherry red, the other two sunny yellow. The carpeting was bright blue, scattered with a profusion of plastic toys in colors that mirrored the red and yellow of the walls. There were two playpens, one empty, one occupied by a tiny child who stood clinging to the side, swaying and grinning at me as though I might be his own daddy just arriving home from work. There were also two toddlers busy among the toys on the floor.

Zera propped one of the babies among pillows in the empty playpen and sat down on a sofa holding the other baby in one arm, patting the cushion beside her with her other hand. "Please have a seat."

Sitting, I said, "I really am sorry to be bothering you at a time like this."

"It is all right. It is good to have some company that is older than three years. But if I start to cry please don't worry. Sometimes when I talk to people who knew him, I can't help it."

Awkwardly, I hurried into the interview, asking her about the rent, telling her that it wasn't a problem but I was trying to figure out the financial records and wasn't sure whether Jonah had been paying it with cash or by check.

"He was paying almost everything," she said. "I was taking classes at night, trying to finish my degree to become a teacher. I paid for that and he paid for everything else. I don't know what I am going to do now."

I didn't know what to say to this frightening observation. I pushed on. "Do you know if he usually paid the rent in cash?

We're trying to find out if there might have been cash that someone was trying to steal."

She looked at me, her eyes wide. "We have a checking
account, but when he would deposit his paycheck he would usually get quite a lot of money in bills. I think he paid the rent with
that."

"You don't remember any checks written on your joint
account for rent payments?"

"I don't think so, but we can look." She rose with the baby and
left the room briefly, returning with a checkbook, which she
handed to me.

"I don't mean to pry into your personal finances," I said, but I
took the opportunity to glance th rough the record of checks written in recent months. I saw nothing not eworthy. Routine month ly
checks for gas and electricity, phone, cable, a few checks to local
retai le rs. No rent checks. Also no credit card payments, no debt service of any sort. The account balance ranged from one hundred to
five or six hundred dollars. It was the checkbook of what appeared
to be a highly disciplined low-income cash-based household.

"You're right," I said, "it does look like he was paying the rent
with cash." I placed the checkbook on the sofa bet ween us. "Did
Jonah talk much about his work — about NHA and its projects —
when he was at home?"

"A little bit. Sometimes."

"Did he talk at all about the new project on Sheridan
Avenue?"

"I'm sorry," she said, "I came up from the city just a year ago
and I have been busy with the child care and the classes so I don't
know...Where is Sheridan Avenue?"

I pointed in a southeasterly direction. "It's the street that runs
down through the low area down there — where the NHA bought
two buildings not too long ago."

"Oh, by the long stair."

"Yes, by the long stairs that go up to Capitol Hill. Did he talk
about those buildings?"

"I know he was spending much time working on that — those
buildings — I think trying to get money to fix them. But we didn't
talk about that very much."

"It must have been a very important project for him."

She looked at me wonderingly. "It was *a l l* important to him."
Her eyes filled with tears, her body slumped and she began to sob.

The baby that she held slid against my shoulder and began to make tentative crying sounds. I reached with my free arm to steady the baby. Zera leaned toward me and I somehow found myself with both arms around the woman and baby. Both of them cried harder.

It was true, as Harry had said, that she was not one to keep things bottled up. The grief that had welled up so suddenly now flowed with all the inevitable force of a river. I was moved by her readiness to let it flow in my presence, but I was also embarrassed, frightened, unready to embrace so much unhappiness and human need. But I had no choice. I held on as her sobs shook the three of us.

After a minute, the baby stopped crying and stared, frowning at the woman's face, then looked up at my face, took a deep breath and began to cry louder than before. At least two other children had begun to cry now as well. Zera separated herself from me and with her free hand patted the head of the baby she held, wiping at her own tears with her forearm as she did so. Gradually, with the attention returned to the baby, the woman and children quieted.

Finally, she rose, deposited the baby in a playpen and left the room. I heard water running briefly. Then she reappeared, one hand full of Kleenex. She plucked the child back out of the playpen, and returned to the sofa. "Poor babies," she said. "When I am alone with them I don't do that."

"One of them is your own?" I asked, making conversation in the calm that had returned so quickly.

"Tiger over there is mine." She pointed toward the child that still stood clinging to the netting in the other playpen. "This little bitty here is my daughter's."

It felt like I had been for a moment at the heart of this woman's life, and yet I still knew next to nothing about that life. Had she and Jonah known each other before she moved to Albany? Was he possibly the father of "Tiger"? And where was the daughter who was the mother of the baby she held? My curiosity was aroused, but I didn't really need to know these things, and I certainly didn't want to stir her emotions again. Getting up from the sofa, I said I had to get back to work and hoped my visit hadn't been too upsetting.

She got up with me, patted my arm, and said, "You should not worry."

On my way out, I heard myself say, "If there's anything I can do to help..."

* * *

Until late afternoon I worked more or less diligently on a spreadsheet and memo, which I then e-mailed to the organization in Rochester.

I waited until after five to call Harry Cooper at home. I had avoided calling him during the day because I thought that, like a lot of state employees, he might prefer not to receive non-work-related calls in the exposed and often zealously supervised environment of a state office cubicle. At five-thirty Harry answered his home phone with the sound of a television and loud children's voices in the background.

I told him I'd noticed that the organization had bought properties on Sheridan Avenue and wondered what stage the project was at and whether there was anything that needed to be done about it right away.

"I did want to talk with you about that," Harry said. "It's kind of a complicated project. There's an application in to the state — for some kind of special money they put out a request for proposals on. I don't know what we should do about it now."

I tried to think of what request for proposals Jonah might have been responding to. The only recent state RFP for housing projects that I was aware of was for so-called "high impact" projects. No one I had talked with had been sure just what kinds of projects DHCR — the Division of Housing and Community Renewal — was really looking for, but it was hard to imagine how Jonah could claim any kind of high impact for a pair of rehabs on Sheridan Avenue.

"It was just the two buildings, seven units?" I asked.

"That's what we own now. Jonah was trying to get more. Some of us were a little worried that it was taking on maybe more than we could handle, but he really wanted to go for it, so we went along with buying those two buildings and putting in the application to the state — on sort of a see-how-it-goes basis."

"Isn't it a pretty tough place to do a residential project?"

"No question. That's one of the things that worried us. But then I guess it's also one of the things that made Jonah want to do it. He wanted to turn the whole block around — and there was something about Sheridan Hollow that was important to him. He kept saying if we could have an impact there it was not just housing. I thought we ought to just go on having our impact one family at a time. For me that's what it was all about, what we were building on. For Jonah, well it was only one of the things it was about for him, and not the deepest down thing. You know what he really wanted was to turn *everything* around." Harry paused. "Which would be great," he said. "I just don't know how to do it."

"Yeah...So he was trying to buy more properties?"

"He hadn't brought anything else to the board. He told us he was talking to some different people and was trying to put something together. I remember he did say it like that — put something together — and I wasn't sure what it meant, and I was looking for a chance to sit down with him and ask about it. Before, we always bought one property at a time and we'd just concentrate on putting that one property together, fixing it up and getting a family into it. But he was talking different this time. I still don't know what to make of it. You don't think it could have had something to do with . . . with what happened?"

"I don't know, probably not," I said. "But it sounds like it had quite a lot to do with how he was spending his time and who he was talking to. I'm wondering how he actually described the project in the application to the state. Did you ever actually see that application?"

"No, it was the usual thing. We passed a resolution on it, but it was pretty general and he did the application himself and none of us saw it. I mean he would have given it to us if we'd wanted to read it, I mean if we'd asked." One of the children's voices in the background rose to a wail. "Charlie, cut it out, leave him alone," Harry said.

"I better let you go," I said. "I'll do some checking and be in touch."

6

I walked east on Orange — past the Salvation Army warehouse across the street, where a truck was unloading used furniture, past the uniform service, past the auto repair shop, past the burned-out house and the two well maintained houses, one of which was an NHA house. At the corner, by the Bridge Diner, I turned right on Lexington Avenue. Then in another block I turned left between Rolf's Pork Store and Yana's Grill and started down the long eastward slope of Sheridan Avenue into the Hollow. In another two blocks I crossed Lark Street at the low point in the dip between Arbor Hill and Capitol Hill. To the right, Lark Street rose toward the affluent white Center Square neighborhood on the west edge of Capitol Hill. To the left, Lark rose gradually into the black neighborhood of Arbor Hill.

Straight ahead on Sheridan was a long stretch where no streets actually crossed through the Hollow to connect the two hills and their contrasting neighborhoods. As you walk that stretch of Sheridan the southern edge of the hollow grows higher and steeper on your right, walling off the world of affluent hustle and bustle that lies just beyond it.

Unlike the higher ground of Arbor Hill — once the home of the wealthy — Sheridan Hollow has been the home of poor people for the better part of two centuries. First Irish, then Polish, and now mainly African American, though not as completely African American as some people assume. But if you live here and you're not a person of color then either your income is low or you have unconventional reasons for living where you do. In fact it's not a place where convention holds sway. It's a jumble of vacant lots, odd buildings and odd uses — run-down single-family houses, larger houses that have been chopped up into crude apartments, warehouses, side-yard auto repair businesses, a few gardens.

Walking eastward deeper into the hollow, I kept an eye out for the buildings recently acquired by NHA, but I had trouble spotting any house numbers on the decaying buildings around me. Ahead of me, however, was the sign in front of the Gander Bay Bar. The sign hangs out over the sidewalk and pictures a gander with its neck aggressively outstretched — the one striking feature of an otherwise dreary little establishment. "Gander Bay" was what this neighborhood was called back when, in the nineteenth century, Irish families had moved with their geese and ganders to occupy the bottom of the ravine.

Between me and the bar was a vacant lot. At the rear of the lot a thicket of ailanthus crowded the base of the steep slope. At the front of the lot, several battered vehicles stood on the packed earth. Nosed up against the bar's peeling asphalt siding were two large motorcycles. The front door of the bar stood open, letting the sound of male voices and the smell of stale beer spill out into the street. I went in. My only previous visit to this place had been once when I was looking for a local mechanic who had promised to do some work on my pickup.

The place was narrow and deep, an old wooden bar in front, and beyond it high-backed wooden booths receding into the shadows. The bar was surprisingly crowded, and the crowd was surprisingly diverse — black men from the neighborhood, some of them familiar, but also some white men, including the leather-clad bikers.

I nudged my way toward the front end of the bar. The bartender was a pale, skinny woman with long bleached hair, skintight jeans and a tee-shirt cut off so it just barely covered her breasts. She appeared to be teasing one of the bikers who leaned across the bar, reaching toward her bare midriff as she shimmied just out of reach. The precise target of the man's reaching middle finger was a metal ring, at least an inch in diameter, which was linked through the smaller ring fixed to the woman's navel. She finally took a step backward, flipped the ring with her own middle finger, and then flipped the finger outward toward the biker.

"Fuck you too," the biker said.

Others at the bar seemed to pay no attention to the interchange. I eased myself between two people to a point where I could rest an elbow on the bar. The man on my left, a tall angular African American, shifted his weight accommodatingly, glancing over his shoulder at me as he did so.

I thanked him, then asked, "Hey, you wouldn't know where number eleven-oh-four is would you — here on Sheridan?"

The man looked at me with surprise, then amusement. " I didn't know places around here even *had* numbers. What you doing — looking to *i n*vest in some prime real estate?"

Beyond him, another African American man — small, light skinned, with a goatee — leaned forward to stare at me. "Why you asking?" he demanded.

This was not a conversation I had planned to have, but, since I was having it, I thought I should see what I could learn. "You know Jonah Lee?" I asked.

"Did know," the man said. "Everybody knowed the dude. Now the dude is dead. So why you asking?"

"You know he bought eleven-oh-four?" I asked. "And eleven-oh-six. For his organization, the NHA?"

"He shouldn't a done it. No need for him to come fucking around this place, buying up stuff right the fuck next door to the Bay."

"Are you saying it's what got him in trouble?"

The man's eyes were still fixed on mine. "What I'm saying is, why the fuck you asking?"

"No big deal," I said. "Just trying to help the organization figure out where it's at."

Other conversations along the bar had given way. Someone I

couldn't see, an older, quieter voice, said, "Tell them to sell, mister. Only thing to do. That's eleven-oh-four across the lot, one of Duber's dumps, no place for decent folks to live."

"You're probably right," I said.

The skinny blond bartender was in front of me. "Get you something, sweetie?" she asked.

"Just passing through," I said.

I went out and crossed the vacant lot to the building beyond, a blocky flat-roofed wood-frame building recently boarded up in what I recognized now as the half-assed Duber manner, with unpainted, not-yet-weathered sheets of plywood nailed slap-dash over the downstairs windows. Intending to make a circuit of the structure, I walked toward the rear of the lot, but found that the ailanthus jungle grew so thick against the back of the building — saplings already growing up through the rotted back porch — that it was more trouble than it was worth to get through. Turning back toward the street, I saw that the man who had demanded to know why I was asking about the building was now standing in front of the bar, hands in his pockets, watching me.

After briefly checking out the front and further side of the building, and then doing the same for the next building, 1106, I headed at an angle across the street past the Gander Bay. From the street, I waved to the man watching me, who did not respond.

It was clear to me now that Jonah had paid more for these properties than he ever would have considered paying if he had wanted them only as affordable housing stock. So why did he buy them? What was it about this neighborhood that had made it so important to him to make something happen here? And what was it he had been trying to make happen?

The questions tugged at my thoughts as I moved on down Sheridan. For a passing moment — then again for another passing moment — it felt as though I was about to remember something that might be a part of an answer, but I missed it both times and it sank back out of reach.

At the foot of Swan Street, I paused to look up at the very long set of stairs that ascended the south slope of the ravine, the one connection between the Hollow and the upper world of Capitol Hill. "The long stair," Zera had called it. It was a stairway that actually got quite a lot of use. There were thousands of state jobs on Capitol Hill, many more jobs than there were parking spaces on the hill, even with all the spaces in the vast parking garage underlying the South Mall. Some of those state workers who were not senior enough to have reserved parking spaces, but who had the necessary nerve and legs, would park on the streets in Sheridan Hollow and climb the long stair to work. Although the streets were almost empty now, they were always crowded with cars during the work day.

But in climbing the stairs to work, the owners of those cars crossed a no-man's land, between neighborhoods, between classes, between races. A notorious place, the scene of muggings, and several rapes, though less dangerous during the rush hours when the commuters used it. Gazing up at the stairway, I realized that the grove of trees to the right of the steps was full of crows, the urban crows whose voices I enjoyed hearing early in the morning. I've always been interested in these birds that belong in a world of fields and woods — at least that's where I first knew them as a boy — but that nonetheless seem to get along just fine in the city, and without changing their style at all.

I stood watching them and suddenly a fragment of the memory that had been teasing me slid to the surface. Jonah had talked about the stairs. The one time we had actually shared a bottle and talked. Deep in the night, near the bottom of the bottle, at a point when I was having trouble seeing straight, he had talked about the stairs, the wooded no-man's land, the fact that no streets directly connected the two hills. He said the place was a product of public policy, an intentionally defined no-man's land keeping the black folks over on the other hill.

Turning around, I climbed the other, more gradual slope, up North Swan. At the corner of Orange I stopped and looked back again at the stairs, hoping I could jog another bit of memory from that alcoholic night with Jonah, but no more would come just then. I would have to set it aside for now. Because right now I was headed for Lisa's.

I went up the final block to Clinton Avenue, where I crossed the street and made my way down to Ten Broeck, that short street along the eastern brow of Arbor Hill where the wealthy once built their elegant town houses, shoulder to shoulder, facing the little park in the center of the Ten Broeck Triangle.

Most of these homes were "historically restored" a decade and a half ago, at a time when it seemed that this whole sector of Arbor Hill would be gentrified. The Ten Broeck Mansion, owned by the Albany Historical Society, was just up the street. Around the corner in the other direction, the Palace Theater was a two-minute walk away. The childhood home of Herman Melville was three minutes away, and five minutes beyond that was the corner of

State and Pearl, at the center of downtown. Gentrification had seemed a sure bet. But it had fizzled out. Some homes were beautifully restored, but the expected wave of new upscale residents turned out to be only a ripple lapping against the base of the hill. A few middle class African Americans chose to live here rather than in the suburbs. And a very few whites, one of whom was Lisa.

* * *

We had taken our brandy to the sofa in the spacious, high-ceilinged living room of her second-story apartment. There had been martinis, followed by a good steak and a good salad, followed by the excellent brandy. In front of the sofa, tall windows looked eastward over rooftops to the river and, beyond it, the high ground cresting into the last of the evening sun. Lisa, in tennis shorts and sleeveless silk blouse, had curled herself into one corner of the sofa, facing me.

I had told her about the Sheridan Avenue properties and my recent stroll through the Sheridan Hollow neighborhood. I hadn't planned on talking about it with her. I had just wanted to enjoy the food and drink and her company, and felt there were now a lot of things about the Jonah affair that I needed to sort out in my own mind before talking to anyone about them. But she had asked, and now her realtor's curiosity was aroused. "So their deal was," she said, "Arnold Duber takes the Clinton Avenue property off Jonah's hands and Jonah takes the Sheridan Avenue properties off Arnold's hands."

"That seems to be what happened."

"It's not too bad a deal for Duber. He paid too much for Clinton Avenue if he couldn't keep the subsidies in place, but it's rehabbed and ready to rent up and he can depreciate it. And he unloads two properties that he's already milked dry, and gets an awfully good price for them. But what the hell does Jonah Lee get out of it? If he had kept the Clinton Avenue property he could have kept the subsidies in place, so it probably would've cash flowed more or less — right?"

"At least for the short-term."

"But he goes and unloads it and in return gets a couple of properties that are going to be — would have been — dead weights tied around his neck."

"According to Harry Cooper, they were part of something larger he was trying to put together."

"If he was going to pay those kinds of prices for *more* of that kind of property in that neighborhood, he had to be *really* insane."

"It's a puzzle. There was something about the place that seems to have been important to him."

"Like what? Why would he care about that place?"

"I don't really know," I said, wondering again if maybe I did know.

"Right there by the Gander Bay Bar, for God sake," Lisa said.

"He was no doubt trying to buy that too. Which is maybe why at least one of its patrons was so concerned about what he was up to."

"As though they couldn't find someplace else to drink."

"The question of where a man drinks can raise pretty serious turf issues."

"If drinking is most of what he does," she said. "Or maybe if it's also where he does business, where he sells his wares. That would make it important."

"So what do you know about the Gander Bay Bar?" I asked.

"Just the rumors. That you can buy anything there."

"You don't happen to know who owns it, do you?"

"As a matter of fact...an odd and unpleasant woman named Janet Rowley. But her son runs it. I think they call him Buddy."

"Buddy Rowley. Okay, I've heard the name. Maybe I'll try to talk with him, or maybe the mother."

"Maybe you should be careful. You know? There aren't many parts of this town where I think twice about walking down the street, but down there...those stairs give me the creeps."

"You do use the stairs though, don't you?"

"Sure, at certain times of day, but let me show you something." She rose from the sofa and disappeared through a doorway into what I assumed was her bedroom.

I stood up too, taking the opportunity to move to the windows and peer out at the view across the river. I envied her the opportunity to stand in her own living room and see clear out of the city into wider spaces.

When she returned she was carrying her purse, which she opened. "When I do walk up those stairs, at least if there's no one else around, I keep my hand on this." She lifted a short-barreled revolver from the purse and handed it to me. "It's not loaded at the moment, but I do carry it loaded at times."

I looked at the muzzle. It was no mere twenty-two or twenty-five caliber lady's gun. It looked like thirty-eight caliber. I myself had never had a handgun. I grew up with rifles and shotguns and still owned a deer rifle though I hadn't touched it in several years. Handguns I associated with the summer people on the hill who, when I was young, would come up from New Jersey for two weeks each year and blaze away incessantly at targets. "Pretty serious gun," I said.

"Maybe you should hang on to it for a while," she said. "It wouldn't hurt if you're going to be nosing around in the things you're nosing around in."

I thought it was quite a dramatic offer, but I really didn't want the thing. "I don't have a permit, and anyway the only handgun I ever shot was a twenty-two. I'd be a threat to public safety. But thank you. I'm flattered that you would..."

"I could teach you. I do target practice once in a while. It's actually a lot of fun."

"I'd be up for some target practice," I said, "but I really don't have any reason to carry a gun. I'm an affordable housing technical assistance provider, not a cop."

"So was Jonah Lee an affordable housing guy." She took the revolver back from me, released the cylinder, swung it out and spun it so we could both see that it was empty, then snapped it back and placed the muzzle against my wishbone. "So listen," she said. "I like you just the way you are—*alive* — and I want you to stay that way, you hear?"

"You are a very fierce lady."

She lobbed the revolver onto the sofa, then stepped up close against me, her hands going to the back of my head. Looking up at me, she said, "Can you handle it?"

I put my arms around her.

7

In the morning we drank coffee at the little table in front of the east windows in the living room. Bright sunlight lit the table between us. The revolver was still on the sofa where she had tossed it. Looking at it, she said, "I'm so glad I didn't have to use it last night. In order to have my way with you."

"Nor will you ever," I said.

"What I like is, it feels like this is not our first morning together."

"Yes, it feels like we've been on the same track all the way, or at least parallel tracks. Things seem to fit."

"I don't know about tracks," she said, "but I think we've

confirmed that everything fits."

"The important things fit."

"And there are a lot of things that don't have to fit."

"Yes, I agree." I liked the acknowledgement that we were still very different people and that neither of us was going to ask the other to change. At least I hoped that was how it was going to work. I felt close to her and, at the same time, free. "I wouldn't mind doing this again soon," I said.

"Yes, soon. But not tonight. I have a meeting this evening that I'm not looking forward to. I will not be very good company afterward. How about tomorrow?"

"I have to be in Syracuse tomorrow, but I should be back by eight."

"I'll pick up a bottle of Jack Daniel's in case you'd like to stop by."

"I would very much like to." I drank the last of my coffee and stood up. "Can I use your phone before I go?"

She pointed to the phone on the stand at the end of the sofa. I looked up Helen Hamilton's number and called her to see if there was a time when I could get into the NHA office.

"I was just about to go over there for a little while," she said, "so if you could, come by soon."

I arranged to meet her at the office in fifteen minutes.

"The investigation continues," Lisa said.

"I just wanted to look for a copy of Jonah's proposal to the state for Sheridan Avenue."

"So shrewd," she said. "What a clever way to find out what he proposed to do with the Sheridan Avenue properties. Read his damn proposal."

I walked up Second Street from Ten Broeck to the office. Helen Hamilton was there when I arrived and we had no trouble finding a copy of the application, which, with all of its attachments, was almost half an inch thick. As the copy machine was warming up, I asked her if she had read it, but like Harry Cooper she said she had not.

She offered to do the copying for me, and while she coaxed the temperamental old machine to work through the thick document, I located the stack of miscellaneous letters that had been the last things Harry and Reilly and I had picked up off the floor on Sunday morning. At the bottom of the stack was the empty "XXX" file folder.

I flipped the folder open to look again at the numbers penciled on the inside, and even before I focused on individual numbers I knew what I was looking at. The two numbers with check marks after them were 1104 and 1106, the Sheridan Avenue addresses of the new NHA acquisitions. The other numbers were 1094, 1096, 1098, 1100, 1102 and 1107, each followed by a set of capital letters. If the vacant lot next to the Gander Bay Bar was a single lot with a single address, then it would be 1102, and the bar itself would be 1100. The letters following both 1102 and 1100 were JR. The letters EMF appeared after three addresses — 1094, 1096 and 1098. Each of the other addresses was followed by a different set of letters.

If the letters were the initials of property owners, then JR would stand for Janet Rowley, who, according to Lisa, owned the Gander Bay. I had no idea whose initials the other letters might be, but if they were the initials of the property owners then there were ways to find out. I copied the list carefully onto the current page in my pocket calendar, right under where I had written "FINISH SYRACUSE PRO FORMA."

Helen had almost finished copying the proposal. I set the stack of miscellaneous letters on the edge of the copier and said, "I'm sorry. I'm afraid I need these too. But I promise not to find any more."

* * *

Back at Orange Street, I made a pot of coffee; then carried my cup and the new stack of paper up to my desk. I really did have to work on the Syracuse development pro forma, but I wanted to look at the application first — at least the narrative section that described the proposed development and its purposes.

The tone was set in the opening sentences of the introductory section. I knew that Jonah was quite capable of writing careful, straightforward prose for certain purposes. But in this case he seemed to have been unable to restrain himself. Or he had decided that it was not an occasion for restraint. He didn't seem so much to be applying to the DHCR bureaucracy for project funding as to be challenging the state itself.

"Where is the Sheridan Hollow neighborhood? It is very close at hand. Standing on the steps of the Capitol you would be looking right into it, just a block away, if it weren't for the fact that it lies conveniently at the bottom of a ravine where the city and state have been content to leave it to deteriorate, out of sight and isolated. So you will have to walk five minutes north and look down the slope to see what a poor neighborhood looks like. What you will see is real, the reality of the problems faced by residents of real low-income neighborhoods everywhere. It is also symbolic, a dramatic symbol of what is wrong with a society that isolates and turns away from those it has come to call "the underclass," even when they live just a block from the state capitol."

I skimmed forward to the statement of "project goals." The first few goals in the list were conventional community development goals, but some of the later ones were not at all conventional:

> To provide decent affordable housing, with long-term security, for low-income households;

> to improve the physical quality of the Sheridan Hollow neighborhood;

> to eliminate threats to the health and safety of neighborhood residents;

> to convert properties known to be the sites of criminal activity to safe residential use;

> to establish a pattern of land use that supports rather than threatens the well-being of the local community;

> to connect Sheridan Hollow to Capitol Hill, and thereby connect this isolated, primarily African American low-income community to the sources of power and resources that drive the prosperity of the rest of this American society;

> to eliminate the embarrassing circumstances of an impoverished and isolated neighborhood within two blocks of the state capitol;

> to demonstrate the effectiveness of an intensive approach to community development that can be replicated in other neighborhoods.

I now had some idea of why this project had been so important to Jonah, but I was still a long way from understanding how he had thought he could pull it off. I searched the application until I found a specific list of properties. All of the properties I knew about on the south side of Sheridan, from 1094 to 1106, were included, as well as 1107 on the north side.

What was surprising was that the application claimed the NHA had site control not only of the two properties bought from Duber but also of the three properties to the east of the Gander Bay Bar,

1094, 1096 and 1098. The application stated that the NHA held an option to purchase these three properties — the three properties that the list in the XXX file identified with the letters EMF. I definitely needed to find out who EMF was as soon as possible.

The application also stated that an option was "currently being negotiated" for 1100 and 1102 — the bar and the adjacent vacant lot — presumably the properties "known to be the sites of criminal activity," which the proposed project would "convert to safe residential use." So I also needed to talk with one or both of the Rowleys as soon as possible.

The proposed redevelopment of the properties included both rehab of existing buildings and new infill construction, for a total of 14 housing units. But the most dramatic feature of the plan was not the residential development but what was proposed for the land to the south of the buildings, the steep slope up to Capitol Hill. In Jonah's words the project would "convert what is now a wasteland separating the poor and disempowered from the rich and powerful into a park to be enjoyed by rich and poor alike." The park would include play areas for small children and a network of attractive walkways and steps winding among flower beds, low hedges and stone walls to a promenade at the summit. The landscaping, Jonah had written, would "invite entry and participation from both the top and the bottom."

I didn't know who owned the wooded side of the ravine, but it seemed likely that such a no-man's-land would not be owned by any private individual — why would anyone want to assume the liability and pay the taxes — and must therefore be public property. The written proposal did not deal directly with the question of ownership, but said that the NHA would "work with the city" to develop the park and was "submitting grant proposals to several foundations to fund the effort."

But the park was not the only way in which the environment of the neighborhood was to be redesigned. There was still more. Jonah was going to liberate Fox Creek, the creek that had once flowed through the ravine and that, like several other streams that had once flowed down through the city to the river, had been paved over, forced into the sewers out of sight. The proposal did not say exactly how the creek was to be restored or where it would flow in relation to existing buildings, street and sidewalk, but it said a planning grant would be sought in collaboration with an organization called Heal the Earth. "Thus the community will be connected once again, at its heart," Jonah wrote, "with the living earth."

It was exciting and disturbing. It was exciting to read something that proposed a dramatic physical response to the underlying problems that are so hard to get at — the problems that most housing and community development projects barely scra t ch the surface of. Nonetheless, the proposal was just way out there. It couldn't possibly succeed. If someone else had written it, I might have suspected it as being a kind of elaborate joke, a sort of April Fool's proposal to give the folks at DHCR a little excitement. But the vision it expressed was no joking matter for Jonah. So why had he let himself get so completely carried away? Even if the bureaucracy was wholeheartedly sympathetic with that vision th ey could fund no more than a f raction of what was being proposed. If he had had a big-time commitment from some foundation then he might have gone to DHCR for the housing development subsidy. But to propose the pro ject this way to DHCR, before he had any thing else committed, was wildly unrealistic. It did not really seem like Jonah.

I couldn't imagine what DHCR personnel would have done with this thing. I thought about calling the new DHCR local rep for the Capital District. The proposal would have crossed his desk, but he was young and inexperienced and I had met him only once and wasn't sure what I could learn from him. I decided to call my old friend Erica Schmidt instead. She would not have been an official reader of the application, but she had been in the Division for years. She knew how things wo rked, and who to ask about what. And she would be interested.

* * *

For once, Erica was neither in a meeting nor on another line. I reached her at her desk. "As a matter of fact I've been curious about that," she said, "since I heard about Jonah."

"You don't know what its status is now, do you? I'm trying to help the organization pull things to gether, and one of the questions is what to do with those buildings on Sheridan."

"I really don't know a great deal. I never saw the application or heard the details, but there was some talk and some raised eyebrows and head shaking. This was a month ago when the application came in. Since then I haven't heard anything about it, which is kind of surprising, actually."

"But you've been curious..."

"Since I heard about Jonah, I've been thinking about asking a couple of people who might know something — since what happened to him gives me an excuse — but I haven't caught up with them yet."

"I do have a copy of the application if you'd be interested. And I do think you'd be interested — it's a pretty extraordinary document."

"You know me too well," she said. "Okay, give me a day or two and I'll see what I can learn."

"Give me a call and I'll buy you lunch," I said.

8

By late afternoon I still hadn't finished all of the work that needed to be done before I left for Syracuse in the morning, but I did want to find out who EMF was, and it would be too late to get into the city and county offices to check tax records and deeds if I didn't get there soon. Besides, I wanted to get away from my desk and out of the house. I decided I would finish the work for the Syracuse project in the evening. Right now I would walk downtown.

I headed down Sheridan Avenue again. At the corner of Lark, Jesse appeared on his bicycle. "Where you headed?" he asked.

"Downtown. Courthouse and City Hall. How bout you, where you headed?"

"Downtown with you."

"Might be boring. You got stuff to do downtown?"

"Just go along, keep you out of trouble."

"As a matter of fact I need someone to keep me out of trouble."

When we passed the Gander Bay Bar, its door again open to the June afternoon, Jesse said, "How bout you buy me a beer?"

"Thought you were going to keep me out of trouble. That's no way to keep me out of trouble."

"You right about that," Jesse said. "They say some serious trouble in there."

We reached Swan Street and turned right, past the homeless shelter to the foot of the stairway. "You ever ride that bike up twelve flights of stairs before?" I asked.

"We going to haul it up."

I did most of the hauling. Halfway up I paused to rest. "You really know how to keep a guy out of trouble. I'm going to be too tired to want any trouble."

"We getting there," Jesse said.

The top of the stairs was still far away, but we were already high above Sheridan Hollow, looking down on the roof of the church, the New Jerusalem Home of the Saved and the adjacent homeless shelter. It was the church where the memorial service for Jonah would be held, though Jonah himself had not been a churchgoer. Up and down the Hollow, on either side of the church, the rooftops were scattered among treetops. There were as many vacant lots as buildings. We could have been looking down on an isolated hamlet in some rural setting.

As we continued upward we met state workers coming down, one at a time, eyes fixed downward on the steps, headed for their cars and then escape from the city. They passed by without acknowledgement, their faces refusing to show any reaction to the odd pair hauling a bicycle up the steps.

Finally the steps brought us onto the sidewalk beside Elk Street, facing Swan Street, which was now an entirely different street from the Swan Street that came down Arbor Hill to the foot of the stairs.

With the Hollow behind us, we faced the other Albany. Diagonally across Elk, to our left, was the Episcopal All Saints Cathedral. Immediately beyond it rose the marble façade of the State Education Building, beyond which, diagonally across Washington Avenue, was the Capitol. To our right on the other side of Swan was a row of brownstones, and, towering above them, the rectangular steel and glass shape of the modern office building that fronted on Washington Avenue. On the far side of Washington was what had at one time been the city's tallest building, the old Alfred E. Smith State Office Building.

Turning left on Elk, we made our way down the block toward Lafayette Park in front of the Capitol. The people on the street now all seemed to be hurrying somewhere, almost all of them dressed in business clothes, and almost all of them white. The only people of color were some men in hard hats clustered around a manhole behind a barrier.

Jesse was quiet, concentrating on keeping his bicycle and himself out of the way of the people hurrying by.

At the end of the block we crossed Hawk Street into the park. The Capitol building was now visible across Washington Avenue on our right. Beyond its intricate Victorian roofline rose the hard-edged vertical shaft of Corning Tower. Ahead of us at the far end of the park were my destinations, City Hall, ornately and distinctively elegant, and the county Courthouse, looking like a thousand other county courthouses.

"You come down here much — to this part of town?" I asked.

"It got nothing for me," Jesse said.

"Ever go to the state museum?"

"One time with my class. But they didn't let us look at the cool stuff. Had to look at the Mancipation Proclamation."

"What kind of cool stuff didn't they let you look at?"

"Dinosaurs."

"I have to try to find some stuff in City Hall and maybe the Courthouse. It could take a while, but if you want to wait — hang out in the park with your bike — then we could walk over to the museum and check out the dinosaurs. Since we're already down this way."

"Sure, cool," Jesse said.

* * *

When I reemerged into the brightness and warmth of the late afternoon, I felt some regret at having promised to go to the museum with Jesse. My brief research had yielded a piece of information that I wished I could carry off, like a dog with a bone, to chew on quietly by myself. I especially wanted to go back to the Hollow and have another look at the Sheridan Avenue properties. By checking tax records I had learned that the property owner identified in Jonah's list as EMF was in fact Eddie McFadden, the somewhat notorious dealer in cheap real estate whom Lisa had insisted was not her colleague. I had then checked the registry of deeds to learn when McFadden had acquired the properties and make sure that he had not recently sold them. He had bought all three properties, from three different owners, not quite a year ago, and apparently still owned them. It was puzzling information.

Jesse came circling on his bicycle out of the park to the edge of Eagle Street. I waved him back, pointed to myself and then to Jesse's side of the street; then waited for the light to change and crossed over.

We made our way across Washington Avenue, looped around the east-facing steps of the Capitol, crossed State Street and went up the steps beside the Justice Building to the Empire State Plaza. The museum, an odd trapezoidal building, wider at the top than at the bottom like an upside-down pyramid, was now a quarter mile straight ahead of us at the far end of the Mall's long central platform. The concrete surface of the platform is a pedestrian runway that seems to have been designed to be as uninviting as possible, to discourage anyone from wanting to linger, any groups from wanting to gather. It reminds me of the lid of a giant casket. Directly under the lid is the main underground corridor of the mall, running from the Capitol to Madison Avenue, with connecting corridors to the surrounding state buildings.

On our left now was the Egg, the one curved shape in an environment otherwise defined by straight lines laid out severely parallel and perpendicular to each other. The Egg is a windowless structure that looks like a giant clam balanced aloft on a kind of pedestal. It houses a performing arts center. Just south of the Egg, Corning Tower rises straight up forty-four stories. Along the other side of the Mall are four identical twenty-three-story towers, each a tall stack of windowed offices clipped to a solid white marble spine. Behind them is the low quarter-mile-long marble building that houses the Motor Vehicles Division.

"Ever been to the Egg?" I asked Jesse.

"Nunh-uh," Jesse said.

"Ever been to the top of the tall building?"

"Nunh-uh."

"Maybe one of these days we can do that stuff. Did they teach you in school about how this place was built?"

"The governor he was all ashamed because the queen came to visit and he didn't want her seeing his old city, so then he had them do this here."

"So the story goes," I said. "When the Queen of the Netherlands came for the anniversary of Albany being founded by the Dutch. Anyway Governor Rockefeller did get them to do this here, though it sure took him a long time. Tore down more than a thousand buildings to make room for it. Something like nine thousand people got pushed out, had to move away."

"Good thing he didn't decide to put it on Orange Street — push us out."

"You know what? I bet Governor Rockefeller never even saw Orange Street. I bet he never even looked down the stairs into Sheridan Hollow."

"Didn't have to," Jesse said. "Big man like that." He stood on his pedals and accelerated the bike, riding ahead and swinging around one of the rectangular islands planted with straight rows of trees with straight-pruned tops.

To the east, between the Egg and Corning Tower, I could now look out over the valley to where the flowing line of a natural horizon offered some relief from the immediate surroundings. I made a point of walking through the Mall this way from time to time, to remind myself of what I like and don't like.

At the far end of the walkway, we descended the steps and crossed Madison Avenue to the front of the museum. The question now was what to do with the bicycle. There was really no place to leave it, certainly no place secure. It was not the most expensive of bicycles, but it was Jesse's most important possession. So I offered to stay outside with it while Jesse went in to check out the dinosaurs. "Just ask the person at the desk up front where to find them," I told him.

"Already know where," Jesse said, heading in.

Rather than wait in the thick of the diesel exhaust from the busses that lined up to transport state workers homeward, I walked the bike a ways down the sidewalk toward Eagle Street. I hadn't been on a bicycle in years, but it was tempting. I swung a leg over and lowered my weight tentatively onto the seat. My legs were too long to pedal without bumping my knees on the handlebars, but I could lift my heels from the sidewalk and coast down the hill.

At the corner in front of the Catholic Cathedral I considered turning right to walk past the Governor's Mansion, just a block up Eagle, but the light changed as I reached the corner and I let myself roll on across Eagle and down into the next block along the little wedge of a park that separates Madison Place from Madison Avenue. Here I stopped. Not wanting to drag the bike back up the hill from further down, I leaned it against the low wall bordering the park and sat on the wall beside it.

In front of me now, hardly more than a block to the north, was the multi-lane highway that swings off I-787 and disappears directly into the side of the Mall, where it feeds the huge underground parking area. At one time I lived just around the corner from here in the Mansion neighborhood, and every day walking downtown I would look up at the great masonry-walled eastern face of the Mall where the highway disappeared and think how much it looked like a medieval fortress standing above the town, shielding the powerful from the townspeople. Before the Mall was built in the 1960s and '70s, a series of streets — Hamilton, Hudson, Jay, Lancaster and Chestnut — had sloped gradually upward through the area on the same plane as Madison Avenue to the south and State Street to the north. There was no vertical wall cutting across those streets then. It occurred to me that Nelson Rockefeller's vision had been exactly the opposite of Jonah Lee's vision. Rockefeller's project created a precipitous barrier in order to wall the untidy town out from the seat of power. Jonah's project was designed to transform a steeply sloped wasteland into something that would link the untidy town with the seat of power.

The idea of the Mall as a huge platform raised above its surroundings had been Rockefeller's own concept, reportedly inspired by, of all things, the hilltop palace of the Dalai Lama in Tibet. In fact the original plan had been to build the complex on a cliff along the Helderberg escarpment some miles to the south, in truly splendid isolation where the untidy town would have been far out of sight and sound.

Jonah was asking the State of New York to contribute several hundred thousand dollars toward his project. Rockefeller's project had cost the people of the State of New York something like two billion dollars. I tried to think of what it would be like to write a proposal and develop pro formas for a two billion dollar project, but I couldn't begin to imagine it.

Of course it had not been proposed up front as a two billion dollar project. In the beginning it was supposed to cost $250 million, but the projections had inevitably expanded, until Rockefeller knew that getting the Philistine voters of the state to approve a bond issue for such an expenditure would be difficult if not impossible. So it had taken a scheme conceived by Albany's mayor of forty years, Erastus Corning, to get the deal done. Title to the land that the state had taken was transferred to Albany County, which issued the bonds itself and contracted with the state to build the project, with a leaseback commitment that would generate enough revenue for the county to service and pay off the bonds, so that in the end both county and state escaped accountability to their respective electorates and the project became such a vast boondoggle that no one could finally say exactly how much it did cost.

Jonah Lee's desire to change the urban landscape might have been every bit as intense as Nelson Rockefeller's, but no politician was going to develop a scheme to fund his project. His only hope of getting it done had been to do his own scheming, his own dealing, with people far less powerful, though maybe just as slippery, as those who had built the Mall. The question was what had the scheme been. What deals had he cut, or tried to cut? How many people had he been trying, more or less secretly, to deal with? Holding out what incentives to each?

Eddie McFadden in particular — what was his incentive? Had he actually sold Jonah purchase options on the three properties? If the properties had belonged to Arnold Duber, as old milked-out rentals, the motivation to sell would have been obvious. Duber would have jumped on any opportunity to unload them and certainly would have given Jonah an option on whatever terms it took to get the deal done. But with McFadden the question was why was he holding them and why had he bought them in the first place. They were not his kind of properties, any more than they were the usual kind of NHA properties. McFadden was a bottom-end dealer-rehabber. He once told me that he was "doing the same kind of thing Jonah does." In other words, they both looked for bargain houses that didn't need a whole lot of work, then rehabbed them as inexpensively as possible. The difference was that McFadden cut corners and covered up problems, plastering over cracked foundations, hiding decayed framing with new sheetrock, and then sold the houses for too much money to inexperienced first-time homebuyers.

But the Sheridan Avenue properties — I had confirmed as Jesse and I walked by — consisted of a vacant lot and two abandoned buildings that looked like they had been boarded up for years. To rehab those derelicts would cost at least as much as building a new house on the vacant lot, which would be several times as much as even a brand new house could be sold for in that location. To do anything with those properties would require a very deep subsidy. The sort of deep subsidy that Jonah had applied to the state for. But subsidized affordable housing was the last thing McFadden would have planned. State money brought with it the kinds of regulations that Eddie McFadden had made a career out of avoiding.

So what was his reason for investing in this real estate? What was his scheme? What did he know that made him think it was a good investment, even with the cost and liability entailed in holding unused property? Certainly he had not bought it on the slim chance that he could eventually sell it to a nonprofit for an affordable housing project, so there must have been another reason. But if there was another reason — puzzle upon puzzle — why had he optioned the property to NHA?

And on top of these questions was the question of what Jonah did or didn't know about McFadden's situation and motives. And, more generally, did Jonah have a potentially workable scheme at all? Or had he just let himself be carried off into deep water where his only chance was a long-shot scheme involving a large and unlikely project? And in any case, with or without a rational scheme, what had he got into that got him killed? That is, if the cause of his death wasn't just some desperate kid looking for cash.

I stood up. I didn't know how long Jesse might spend looking at dinosaurs, and I didn't want him to come out of the museum and find both his bike and his companion gone, so I started back up the hill, half dragging the bicycle with its front wheel lifted off the sidewalk.

* * *

Back at home I opened a beer, made myself a salad and an omelet, then turned on the radio and listened to All Things Considered as I ate. When I finished, I washed the pan and salad bowl and plate and fork and left them to dry in the drainer that was their regular everyday place. Then I went upstairs to my desk with the intention of finishing the Syracuse work, but before getting back to that task I picked up the folder of miscellaneous papers that Helen Hamilton had copied for me that morning, and began leafing through them.

I was halfway through the stack before I found anything of interest. But what I then did find was interesting indeed. It was a brief handwritten letter on a plain sheet of paper, no name or address at the top, dated March 27. The message was a single sentence.

"Jonah — your offer for the options ($3000 for 3) is a lot less than I need but if you still think we have something to talk about I will be glad to meet as you suggested."

It was signed "Eddie."

I set it aside and hurried through the rest of the stack of papers, hoping to find something more that related to Eddie McFadden or the question of purchase options, but I found nothing. I would have to get back to the NHA office as soon as I could, to check with Helen Hamilton — to ask her specifically if she knew anything about purchase options or anything at all about the Sheridan Avenue properties — and to look for any files that might relate to the project. I also needed to talk to Charlotte Wolf, the bookkeeper, to see whether there was any record of expenditures for Sheridan Avenue purchase options, as well as to ask her about the rent for Zera's apartment.

I felt I should do these things before trying to talk to McFadden, or to the Gander Bay owners, the Rowleys. But none of it could be done tomorrow. I had to leave early for Syracuse and wouldn't be back until evening. And the morning after that, Friday, was the memorial service for Jonah. I felt a wave of frustration. There were so many things that needed to be done one step at a time — so many steps, so little time to get it all done. I wanted to do something fast and decisive to try to break something loose. Just pick up the phone and call Eddie McFadden at home and say, "Look, we need to talk about those Sheridan Avenue properties you optioned to Jonah," and see what it would lead to.

There would be no reason *n o t* to make that call right away if it was just a question of helping the NHA to wrap up the loose ends of a would-be project. But there was too much that was strange about McFadden's ownership of those properties, and I couldn't shake the feeling that Jonah's death was somehow connected with everything that was strange about the Sheridan Hollow project. I wanted to know as much as possible before I made that call. I had to be patient.

9

I had come straight to Lisa's after a long day — long meetings and five hours of Thruway driving. She met me at her apartment door with an embrace and a long kiss that was a powerful reminder of why I was here.

But the kiss ended and she stepped back, saying "Bye and bye. Let me get you a drink." Taking my hand, she led me into the kitchen. "Did you hear the evening news? About the police arresting a suspect in Jonah Lee's murder?"

"What? Did they say who?"

"There was a name I didn't get. Someone described just as a young African American male, charged with armed robbery and murder."

"Shit."

She looked at me with surprise.

"I'm sorry," I said. "I don't know. I need to know more, but I have a hard time believing they have the right person. I don't really believe robbery was what it was about."

"Whatever it was about, they apparently had a reason to arrest this guy." She had lifted a bottle of Jack Daniel's from a kitchen cupboard and now poured me a generous drink and herself a modest one. "I would think what matters is that they catch the guy that did it, no matter who it is. It sounds like you think you have a theory you want to have confirmed...Let's go sit." She handed me the drink and led the way into the living room.

I felt ambushed by the news and was annoyed at having my response so quickly analyzed. I had spent the last several hours on

the Thruway trying to think my way through various scenarios
that might connect Eddie McFadden with Jonah's death. I had not
really come up with much — and I couldn't really believe that
McFadden himself was a murderer, even if his business practices
were on the slimy side — but I had let my thinking gravitate further and further away from the idea that it was just a robbery that
had killed Jonah.

"I didn't mean to sound critical," Lisa said, settling into her
corner of the sofa. "But it does seem like you see Jonah Lee as
standing up for all the downtrodden, so the killer has to be someone from...well...the other side, not just another one of the
downtrodden. Is that it?"

"Something like that," I admitted, still standing. "Actually
very much like that. But I also do think there were some strange
things going on around that Sheridan Avenue project." I knew
that it didn't necessarily follow — that the strangeness of the
Sheridan Avenue project didn't necessarily say much about the
likelihood of Jonah being killed by a young black male in the
course of an armed robbery.

"What kind of strange things?"

"Jonah's application to the state...it's maybe not strange, but
it is a pretty amazing proposal nonetheless. Then there's the fact
that Eddie McFadden owns three of the properties on Sheridan, a
vacant lot and two shells. Bought them almost a year ago and I
have absolutely no idea why, but it looks as though he may have
optioned them to Jonah."

"Come sit," she said, patting the sofa beside her. "Tell me
what you've been up to. It sounds at least more *interesting* than
some armed robbery."

I sat down and told her about the proposal. She had many
questions. I drank my drink and answered as many of the questions as I could.

"But I still don't understand what he thought it would prove
even if he could pull it off," she said.

"Connecting Sheridan Hollow with the Capitol...you have to
admit it would be some kind of accomplishment."

"But what does that mean? What kind of connection, really? I
mean, as it is, if someone living down there actually has business
at the Capitol, all they have to do is walk up the stairs. But how
many people in Sheridan Hollow have business at the Capitol?"

"I guess his point was that they *should* have business there. Or,
more to the point, the state *should* have business in Sheridan Hol-

low — or at least stop ignoring Sheridan Hollow and all the places like it. Or do more than pay lip service to the needs of such places. But I agree, it mostly seems like a symbolic statement, and like he was going to an awful lot of trouble to make a symbolic statement. There's a whole lot I don't begin to understand."

"Like why Eddie McFadden bought those Sheridan Avenue properties," she said.

"Do you have any idea why he might have?"

"Certainly not to develop. He had to know something we don't know...but what? He's a bottom feeder. He just works with what sifts down to the bottom. Not exactly an insider who hears about opportunities before other people do."

"He must have known something though. I figure he had to have a buyer in mind."

"Could be the deal was already done. Maybe he bought them for someone who needed to stay out of sight."

"So why did *that* person want Sheridan Avenue property?" I asked.

"Good question."

"And if he bought the property for someone else, why did he option it to Jonah?"

"Another good question. My kind of question. Snooping into other people's deals turns me on. I will work on it."

"I didn't know you were such a voyeur. I thought it was *doing* deals, your own deals, that turns you on."

She laughed. "Oh, it's no substitute for the real thing. But there is a kind of kinky pleasure in finding out what deals other people are up to." She slid across the sofa and snuggled against me.

I felt her warmth and the warmth of the whiskey spreading through me. "You know what turns me on?" I asked.

"I'm making a list. Tell me."

"Real estate ladies who're turned on by doing deals, and snooping, and other things."

"Good to know," she said.

10

I drove home from Lisa's early in the morning. I would have liked to linger over coffee with barefoot, dressing-gowned Lisa in her sunlit living room, but I had more work to do now for the Syracuse organization, and phone calls I wanted to make. Then the service for Jonah was at eleven.

At eight o'clock I began trying to reach Detective Reilly, without success. At nine I called Erica Schmidt. She told me she was about to rush off to a meeting in the Legislative Building but she would like to have lunch. We arranged to meet at one o'clock in "Cafeteria A," off the main concourse in the Empire State Plaza.

It was after ten when Reilly returned my call.

"So you have a suspect," I said.

"Yes, in custody."

"*Times Union* says you arrested an eighteen-year-old African American guy named Ronald Burns, for armed robbery and the murder of Jonah Lee. I guess that's all you've told the press."

"We're doing our job, checking alibis. Know more pretty soon I hope." He was steadfastly uncommunicative.

"I have more information than the last time we talked," I said. "It may or may not be relevant but I think I should pass it along to you, and I'm hoping you can fill in a few things for me while we're at it. I wondered if you have a few minutes later today."

"What kind of information? If you found any cash missing I need to know."

"It's not the kind of tidy evidence you're looking for. There is no evidence of any missing cash. But there's an unusual situation suggesting that Jonah *might* have been bankrolling a fairly large amount of cash, which could have been stolen or could have been used by Jonah on a complicated deal he was trying to put together." I hoped that Reilly would be interested enough in the possibility of a large amount of cash to agree to meet with me.

Reilly sighed. "I need to go by the NHA office late in the afternoon, between four and five. If you want to meet me there, we can talk."

* * *

I chose a pew toward the back of the church where the only other occupant was a young man who looked as though he felt as much out of place as I did. The man nodded to me as I sat down, then turned back to face the front of the church. In profile he had distinctly Native American features and a long pony tail, jet black against his white shirt. He sat very still. I assumed that, like me, he was paying his respects to Jonah by the simple act of sitting in a place he would otherwise never sit.

Of course Jonah himself would never have sat there either, except for similar occasions — funerals, and maybe weddings, but mostly funerals. This thought helped me feel a little closer to Jonah, but it didn't help me feel any closer to most of the people around me — for whom this was a natural place to bring their grief — and I *wanted* to feel closer to them. There appeared to be more than a hundred and fifty people. Most were African American. At least half, I thought, were NHA members, people who in some sense owed their homes to Jonah, people whose lives had been affected by Jonah in real ways.

The service began with a lengthy invocation by the pastor who had agreed to make the church available and to let the NHA people — mostly Helen Hamilton I thought — plan the service. Then, after a brave little choir had sung, there was a long address by a man whose reputation I knew somewhat — a college professor and lecturer who had known Jonah and seemed to think of himself as Jonah's mentor. It was a proper address. The man was sincere and he had an impressive voice. But for me the words didn't connect with the Jonah I had known, or the Jonah I wished I had known better, and after a minute I lost the thread of the man's speech, and then no longer heard the words at all. Instead I thought about Jonah's Sheridan Hollow project — right here, just up the street — and what it meant and all the questions it raised.

By the time the man finally sat down, I was busy trying to plan who I needed to talk to about which questions, and when I could make the time to see them all. I was only half aware of a tall woman standing up from a front pew, moving slowly up the steps of the dais, turning and waiting quietly as a piano began to play, then beginning to sing. Gradually the voice lifted me out of my thoughts. It was a beautiful voice and, unlike the earlier efforts of the choir, it seemed to come out of the heart of the occasion, expressing sorrow, grief, longing, praise. The music was unfamiliar to me, but whatever else it was about I knew it was about Jonah.

Then I realized who it was. The singer was Zera. I was seized by the memory of holding her and the baby, and unexpectedly I felt myself begin to cave inward. Her voice soared, and I hunched forward and shut my eyes tight and tried to hold back a surprising surge of emotion, but I couldn't keep my shoulders from shaking.

Then a hand came to rest on my left shoulder. Someone in the pew behind me. A small hand with a light touch. I put my own right hand over it, grateful and embarrassed, and amazed at myself for acting this way, until I could pull myself together enough to sit up straight. Out of the corner of my eye I could see the man beside me still motionless, gazing straight ahead.

The service lasted for another fifteen minutes. I was mostly oblivious to it. I was aware of an empty space inside myself, and I was aware of the people around me. I could hear the emotion in the breathing around me.

At the end, Harry Cooper stood in front of the congregation. "There is so much I wanted to say," he said. "I was up all night trying to write something. But I couldn't. I can't. Some of it we'll have to say by going on with the work." He looked down and was silent for a long time. When he looked up, he said, "Jonah, we'll miss you. Goodbye brother."

"Amen," said a hundred voices.

People were rising to go. The man with the ponytail stood up. I stood and turned and saw Helen Hamilton departing from the pew behind me.

I made my escape quickly — outdoors and then around the corner away from the people clustering on Sheridan Avenue. I walked to the long stair and began climbing. No one else was coming this way. At the halfway point I stopped and sat down on a step, looking down on the church and the people gathered far below me, the people who were not mine the way they were Jonah's people, though I might wish they were. The midday sun was hot on my back. I would sit here a while before going on up to meet Erica. Talking with Erica, I thought, would be a good antidote to all of this emotion, a good way to refocus on what had to be done.

* * *

I found Erica sitting at a small table against the west wall of the huge, windowless cafeteria. A strong-featured middle-aged woman with short, gray-streaked hair, she was working vigorously on a fat roast beef sandwich when I sat down. "I hate this place," she said. "I used to eat here way too often back when we had our offices up in Corning Tower. I don't miss it."

"You should have said. We could have met anywhere."

"Nah, this is fine. It's a good place when you want to meet with someone anonymously. Here, I'm just one of three hundred anonymous state workers having their anonymous lunches in a place so damn anonymous it's named after a *letter* for christsake."

"I would imagine that the full name is actually the Nelson A. Rockefeller Empire State Plaza Cafeteria A."

"Cute," she said. "Is that the missing proposal you brought with you?"

"It's a copy of Jonah's proposal I made for you. What do you mean, missing?"

"It's missing. Gone. DHCR has lost it."

"I didn't know DHCR just lost things. The feds lose things. HUD is so used to losing things it doesn't even embarrass them. 'We are unable to locate your application — please resubmit.' With DHCR it's, 'We have received your application but must inform you that Form 23e is no longer current. Please resubmit on the enclosed Form 23f.'"

"It's gone. Listen, this is all I can tell you. I was told — by someone who should know — that the application was lost and is therefore no longer available to the Division."

"Those exact words — no longer available to the Division?"

"That's right. Interesting way of putting it, huh? I was also given to understand that I shouldn't ask any further questions about it."

"In so many words?"

"Not in so many words. In hardly any words. But I've been around too long to miss that kind of message." She reached for the manila envelope that held the proposal and pulled it across the table. "So I sure as hell am interested in reading what I'm not supposed to ask about."

"I think you will be. It's not the kind of proposal you read every day. And I'll be interested in talking with you after you've read it. I'm going to have to figure out what to advise the NHA to do with this thing. As long as the application hasn't been rejected — and we have the copy — we can try to put the thing back in play if it still makes sense for the NHA to go after it. But it would be helpful to know what we would be up against if we resubmitted." I paused and watched Erica chewing vigorously on her sandwich. "I don't suppose you have any suspicions at this point...about who might have taken it and why."

She swallowed and wiped her mouth quickly on the back of her hand. "I'm suspicious of most people most of the time. But no, I really don't have a clue. I have to assume someone thinks it would be convenient if the Division didn't have to take action on the application, but I have no idea where that's coming from. Or possibly someone just thought, Okay Jonah's dead, don't have to deal with this one now." She picked up the application and made as though to chuck it on the floor. "Actually it would be convenient if we didn't have to deal with *any* applications."

"You could do like the feds. Devolution. Just make block grants to the cities and counties and let them worry about who actually gets what — and be the ones to screw up and take the heat."

"I like that. So we in the Division could just do what we're really good at — design forms and write regs." Her sandwich was gone. She picked up the proposal. "So what else are you up to these days? You still do those godawful flybitten canoe trips up north like you used to do with Barney?"

"Absolutely. I'm headed north at the end of the month. And speaking of Barney... how is he? Do you hear from him any more?"

"It's been a while. Last I knew, Barney was working for Alaska Housing Finance — as far away from me as it's possible to get without leaving the affordable housing world. And you — *your* ex — do you hear from Martha?"

"No, but as far as I know she's still right there in Colonie, and married of course."

She stood up. "Some things change, some things don't. Can I call you over the weekend, after I've read this?"

"Please do."

*　*　*

I was partly disappointed, partly relieved to find Reilly already at the NHA office with Helen Hamilton when I arrived. I had wanted to ask Helen if she knew anything about Sheridan Avenue purchase options, but, after the memorial service, I felt awkward about seeing her. Reilly's brusque presence covered the awkwardness for the time being. Helen sat unobtrusively at the desk in the corner, opening mail. Reilly was slumped in the swivel chair at Jonah's desk, looking tired as usual. I sat down on one of the folding chairs by the file cabinets.

"So," Reilly said, "what's this about some chunk of cash that was maybe lying around here?"

"I don't know if the NHA had any cash lying around anywhere," I said. "I might know more after I talk with the bookkeeper. There's some income unaccounted for — or possible income. But it might never have been received. Or if it was received it might be in a separate bank account that I haven't caught up with yet. Or if it was in cash it might not have been in the office."

He shook his head impatiently. "How much are you talking about?"

"The equivalent of about a year's rent, at most. So maybe as much as five thousand."

"Are you saying Jonah Lee was playing fast and loose with rent receipts?"

"Not the way it sounds. It was his own money. That is, it was rent for his own apartment, which he actually wasn't required to pay. The board wanted to give him the apartment rent-free as part of his compensation, which was not a lot, but he said he wanted to pay it, and his partner says he did pay it, but not out of their checking account. But I haven't been able to track the money yet. It's possible Jonah was using it as a kind of slush fund to move a complicated project forward. Maybe using it to buy purchase options on some property." I looked toward Helen Hamilton, who lifted her head briefly from the mail on the desk, but did not look at me.

Reilly was staring at me. "Does any of this matter?"

"Five thousand dollars in income makes a difference for the organization. I don't know if it matters for your investigation."

"It would matter for sure if anyone could say five thousand dollars disappeared from this office when Jonah Lee was shot. Or forty-nine-hundred dollars, with one hundred left on the floor."

"The paper said your suspect was charged with murder and armed robbery. But I assume you still have no actual evidence of anything stolen — or did you find something in this guy's possession?"

"We are investigating it as an armed robbery. He has not been charged with armed robbery at this point. The *T-U* article was inaccurate."

"But you do have some kind of evidence that this Ronald Burns shot Jonah, or was seen leaving that evening...or what?"

"We have a very nice thumb print on the hundred dollar bill we found in this office — on the tape that was on it, as a matter of fact. Only way to explain that print that I can think of is that the guy was here pulling hundred-dollar bills out of that filing cabinet when Jonah came in...and one of the bills got away from him."

"Maybe the easiest way to explain it," I said. "But not the only possible way."

"He was not one of your tenants, or living with one, if that's what you're thinking. No way the print could have been made before the hundred came into the office."

"Unless he bought something from an NHA tenant for a hundred dollars. Or..."

Reilly waved a hand impatiently. "Sure, we have work to do. But this is the guy. Ronnie Burns. 'Loosh,' they call him. We saw a lot of him as a juvenile, and if someone had asked me back then, is this kid going to shoot someone some day, I would have said most likely yes, if someone doesn't shoot him first."

"But he has some kind of alibi that you're checking?"

"If you want to call it an alibi. Some members of that sober responsible bunch that hangs out at the Gander Bay Bar say he was there Saturday night. Because he's, quote, usually here, and hey it was Saturday night — where else would he be? We're still talking to people who were there and we've already got conflicting stories. As evidence one way or the other it's not worth much."

"Gander Bay Bar is an interesting coincidence," I said. I was thinking about my encounter with the Gander Bay clientele, and wondered whether the Gander Bay connection suggested a different motive for this Loosh — if in fact he was the killer.

"It's no coincidence that a piece of scum hangs out there," Reilly said. "If you want scum, it's one of the places to look."

"I believe Jonah was trying to buy the place, along with adjoining properties on Sheridan. I don't think it made him very popular with the people that hang out there." I watched Helen again raise her head and gaze at the wall in front of her for a long moment.

Reilly, too, gazed thoughtfully straight ahead, until eventually he shook his head. "Loosh was looking for money, no question. And we'll get what we need to convict him. We're not sure yet who he was living with or where he was staying, but when we find out, we're going to learn what we need to learn. He's just a punk. He's not smart."

Getting up from the swivel chair, Reilly winced, froze in a stooped position, and muttered "Shit," before cautiously straightening himself an inch at a time. "So any information about cash on the premises is top priority," he said sternly, as he moved slowly toward the door.

When he was gone, I asked Helen if she knew anything about Sheridan Avenue purchase options. She seemed troubled by the subject but was unable to tell me much. "We knew he was talking with people down there, owners of other properties around the ones we already bought, but he hadn't given us any details yet. He was working on it..."

"You knew that the Gander Bay Bar was one of the properties?" I asked.

"I don't go down in that neighborhood. But yes, I knew."

"Do you know if there was a file for purchase options?"

She shook her head. "Purchase contracts went in the Possible Acquisition files — there's different files for the different ones he was looking at — but I don't know about options."

"Where would I find those Possible Acquisition files?"

She pointed to the second file cabinet, the one that hadn't been disturbed on Saturday night. "Top drawer."

I didn't think I would find neatly labeled files for the problem properties on Sheridan Avenue, but I looked anyway. There were several dozen folders in that section of the file drawer, each labeled with a street address representing a property that the NHA had looked at and considered buying at some point but had not actually acquired. The properties actually acquired by the organization were filed elsewhere.

I looked quickly through the folders. Most of them contained only a single sheet of paper, with contact information and rough, penciled notes relating to potential rehab costs. A few contained copies of purchase and sale forms that had been filled out by Jonah and presented to owners who had not accepted the offered terms. None of the files contained purchase options, which was not surprising. With the small buildings that the NHA normally acquired, there was usually no reason to deal with options; if the numbers worked Jonah could get a contract and close the deal up front with funding already committed by the city and debt financing from the Community Loan Fund. There was no need to negotiate options.

There was just one file with a Sheridan Avenue address — 1107 Sheridan, on the north side of the street. The only property on that side of the street that was included in the DHCR proposal. In the folder there was just a single slip of paper with the name Greta Green, written in Jonah's hand, and a phone number. I showed the file to Helen. "Know anything about this Greta Green — 1107 Sheridan?"

She glanced at it and shook her head. "I only know he was talking to people down there. I don't know any Greta Green." She seemed uncomfortable with the whole subject.

"From talking with you and Harry I have the impression that the board wanted to support Jonah on this thing but you all didn't really share his enthusiasm for it."

She nodded.

"I've been wondering if we should push the application for that project with DHCR. I don't think they'll do anything with it now unless we do push it, and even then I don't know. The obvious thing would be to just let the whole thing go — except for those Duber buildings. It'll be hard to do anything with those buildings without the state money."

"But they're still right next to that ugly bar. No place for kids.

So we'd have to go ahead and try to buy the bar too. Lord help us."

"Yeah, it's a tough one," I said. The board will have to talk about it."

"We're trying to schedule a special meeting for next week. Harry was going to call you. We're hoping you can come."

"Sure, I'd like to do that." I copied the phone number for Greta Green into my pocket calendar and replaced the file in the cabinet. Helen was still sorting the mail she had opened. "So I guess I'll see you next week," I said.

"Goodbye, Warren," she said.

* * *

I got back from the NHA office a little after five and found myself suddenly at loose ends. Lisa was spending the evening with her sister in Troy, and I had actually looked forward to a quiet evening at home without company and without work — a chance to sort through the week's accumulation of surprises. But at the moment I wasn't sure where to start, or whether I wanted to. The house was hot. I wished I were elsewhere.

I poured myself a drink, sat down at the kitchen table and stared out into the leaves of the silver maple that grew in the tiny yard behind my neighbor's garage. There was no breeze and the leaves hung almost motionless above the garage roof.

When the drink was gone, no useful sorting had been accomplished. I stood up, poured another drink and took it up to my office, where I turned on the computer, more or less out of habit, and then went on line to check my e-mail. Amidst several commercial "newsletters," there were four messages.

One was a note from Lisa with the subject identified as "Saturday night on the town." The message was, "How about Saratoga? Dinner and then some music somewhere?" In reply I typed, "Sounds good. If we don't talk before, I'll pick you up between five and six." I clicked the SEND button, thinking how easy this relationship was.

The next message was from Syracuse: a question about their development budget that had a clear-cut answer. I typed a sentence and sent it off.

Then there was a message from my friend Dave Potter in Saranac Lake, with whom I was going to share a canoe, a small tent and a number of campfires in the month of July. The subject was "food list." The message read, "Proposed menu and food list attached. Can you get the flour, oatmeal, rice and lentils and other such stuff at Honest Weight?"

A cool breeze out of Labrador on a warm Albany night. I downloaded and printed the attachment, then typed, "I'll go over the list this weekend and yes I can get the stuff at the co-op here. I am far from ready work-wise. Very ready otherwise. Summer is settling down on Albany. Definitely time to go north."

The final message was from Erica. "Holy Crimoli. Was the guy serious?"

I typed, "It's about the only thing I'm sure of. He was serious. More later."

I wanted to have another look at Jonah's Sheridan Hollow proposal — not because I doubted Jonah's seriousness but because when I had read it the first time I'd been in a rush, jumping from one section to another in amazement.

Now I read it slowly and carefully all the way through. It seemed a little more coherent than it had the first time — still an amazing concept to be proposing, but, given that concept, not badly put together. The numbers actually worked — if you could believe it was possible to get both major foundation funding and a major commitment from the city to support the elaborate site design, as well as the requested funding from the state for the housing. All of the attachments seemed to be in order: copies of newspaper clippings and other promotional materials, copies of the organizational bylaws, the IRS letter recognizing NHA's 501(c)(3) tax-exempt status, reports to the State Charities Bureau, the completed federal Form 990 and auditor's report for the previous year. There were also copies of the deeds for the two Sheridan Avenue properties that the NHA owned. But I found no copies of purchase options for the McFadden properties.

Turning back to the cover letter, I checked the list of attachments and noticed something I hadn't taken in before. The next-to-last item read "Site control documentation: deeds, purchase contracts, options."

It could be just generic language, as might have appeared in some other word processor file that Jonah had copied and edited for this purpose, without bothering to delete the specific reference to purchase contracts and options. For that matter, I had no reason to think that Jonah had purchase contracts for any new properties at the time he had submitted the application.

Did he not really have the McFadden option agreements either? Was he still negotiating with McFadden when he submitted the application, claiming site control that he expected to have but did not yet have? Or did he in fact submit copies of signed option agreements with the application that actually went to DHCR, even though no such copies were attached to the copy of the proposal in my lap? If copies did go to DHCR they had disappeared with the application. And I hadn't been able to locate the originals of any such documents in the "Possible Acquisition" files.

I would just have to go and talk with McFadden and see what I could learn. But not until I had talked with Charlotte the bookkeeper, which I hoped I could arrange to do tomorrow morning.

II

I poured one more cup of coffee. It was already after eight, and I was scheduled to be at Charlotte Wolf's house at nine, and she lived way down in the South End on Teunis Street. Of course I could drive there in a few minutes, but I wanted the walk. It was a sunny-sweet June morning, and one of the good things about living in this city is that it's compact enough so you can get most places on foot. I had hated living in the subdivision in Colonie, where almost nothing was within walking distance, and where, in any case, there were no sidewalks. Walking around the subdivision meant walking in the street. And if you walked out to Central Avenue, then the only way to move along the strip was from one parking lot to the next. But in Albany, walking is practical and pleasant. This morning I would walk to the South End and back. And later in the day I would get out on the river for a while, before going to Saratoga with Lisa for the evening. A welcome agenda.

My route took me diagonally through Washington Park to Delaware Avenue, then down through Lincoln Park and into the South End by way of Third Avenue. Walking down Third Avenue, I met a tall, angular African American man, someone I saw from time to time on the street but didn't know by name. He grinned and extended an arm. I held out a hand, palm up, and he slapped it neatly and passed on. It was what he did whenever we met. I liked the idea that it was just a friendly ritual greeting between fellow travelers of the street, but I wasn't sure that was what it was. I didn't know whether he might know who I was, or something about me, and whether I ought to know who he was. Anyway, I liked his wordless grin.

Teunis was a block-long residential street off of Third Avenue.

Charlotte's home was a modest fifty-year-old bungalow, set further back from the street than the neighboring houses. Two small children — a boy and a girl, both apparently less than five years old — played in the front yard under a maple tree. Charlotte sat on the steps of the deep front porch. She watched me come up the walk, her face serious until, when I was only a few yards away, she smiled shyly and said, "Hello there." She nodded toward the children. "They were supposed to go to the lake with my dad, but he's under the weather. So we're all here." She stood and went up the steps. "I've got the NHA stuff out here."

In the shade of the porch there was a card table with two straight chairs beside it. On the table, papers were piled neatly beside an open laptop computer. Charlotte sat in one of the chairs and sorted through the papers. "Have a seat. I printed out May thirty-one financials for you." She looked at me for a long moment — one of the long careful pauses that periodically interrupted her speech. "For between then and Jonah's...when he died...I've posted what Helen and I could find...but it's hard to be sure without him there."

"I know," I said. "The end-of-May reports will be helpful. But what I'm most interested in right now is something you either know and can tell me or it's information that Jonah never gave you."

"If he didn't give it to me I certainly don't know it."

"Right. I'm trying to find out if he bought purchase options on some properties on Sheridan Avenue. I don't know how you would have booked an option but..."

She shook her head. "There were those Sheridan Avenue properties he bought a few months back. But you mean paying just for an option to buy...I don't think he ever did that...I mean it would have been done with a check, wouldn't it?"

"You would think so, but I've been wondering if possibly he used cash. These are three properties — two shells and a vacant lot — owned by Eddie McFadden. Jonah wanted to develop them, along with those buildings he got from Arnold Duber and some other adjacent properties. He put in a funding application for the project to the state, and in the application it says NHA held an option on the McFadden properties."

She looked at me wonderingly. Then her focus shifted and she was looking past me. "Billie, don't do that," she said, her voice only slightly raised. "I'm sorry. He's mostly pretty good with his little sister, but once in a while...But an option...it's not something you would pay for out of petty cash, is it?"

"Maybe with a friendly seller who might give an option for a dollar so you could go after the funding you'd need to make the deal work, but that wasn't the case here. I found a note from McFadden refusing an offer of three thousand dollars for options on the three properties but agreeing to meet Jonah to talk further."

"NHA does petty cash a hundred dollars at a time... and it usually lasts a couple of months."

"It's possible he used his own money, or cash he was accumulating in lieu of rent, as it were, for the apartment he shared with Zera Kay. I don't know what information he might have given you on that."

"None. I don't know anything about that. Billie, Mom said don't do that."

Whatever Billie was doing to his sister had to be quite subtle. I hadn't seen anything and hadn't heard any complaint from the little girl, who looked three years old at the most and was even quieter and less demonstrative than her mother. "I'm in no hurry," I said, "if your kids need your attention. And I appreciate your taking the time on a Saturday morning."

"Oh they're fine. He just likes to tease a little. And Saturday's not a bad day. I thought it would be a good day because I thought they would be off with their grandfather. Would you like some coffee? I should have offered."

"Thanks, I'm fine. The situation with the rent, as I understand it, was that the board told Jonah that he and his partner could have the apartment rent-free, as part of his compensation, but he told the board he would rather pay rent. However, I couldn't find any evidence that he did pay except that the rent roll shows them paid up to date. So one of my questions was whether you determine the amount of rent receivable from the rent roll, or if..."

"Oh, no," she said. "Maybe I should...I don't know...but I just have a list of all the rents, totaled, and if I get a note saying an apartment is vacant I subtract that from the total. Then the rent receivable is just that amount minus the rent received as it shows up on the cash receipts journal."

"So it wouldn't create a problem with your books if the rent roll showed rent being paid that didn't actually come in and get recorded in your books as received?"

"No, I just don't work from the rent roll. Do you think I should? I never have. I mean the organization does need to know *whose* rent is receivable, but Jonah always did know that."

"I'm no accountant," I said. "I don't know how it's supposed to be done. I just thought that if you did do it that way and the rent roll was inaccurate — if Jonah's rent wasn't actually received and deposited in the bank — then your books wouldn't balance. But as it is he could have been accumulating that money off the record and using it to buy purchase options."

"I guess so." Her eyes were on her children. Color rose in her cheeks and she was silent for some time. Finally she said, "I used to do Mr. McFadden's books for him. But I don't any more... because he wanted to keep too much of his business off the record and it made me uncomfortable. But Jonah wasn't like that."

"No, he wasn't. Not at all. And if he did have a little slush fund to move the organization's project along it was from his own money that he didn't have to pay to the organization in the first place. Anyway, I guess you weren't aware of any large amounts of cash lying around unaccounted for."

"No."

"The police would be delighted if you said yes."

"Oh, I know. One of them came by. I guess they think the office was being robbed...and that Jonah came in when it was going on...and that was how it happened."

"Yes, they think that."

* * *

When I got home I made a salami and lettuce sandwich on whole wheat, and poured a large glass of tomato juice, which I enhanced as usual with hot sauce and horseradish. Finishing the sandwich at my kitchen table, I decided to go ahead and try to set up a meeting with Eddie McFadden. I had exhausted the other possible ways of gathering information about his Sheridan Avenue properties, so there was no longer any very good reason to delay a meeting. I had no idea how long it would take to catch up with him. I saw Eddie occasionally around the neighborhood, usually at one of his rehab sites. Otherwise I knew nothing about the man's habits.

But when I checked the phone book there was a home number, and a home address in West Albany. I picked up the phone and dialed, and the call was answered almost immediately with a toneless "Lo" that I recognized as Eddie's flat voice.

I said, "Eddie, it's Warren Crow."

McFadden said, "Yeah, lo," still without inflection.

"Eddie, I think you and I need to talk."

"What about?"

"I've been trying to help the Neighborhood Housing Association deal with some things since Jonah's death. In particular I'm trying to sort out that Sheridan Avenue project Jonah was working on, which could have involved three of your properties."

"The options aren't renewable," McFadden said.

"I don't know that anyone *wants* them renewed. But the project could still go forward in some form and I thought we ought to talk about how your properties might be affected, one way or the other." I wasn't sure what "one way or the other" meant and I assumed McFadden wouldn't be sure either.

"If you want, but no way I'm going to extend those options," McFadden said.

"Okay, I won't even ask, but I'd still like to talk. I wondered if I could stop by your house tomorrow evening for a few minutes."

There was a long silence. Finally McFadden said, "Make it early. Five." He hung up.

I stared out through the window at the leaves of the silver maple, which now stirred in a midday breeze. I had learned that the options did exist — or at least had existed. I didn't think Jonah would have bought options that would expire before he had a reasonable chance to get project funding lined up, so it seemed unlikely that they had already expired, but I didn't know how long they might run. I only knew that McFadden was saying he would not renew them. I would have some time now to think about the situation and decide how to deal with McFadden when we met.

I rinsed my tomato juice glass in the sink, then got my rain gear from the closet and went out the front door and walked next door to Jesse's parents' garage where I kept the canoes. I took the solo canoe — all thirty-eight pounds of it — from where it hung from the rafters above the Buick and carried it to the street and slid it onto the pickup's rack and tied it down. I was feeling guilty because I was not taking the larger canoe and not looking for Jesse to go with me.

If Jesse had turned up I would have taken him and planned on some fishing, because Jesse would quickly become bored if all we were going to do was paddle up the river and back. But I just wanted to get out on the river and go, use my body and be alone on the water with my own thoughts.

I drove up the river on I-787 to Cohoes, the one-time milltown where the Mohawk River spills into the Hudson. The old mills themselves are up the hill to the west where the Mohawk drops over a series of ledges to the bottom of the Hudson Valley. I turned away from the mills, eastward, to where the lower town spreads out onto Van Schaick Island. Then, just before reaching the bridge that crosses the Hudson to the Lansingburgh section of Troy, I turned off to the left on the little road that runs up along the river and eventually crosses an old bridge and ends in a parking lot on Peebles Island, which is owned by the state as an undeveloped park. Peebles Island is a good place to walk or jog or poke around and listen to the birds. It's also a good place to launch a canoe if you want to paddle upriver into an undeveloped stretch of the Hudson.

I put in on the north side of the island, across the channel from where the Erie Canal begins the westward course that takes it up a stairway of locks out of the valley. From there I let the fading current of the Mohawk carry me out into the Hudson, where the boat veered suddenly south, pushed not only by the mainstream force of the larger river but by a stiff downriver breeze. Then I settled myself to propel the slender Kevlar boat upriver — five or six quick strokes on the right until the bow swung left, then a flip of the almost weightless graphite paddle to the other side for the next five or six strokes. Back and forth. I leaned into the strokes and felt the muscles of my back and shoulders stretch pleasantly as I carved my way into the wind and current.

Beyond the Waterford Bridge, on the east bank a large supermarket stands on the northern tip of the long, skinny city of Troy. The east bank is then rocky and undeveloped for a way, until you begin to see the houses of Pleasantdale scattered among the trees — the little houses in tight clusters, with a few larger houses in between. The place was originally developed as a working class summer colony, with the land subdivided into tiny lots, on some of which people built small cottages which then accumulated various owner-built additions over the years. But development had been slow and incomplete, so clusters of undeveloped lots were eventually bought up as sites for larger houses with oddly shaped but spacious yards. The result is an unplanned jumble that I like. I've sometimes thought that if I were ever going to live anywhere between the inner city and the wilderness I would like to live in a little house on the river in Pleasantdale.

Beyond Pleasantdale the east bank is steep and densely wooded — the old River Road abandoned, washed out and overgrown. Across the river, the west bank is also undeveloped, except for a chain link fence. But out of sight beyond the fence and a rim of woods is a General Electric plant. I stayed close to the east bank. It felt a little like sneaking past an enemy camp.

It was GE that poisoned the river with PCBs — not from this plant in Waterford but from the Fort Edward plant upriver. Active pollution has long since stopped. In fact, GE has long since moved most of its operations — and thousands of jobs — out of the region to cheaper labor markets. But the PCBs remain embedded in river bottom sediments, poisoning the base of the food chain and producing a rancorous public debate over what to do about it. GE's professionally orchestrated and expensively publicized position is of course that nothing should be done — that any effort to dredge the contaminated sediments will stir up the PCBs and make things worse. The opposing view is radical in the fullest sense — that General Electric should damn well root the poisonous stuff out of the river at whatever cost.

It drives me crazy. My parents — who live on the other side of Rensselaer county near the Vermont border and haven't even seen the Hudson in at least five years — have a sign on their front lawn proclaiming, "We oppose dredging." It's their kind of issue. They have always opposed the dredging up of anything unpleasant and have always condemned those who "stir up trouble." It drives me crazy that they see the environmentalists, not the corporation, as the troublemakers. Of course it's true the river is recovering in some ways, but only because troublemakers like Pete Seeger have fought for years to force a major reduction of the ongoing pollution.

As for me, although my parents think I'm a radical, I'm afraid I've been only marginally supportive of those radical efforts. And now here I was sneaking along the far shore in my high-tech Kevlar boat. Kevlar, I've been told, is hazardous to the health of the workers who make it.

But these things were not what I had come here to think about. I focused my gaze ahead on the water and paid attention to the clean force of the wind on my face and the movements of my back and shoulders. Gradually the GE plant and the unwelcome thoughts it roused slipped away behind and for a while I thought about little more than the way the boat moved. I tried to hold to a steady six strokes per side, but the wind was variable, twisting among the islands ahead of me, so my paddling couldn't be completely symmetrical. The physics of the situation was enough to fill my mind — until eventually I found myself thinking about Jonah.

Not about Jonah as a part of the current puzzle, but about the man I had begun to know during the time I was working with him.

I thought about the nearly night-long conversation that had begun in the NHA meeting room after a board meeting and had then moved eventually to my own kitchen table, where a bottle had taken us far beyond the practical questions we had started with, and finally into a hazy realm where it was still hard to remember the details. It was the only time I saw the anger in Jonah. Anger at the prejudice and exploitation around him, and at all the ways that prejudice and exploitation were rationalized and denied. Anger at the hard surface of the system that he so badly wanted to crack.

But even then it was a contained anger. He didn't rage against the system, and he was scornful of those who did. He talked about the need to be cool, by which he meant being patient and strategic, not trying to force things and not getting out ahead of your constituency. He was a student of community organizing, and a believer in the iron rule of organizing: never do for others what they can do for themselves.

It was from Jonah, not from Harry Cooper, that I first heard the NHA agenda described as "one house at a time, one family at a time." And that night, I now remembered, Jonah had criticized the whole idea of "projects" — meaning larger projects — in no uncertain terms.

I found myself no longer paddling. Jonah's rhetoric might have been heightened by the bourbon, but he did say, *projects never fix your problem or my problem; they're someone else's idea of how to fix what someone else has decided is the problem.*

So why had this man who was so scornful of projects thrown himself into the Sheridan Avenue redevelopment idea, which was a project in the fullest sense. Who had asked for it? The NHA board had not asked for it, let alone others in the Sheridan Hollow neighborhood. It was Jonah's project aimed at what Jonah saw as the problem — which was exactly what he had said was the wrong approach.

The memory brought into focus what had seemed so strange about Jonah's proposal from the time I first read it. It was not just the flamboyant, not-so-cool rhetoric. It was the whole idea of the project. What had made Jonah do this? There had to have been something besides the wild utopian idea of connecting Capitol Hill and Sheridan Hollow.

The boat had swung broadside to the wind and current and was drifting back downstream. I flipped the paddle to the downstream side and paddled hard to drive the boat forward into a long arc that headed it eventually back into the wind and current.

Jonah had to have had some motive that was as strong as it was hidden, just as Eddie McFadden did. Quite possibly it was the same thing that gave them both an unaccountable interest in Sheridan Avenue real estate. Maybe Eddie would at least give me a clue as to what it was.

I had reached the foot of the big island, coming up in the slack water below the downstream sandbar, then angling across the right-hand eddy line and pushing up along the east side of the island close to shore. The GE plant was out of sight in this sheltered place. There were robins busy along the bank. A thrush was singing somewhere in the center of the wooded island. Redwing blackbirds whistled from the cattails on the eastern edge of the channel. And I thought I heard, just barely, the sound of thunder off in the northwest.

I pushed all the way up around the east side of the cluster of islands with the thunder gradually growing louder. Above the islands I approached the dam in the slack water tight to the east shore, then spun out to the left, caught the fast water and rode it down across the rocky mid-river shallows, until I could catch the channel along the west side of the big island. When I felt the first raindrops on my back I pulled up on the island's gravel beach, slid the boat into the woods out of the wind, and put on my raingear. Then I sat on a log and watched the rain come sweeping in across the wide shallow stretch of river below the dam, rinsing and cooling the afternoon.

12

"Are we finally having that argument?" Lisa asked. She was sitting cross-legged on the floor, surrounded by the Sunday *Times* and wearing only the faded pink tee-shirt that she had pulled on when she got out of bed.

"Hard to argue with someone dressed like that," I said. I was sitting on the floor with my back against the sofa, wearing only a pair of jeans.

"You mean all I have to do is give you a glimpse of my ass?"

"I'm weak and easily distracted."

"That's a cop out. You're just afraid you'll lose. I'm ready to debate."

I got to my feet. "Let me get some more coffee then." I went into the kitchen, brought out the pot and filled our cups.

"So point number one," she said, "projects are not a bad thing. Projects are how you get things done."

From the kitchen, where I was returning the coffee pot, I said, "Projects are how you get *projects* done. Anyway Jonah's point wasn't that projects don't make something happen; his point was that projects are how people make things happen to other people who haven't asked for it. The way Nelson Rockefeller made the South Mall happen to a whole neighborhood. To the ten thousand people who were displaced."

"Oh come on. That's such an extreme bizarre example. How many Empire State Plazas are there anyway? It doesn't prove a thing, except maybe that Rockefeller was incredibly arrogant, which we already knew. But even that project doesn't deserve all the complaints it gets. I *like* the fact that Albany has a dramatic skyline. Where would this town be now if no one had decided to *do anything* with it? It had been slowly falling down for at least a hundred years, and something big and dramatic was needed to change that."

I sat back down on the floor against the sofa, extending my legs straight out past her hips. "I hate the Mall. But you're right, it's too extreme an example to say anything about our everyday projects. Let's talk about the Henry Johnson Boulevard project."

"Okay, let's. It's another one that gets a bad rap from you and your ilk."

"My *ilk*?"

She grinned. "Wishy-washy liberals."

"I'm not a wishy-washy liberal. Liberals love projects. I'm a tough-minded community development specialist — even if I'm no match for my tough-minded friend the real estate lady."

She stuck her tongue out at me.

"Whose bare-naked bottom is still very distracting."

"You're not going to sneak out of this argument. The Boulevard project — you guys complain about it because it's about redeveloping the Boulevard commercial strip instead of the neighborhoods on either side of it."

"No, because it's about improving the scenery for commuters headed *through* Arbor Hill on their way downtown, instead of improving conditions for the people who *live in* Arbor Hill."

"But it does improve conditions — or it can and will improve conditions — by creating more shopping opportunities and more jobs for Arbor Hill residents, which is exactly what's needed."

"If I thought it was really doing that I might agree with you.

Those things *are* needed. But you know what's really driving it is the concern with appearances. It's like Rockefeller being embarrassed by having visiting royalty see his run-down state capital."

"But it's *not* like the South Mall. It doesn't replace a neighborhood. It injects capital into one of the main arteries of a neighborhood."

"That's kind of a scary image, but maybe appropriate. An injection when what's really needed is steady nourishment for the neighborhoods on either side of the Boulevard. Instead of nourishing those neighborhoods, the project is sucking resources out of them."

"What do you mean? What resources is it sucking out?"

"Public funds. CDBG money and other subsidies that the city is pouring into the Boulevard project and that should be going into real neighborhood improvement and affordable housing efforts in the neighborhoods themselves."

"Oh, so you're *not* saying projects are bad. You're just saying they're being done in the wrong place." She was enjoying herself. Still cross-legged on the floor she rocked her upper body forward and back excitedly, nipples nudging the pink tee-shirt.

I pressed the calf of my extended leg against her hip, feeling her warmth and connecting with her energy. "I'm saying public money is being used the wrong *way*. I would like to see more public resources going into the kind of work the NHA is doing. The patient, gradual work, one house at a time, one family at a time, as they say. I think the big projects, the big injections of money that are supposed to bring about a quick cure, a sudden change...they almost never work the way they're supposed to, almost never help who they're supposed to help."

"But sometimes any change is better than no change, better than just letting the gradual decay continue. I think the public subsidies you scatter in the neighborhoods one house at a time have absolutely no lasting effect on those neighborhoods. It's never enough, so the money's simply absorbed in the general decay. It's like throwing dust. No impact. Investment has to be concentrated or it can't make anything happen. It's wasted."

"It can be wasted. It often is wasted. But it's not wasted if it's put in the hands of people who are trying to improve their own lives, their own homes, their own neighborhoods, and who can't do it without some resources. I can't believe the Boulevard project is a better use of public money than making that money available to self-motivated groups in the neighborhoods. Even if some of the money that goes to those groups *is* wasted, in the sense that it doesn't make anything tangible happen. Because you're not really just funding a product; you're funding experimentation, trial and error, learning experiences. You're funding hope. It's messy and even wasteful — the way it's wasteful to build rich soil as opposed to just injecting concentrated chemicals into your crop rows — but it's what's needed if communities are going to develop in a positive sense. We need to renew the soil in those neighborhoods so individual initiatives will be nourished wherever the seeds happen to fall. So we need to be patient. People have to be able to try things and learn, and they need to have access to capital in order to do that."

She grasped my calf and pulled it tighter against her hip. "How you talk," she said. "I like how you talk — even if I don't agree and even if I don't understand the farmer stuff about soil and seeds." She paused and lowered her voice. "But actually I do agree with a lot of what you're saying. I just don't want to give up on big projects. I want people to be able to try big things as well as little gradual things. Even Jonah's big project, which was a lot more than one house at a time...It's crazy but exciting and I think we need that. The excitement."

"I don't know," I said, "Jonah's *proposal* is exciting. Because of the extraordinary way it spotlights a problem people would rather pretend doesn't exist. But that's not the same as saying his proposed project has any chance of fixing the problem, and I think Jonah knew that."

"So why..."

"Why did he re-direct his one-house-at-a-time organization to a crazy thing like that? Did he just run out of patience and let his anger and frustration overwhelm his better judgment — or was there something else?"

"Something else like what?" she said. "From what you've said it sounds like the project was aimed more at the state than at the neighborhood, so, if the something-else was political, then I have to agree it's not a very practical way to lobby the state. I mean he had to have known that the proposal would get lost at DHCR. Even if someone didn't literally lose the thing itself the way you heard, they would have found some way to bury it so he wouldn't get any politically useful PR out of it."

"Right. He was not naïve. He knew how things work. And he was coming off the Clinton Avenue project, which he said had taught him a lesson. Which was to beware larger projects and go back to doing smaller buildings one at a time. And yet he turned right around and bought those two properties that could only work as part of a big project."

Lisa lifted her coffee cup and sipped, then shook her head and shrugged. "Truly strange," she said.

"And not long before that, Eddie McFadden bought three buildings just down the street that made no more sense for him than the others did for Jonah."

She lowered her cup to the floor and stared at me. "You don't think it's a coincidence." It was an observation, not a question. "I mean I wondered if there was a connection, but it seemed kind of far-fetched. But you're suggesting it's not."

"I'm convinced it's not a coincidence," I said. "It's taken me a while to take it seriously, because the whole thing does seem so far-fetched, but the *most* far-fetched, hard-to-believe scenario would be one where there is no connection whatsoever between two people each buying seemingly worthless properties for seemingly no good reason on the same block in the same year and then haggling around an effort by one of them to buy purchase options from the other. They had to have *both* known something we don't know."

"But it would make a lot more sense if Jonah was just another opportunist like Eddie, and they were both just trying to cash in on some piece of inside information they both had. I mean Eddie McFadden, yes, should he be so lucky as to have that kind of information, but Jonah Lee — the Jonah Lee you've been telling me about — no. And it's still a problem that neither one of them was what I would call an insider. If they knew something, how did they know it and why didn't other people know it. No one else has been buying up property in Sheridan Hollow that I've been able to find out."

"Unless, as you said before, Eddie was buying *for* someone else."

"Which is what I told you I would snoop into," she said. "Or at least keep my ears open. Well I have kept my ears open and I've tried to steer a couple of conversations with some knowledgeable people around what kinds of deals might be happening north of downtown. But so far I haven't picked up a thing."

"Yesterday afternoon," I said, "sitting on the island in the rain, I tried to think through some possibilities that I could put to the test with Eddie — that I could somehow suggest and see how he reacts to them. I didn't get too far, but one piece of an idea that just feels like it fits is that Eddie was buying for someone else, or buying to sell to someone else, and that Jonah found out about it and wanted to *block* whatever the someone else was up to. Whatever use that person had in mind for that property, Jonah must have hated it so much that he went after it to stop it, to replace it with his own kind of use. It makes a lot more sense that Jonah's proposal would come out of something like that than that he would just out-of-the-blue decide to do the kind of project he proposed."

"So we need to think about what possible use someone else might have had in mind for that location that Jonah would have hated."

"Right. What possible uses are there for Sheridan Hollow property?"

"Well, besides low-cost residential," she said, "it's pretty much just the mix of low-end uses you see there now. None of them a big deal. Nothing expanding."

"Suppose you're not a Sheridan Hollow type of person at all. Suppose you're a Capitol Hill type of person and you're looking for space close to Capitol Hill. What would it be for — space for what?"

"I don't know," she said. "Parking I guess. That's all the Capitol Hill types have ever done in Sheridan Hollow — park and walk up the stairs."

"Which is really a pretty significant use. Parking space for those folks is not cheap."

"I suppose. You've already got the little lot at the foot of the stairs on the east. I suppose you could develop another little lot up the block to the west, where those properties are, by the Gander Bay, but it wouldn't be a *b i g* lot, and the bar is right in the middle of it, and if you ask me, grubby as it is, the bar is already the highest and best use for the land it sits on. Anyway, how many people really want to park down there? I'm telling you, people are scared of the place and scared of those stairs."

"There's also the larger state lot at the top of the slope, right up above those properties."

"Sure, all the way up. Right there on Elk. In a different world."

"And in between is the slope that Jonah wanted to convert from a barrier between the two worlds to something that joined them, something natural, green-growing, healing, uniting."

"That environmental piece of Jonah's grand design that you can't help liking."

"Which was maybe Jonah's answer — his alternative — to someone else's *different* design for that land."

"What? For the *hillside*? You think this is about the *hillside*?"

"I don't know. The top of the hill, I think."

She laughed. "I've got it. There was even something just like it in Vermont a couple of years ago — where these environmentalists were fighting to keep this mountainside from being turned into a ski area. And now someone has a secret plan to develop a ski area in the middle of Albany. I love it."

I laughed with her. "Maybe so. With a lift going up the slope from right beside the Gander Bay. The old clientele might be a little upset — their bar filling up with yuppie skiers. But seriously, I still don't know what the answer is but I'm beginning to think I should turn around and look at the top of the hill, not just at the bottom."

She looked at me thoughtfully. "That does make it quite a lot more interesting," she said.

13

I drove west on Clinton to Central Avenue and then on out Central until I'd crossed the I-90 corridor and could make my way north into West Albany. I found Eddie McFadden's house, a smallish older ranch in only slightly better condition than some of the houses Eddie bought and sold in the city. It was a few minutes after five when I pushed the front door bell.

I heard nothing, neither a bell nor the sound of footsteps. I knocked hard on the door and waited, and still heard nothing. The smell of barbecue wafted from somewhere behind the house. I was about to walk around the building to check the back yard when the door was opened by a stocky, dark-haired young woman, wearing a tank top, stained khaki shorts, and no shoes.

"Hello there, are you Crow?" she asked in a startlingly loud voice.

I recognized her as someone who had been pointed out to me as working for McFadden, going door to door in the neighborhoods looking for homeowners who might be hard-up enough for cash to consider selling their homes for bargain prices. I had wondered just how those conversations would go. How did you lead up to asking people you had just met if they wanted to sell you their home? But there seemed to be nothing subtle about this person. Maybe there was no lead-up. Maybe it was just "Hello, want to sell your house?"

"Yes, I'm Warren Crow," I said. "Sorry if I'm a little late."

"Linda Bettleman," she said, extending her hand abruptly. "He's out back."

She shook my hand solemnly; then led the way back through the house and out the kitchen door. McFadden was sitting in an old lawn chair beside a meat-laden charcoal grill. It looked like enough meat for half a dozen people, though there was no one else there. Like his companion, he was dressed in tank top and old khaki shorts, a small man with bony knees, narrow bony shoulders, and a mostly bald head. He drank from a can of Budweiser as he watched me approach. Lowering the can, he said, "You're wasting your time, Crow."

"If I am it's okay. How are you Eddie?"

McFadden burped. His friend Linda moved to the cooler that sat on the ground beside the grill and opened it. For a moment I thought she was going to offer me a beer, but she took only one can from the cooler, opened it and carried it back toward the house. I laughed. In a way they were making it easy for me.

McFadden said, "We don't have anything to talk about. What's the point?"

"I think we do," I said, "but I understand what you're saying. I guess your, uh, client wants the properties after all, and I guess you feel some obligation there, but that's not my problem. I'm not talking about that, and I'm not talking about extending the options." I sat down in a lawn chair to one side of McFadden. "I want to talk about exercising the NHA options as they stand."

McFadden's head turned sharply and he stared belligerently, but he had not quite been able to keep surprise — and I thought a flicker of fear — from showing on his face. "What the fuck you talking about?"

"The obvious. The NHA is interested in exercising the options, buying your properties. They've already got the Duber properties. It doesn't make sense for them to stop halfway. Makes sense for them to follow through. I'm here to talk about how we're going to close."

"No way."

"Why not?"

"Just can't be done."

So I thought I had cleared one hurdle. Though he was claiming the options couldn't be exercised, he was not saying they didn't exist and he was not saying they had expired. "Of course it can be done," I said. "You own the properties. You sold a purchase option to the NHA, which they want to exercise. Seems pretty straightforward. Maybe you have reason to regret selling those options. I'm sorry if you have regrets, but you did take payment for them."

"Look," McFadden said. "It was a kind of side deal between me and Jonah, and now Jonah's dead so the deal's dead, all right?"

"Jonah represented an organization that is not dead. You sold the options to the NHA, not to Jonah."

"Whatever. But they weren't recorded, and it's not like you're going to be pulling them out of your pocket."

I didn't know how to take this statement. Was he bluffing? Or did he know for a fact that the NHA did not possess signed originals — maybe because he knew for a fact that the originals had been stolen from the NHA office? And if that was the case, could he possibly know whether the originals had been photocopied? I said, "No, I'm not going to pull them out here and now, but even if I didn't have the paper, I could demonstrate that you took payment for purchase options. You'd better be prepared either to honor those options or be sued for knowingly taking money for what you did not intend to deliver, which is fraud." I hoped that, even if he knew I didn't have copies of the option agreements, he wouldn't know what the NHA financial records would show.

McFadden got up and, with a long fork, began turning over meat on the grill. There were a number of pieces of chicken as well as a rack of ribs and some sausages. After turning over each piece with the fork, he picked up a jar of barbecue sauce and a long-handled brush and began brushing sauce on the pieces. He did it deliberately, taking his time, with his back to me. Finally he said, "I wish you'd just get the hell off my back, Crow."

"Eddie, if you had a signed purchase and sale contract from someone who changed their mind and decided they didn't want to sell you their house after all so they said to you 'Just get the hell off my back, McFadden...' I guess you would just apologize and walk away, right?"

"Fuck you," he said. He was still brushing sauce onto the meat, as carefully as if he were brushing paint into every corner and crevice of some intricate piece of woodwork.

"You're going to have to deal with this, Eddie."

"Fuck you."

Eddie's fuck-you strategy was going to deny me any further information — which left me still with very little to work with. I still didn't know when the options expired, or what purchase price they specified for the properties, or anything else about the terms of what McFadden had signed, or what had happened to the signed document. But I had seen the flicker of fear on Eddie's face and I wanted to keep that fear alive. I took a deep breath and said, "Listen carefully. I want you to think about what I'm going to say because it's something you won't be able to avoid. There is something very nasty going on, which you are aware of. There are some things I know and some things I am going to find out, because what is going on got a good man killed, and I am not going to just forget about it and go away. I am not going to leave you alone. I am going to stay tight to your ass until we get some things worked out."

McFadden spun toward me and screamed "You stupid son-of-a-bitch." He raised the barbecue brush and for a moment I thought he was going to attack me with it, but instead he hurled the brush against the back of his house, where it left an angry fire-red streak on the peeling paint.

"I'll be back tomorrow," I said as I left.

Driving home I reviewed the odd little scene in as much detail as I could remember, hoping I could recover some bit of information I'd failed to recognize at the time. But I could glean nothing further. The only important information was that the usually cold-blooded, thick-skinned McFadden had completely blown his cool. Whatever the exact circumstances of Eddie's situation, he clearly felt trapped by them. And he was frightened. The question was how to keep the pressure on and take advantage of this fear to find out what was behind it. And not make a mess of things in the process.

I parked the pickup on the street in front of my house, but didn't go in. I needed to think. I needed to walk. Without a destination in mind, I walked down Orange Street, crossing Lexington, then Henry Johnson. At Lark I turned right. Then after another block I turned left on Sheridan Avenue and headed on down into Sheridan Hollow.

I was thinking it was time to focus on this thing and push harder. I'd been trying to keep it in its place, along with all the other things. The various pieces of paying work as well as the work for NHA. Plans for the upcoming canoe trip that claimed my thoughts along the edges of all the work. And of course Lisa. But the questions around the Sheridan Avenue project and Jonah's death kept looming larger and larger. I was going to have to do more than just gather information as opportunities offered themselves. I had pushed Eddie McFadden and had learned some things. I needed to keep pushing.

I could see the Gander Bay sign ahead of me and decided I had a destination after all.

A half dozen people sat at the bar, most with heads tilted back watching a baseball game on the television mounted above the bottles. The skinny blond was again behind the bar. I ordered a pint of Killian's, and when she put it in front of me I said, "Tell me — where would I find Buddy Rowley or Janet Rowley?"

"Don't know why you'd want to find the old lady." She jerked her thumb in the direction of the booths in the shadowed rear of the room. "Buddy's there. Like always."

I carried my pint toward the booths, only one of which was occupied. The person I assumed was Buddy Rowley — the son of Janet and "manager" of the Gander Bay — was a pudgy-faced man with a large beard and an equally large belly. He was hunched in the corner of the booth in a position that brought beard and belly into contact. The blond woman across from him looked as though she might be the older sister of the bartender — and probably used the same hair color product.

"You must be Buddy," I said. "I'm Warren Crow. If you have a minute there's something I'd like to talk about."

Buddy peered at me with small eyes set deep behind the pudgy cheeks; then looked at the woman and moved a thumb slightly toward the outside of the booth. She made a face, picked up her beer and slid out of the booth. I sat down.

"What can I do for you?" Buddy asked. He didn't sound as though he much cared.

"It's a real estate matter," I said.

"Not my line of work. I run a bar."

"Yes, but I understand there's been someone — or more than one someone — interested in buying your bar. Buying this property and the lot here beside it."

"Don't know where you heard that."

"I'm doing some work for the organization Jonah Lee was with. I know Jonah was interested in this property and I know he wasn't the only one. Same as with Eddie McFadden's properties over here."

Rowley frowned and said in a half-whisper, "Not so loud. You must be the guy they said was in here the other day. Got some of the guys worked up. They don't like the idea of being evicted."

"They're not exactly tenants," I said.

"Might as well be. And I got no interest in being the one to tell them they're out of here."

I sipped my beer and thought about what I had just heard. "So maybe one day they just find the bar isn't open any more."

"Maybe."

"And how about you — make you sad if the bar is sold? It seems like you've been doing all right here, without having to work too hard at it."

"Yeah, right. You think there's no sweat running a place like this? You think there's someone else I can trust to keep an eye on things seven days a week, count the cash every night down below at closing, with a gun on the table, lock up the money, get it to the bank next day?"

"So raking in the dough is pretty heavy work?"

"It ain't *safe* work. You got to watch yourself all the time. You seen what happened to Jonah Lee." Buddy reached to his left side, beside the big beard, and lifted the edge of the leather vest that he wore unbuttoned. Beneath the vest was an automatic in a shoulder holster. "I don't keep it a secret," he said. "They know it's here. Just like they know the money's here."

"I can see how it might not be a restful occupation," I said. "I guess I don't blame you for wanting to sell. I'm surprised you haven't done the deal already."

"Don't I wish. But the place is in the old lady's name and by God she was going to squeeze the last penny out of it. But the greedy old battle-ax missed her chance."

"Maybe not. There's still some interest in the property."

"Sure, but as soon as Jonah got killed it was just Brison's offer, which he right away lowered, and now he's just waiting us out. And Ma thinks she can wait *him* out. So here's old Buddy still sitting in the back of the bar seven days a week."

"You do have a problem." I wanted to sound sympathetic. I wanted to keep Buddy talking. In particular I wanted him to repeat the name. Was it Brison? Briston? "So which of them had the better offer on the table?" I asked. "When Jonah was killed."

"Brison's was the one she should've taken. The money was right there. Penny-pinching bastard could've paid ten times as much. Jonah said he'd beat Brison's best offer, but where was he going to get the money?"

"He'd put in an application to the state. If it was funded there'd be quite a lot to work with."

"Like how much?" Buddy asked.

"How much would he have needed?"

Buddy shrugged. "Not for you to know, not public information. Anyway it don't matter. Jonah got himself blown away."

"But the organization is still here and functioning and they're still interested, and the application to the state could still be funded. This isn't public information either, but it's why I'm here."

Buddy lifted his beer glass to his lips and his little eyes peered at me over the rim. "You ain't shitting me?"

"No, I'm not. Maybe you and I should have a talk with your mother. Maybe I could help move things along the way you want them to move."

"She don't listen to me," Buddy said. "But if you want to talk to her...It don't hurt for her to hear from someone else who wants to buy this dump. You know where she's at?"

"Hadn't checked yet. I came here first."

He reached into an inside vest pocket, on the side opposite the gun, and pulled out a pack of business cards held together with a rubber band. He extracted a card from the top of the pack and another card from the bottom. With a funny little smile he laid both cards on the table as though laying down a winning poker hand.

I picked them up. One card was headed *The Gander Bay Bar*, with a miniature version of the picture of the attacking gander that appeared on the sign out on the street. The address was printed under the picture: 1100 Sheridan Avenue. There was no phone number. At the bottom of the card was printed, *Janet Rowley, Proprietor*. The other card was headed *Exotic Birds*, and pictured two parrots facing each other on either side of the heading. There was a Sherman Street address and a phone number, and at the bottom again, *Janet Rowley, Proprietor*.

"She's got a thing about birds," Buddy said. "You won't get very far with her unless you can show her a bundle."

I decided he was talking about a bundle of money, not a bundle of birds. "Or maybe give her some leverage with Brison," I suggested.

"Maybe. Wish you luck."

"I guess you know why Brison wants the place?"

Buddy's eyes flicked away from my face. "None of my business." He raised his glass, in which only a half inch of beer remained. "Hey Margie..." He waited, staring over my head toward the bar. "Aileen, where'd Margie go?"

"Out," came the blond bartender's voice. "Went home."

"Then get your own ass back here. I need another."

I sipped at my still almost full glass and waited until Aileen brought Buddy's beer. She set it down hard on the table and clacked back toward the bar on stiletto heels.

"One more thing I wanted to ask you, Buddy," I said. "This Ronald Burns they call Loosh, who either was or wasn't here the evening Jonah was killed..."

"They got him locked up."

"Yes. And I guess they asked you whether he was here the evening Jonah was killed. During the time when it happened."

"Me and everybody else."

"I'm interested in your version. Like you said, you keep an eye on things in this place."

"He was here. Running his mouth like he always does."

"But I guess it would be hard for you to say he didn't ever go out and come back at some point."

"I would've noticed. He goes out, it gets quieter in here. Anyway he was here till closing and — like I told the cops — I don't see that asshole just running up to Second Street to pull off a robbery and shoot somebody and coming right back before someone noticed."

"It does sound unlikely."

"Not that I give a shit what they do with him. It's real restful not having him around all the time."

I wondered what Buddy knew about how Ronald Burns made a living, but didn't want to suggest that he did whatever it was on the premises of the Gander Bay. "As far as you know," I said, "the guy's always able to pay his tab without running off to rob someone every so often?"

"No one runs a tab in here," Buddy said. "Does Loosh come in with money in his pocket? Yeah, he does. All I know."

"One more question. Maybe this is out of left field, but have you wondered what Jonah's death might have to do with what was going on here — all the interest in these properties?"

"If I did, I sure as hell wouldn't be blabbing about it to someone I never met before."

14

"Brison," Lisa said. "Not anyone I know around here. It's someone's last name, not a first name?"

"It seemed that way but I can't say for sure," I said. I had come here directly from the Gander Bay, hoping the name would mean something in the real estate world.

"But you know it's a person, not Brison, Inc.?" She dumped ice into a martini shaker, covered it and, turning away from the kitchen counter, shook it vigorously, one small palm under the base of the container, two fingers of the other hand holding the top on, and the movement so rapid it sounded like a high-speed machine suddenly switched on.

"I don't even know that for sure. Is there a Brison, Inc.?"

"I don't know. But it sounds like it could be the name of a corporation. Or someone's last name. Or first name."

"I was hearing it as the last name of a male person. I don't think Buddy ever said *he* or *him*. But it didn't sound like he would be on a first name basis with this person. It sounded like he didn't like him, or was scared of him."

"So you assume it's a big scary man?"

"I admit it could be a small scary woman. I know one of those."

"And I know a big dumb man." She filled two martini glasses from the shaker. "Come on, let's go sit."

We went into the living room and sat by the windows, looking out over rooftops and the river beyond the roofs to the Rensselaer horizon.

"Brison, Brison, Brison," she said. "Doesn't ring a bell. Not someone around here. But there's a little echo — it's *almost* familiar."

"It could be more like *Bresson* or even *Breston*. It was hard to tell with Buddy. He was kind of spitting the name out like he hated the taste of it."

She opened her eyes wide. "Oh. More than an echo. Oh my." She stood up.

"Who? What?"

"A who and a what. There's a developer down in the mid-Hudson valley — I think based in Poughkeepsie. His name is Thomas Breston. His business is called the Breston Company. I don't think he's ever done anything up here, but he's done malls and stuff, I think, down there. Big stuff. He has a reputation for playing hardball."

"Playing hardball with who?"

"You know, malls get to be big local issues. Not everyone wants one in their backyard, or all the traffic going by their front door. There can be real battles."

"But a developer wants to avoid the battles. Wants his deal

sewed up before the opposition can organize to make a public issue of it. Which might mean playing hardball with a few key players up front, to get there as fast as possible. Is that the kind of thing you mean?"

"I don't know any of the specifics of what this guy has done. But I can find out. That's the kind of thing I *can* do, once I know who or what I'm aiming at. The Breston Company is not a small target. I'll work on it."

"If this guy is really the other player in this thing, it would sure help to know something about who he is and how he works. And if he has any connections up here in Albany."

Putting her drink down, she sat on the arm of my chair, where she became very still, staring out the window.

"You're working on it already," I said.

"Actually, I was wondering if you're going to spend the night. We hadn't planned on it."

"Do you want me to?"

"I would hate it if you left right now."

"Then I won't."

* * *

In the morning she was up ahead of me. By the time I had showered she was at the kitchen table, fully dressed, with telephone and calendar in front of her, muttering to herself as she rearranged her day's schedule. I poured myself a cup of coffee and sat across from her.

"I'm trying to set up a dinner date with someone," she said. "It'll probably mean spending the whole evening with them."

"Them?"

"Him."

"One of your admirers?"

"I hope at least a little bit. At least that's what I'm counting on." She looked at her watch. "I have to get to the office. Can you come tonight — spend the night — even though I might be late getting home?"

"Do you really want that? It sounds a little awkward." I didn't say that I was feeling crowded by her schedule, but I was.

"I really want that," she said. "And maybe I'll have some information about Breston."

"Then I'll be here. Whether you have a Breston report or not."

When she had left, I used her phone to dial Eddie McFadden's number. As I had hoped, I reached Eddie's machine, but the recorded message was not in the flat McFadden voice I had expected. It was the surprisingly loud voice of Linda Bettleman that said, "You've reached the McFadden home and the home of McFadden Homes. We're not here. Leave us a message."

I had decided to wait a few days before visiting Eddie again, but I didn't want him to think I was backing off. I wanted to keep the pressure on. After the beep, I said, "Eddie. Crow here. Wanted to let you know NHA should be able to close later this week. I'm wrapping up the financing. Be in touch soon." The phone at the other end was picked up. I hung up.

Next I called Harry Cooper at home. Harry answered, with the usual children's voices in the background. "Sorry to bother you at this hour," I said, "but I wanted to check with you about a couple of things — the board meeting for one."

"Yeah," Harry said, "the board meeting. Wednesday. I wanted to talk with you about that too. Can you come? I'll have to check on the exact time and let you know, but does Wednesday evening work?"

"It works and I'll be glad to come if you want me there. I can also try to put together a financial report — at least give some sort of overview to help people think about what needs to be done. Unless your treasurer is going to do that. But as I remember Jonah used to report on the finances himself." I knew that, as was often the case with community-based housing organizations, the volunteer treasurer didn't really understand the finances of what was after all a rather complicated little real estate business.

"That's the trouble," Harry said. "Jonah did everything himself. We can use all the help you can give us. With Jonah gone we need to hire someone, and we don't really even know how much money we've got to hire someone *with*."

"I don't think you're in bad shape. But you may be right that cash is going to be pretty tight. I'll do a cash flow projection, as best I can with what I know."

"Got to do something. Bock Calloway called from the city. He's saying with Jonah gone he doesn't see how we can fulfill our contract for the money they give us each month. Says maybe they'll have to hold up the payments. I said if they don't give us the money how are we going to hire someone to get the job done. He says, well, they're going to have to look at it."

"Bullshit," I said. "Don't worry about it. We'll get the money if we have to..." I stopped, wishing I'd said *you'll* get the money.

"I hope you're right," Harry said.

"Look," I said, "the other thing I wanted to tell you...those buildings on Sheridan that Jonah got from Duber...I'm still trying to find out what was going on, but *something* was going on, and still is going on. Someone else is trying to buy up property in that neighborhood, and sooner or later you're going to hear from them."

"Good. A buyer? Who is it? I'll call *him*."

"That's the big question. Someone who's been working through other people. I don't think you'll hear from the guy himself. But if anyone asks about those properties, call me before you do anything else."

Harry was silent.

"I could be completely wrong," I said, "but I'm coming to think whatever is going on around those properties is what got Jonah killed."

"Then if I hear anything I'll call you right away," Harry said.

* * *

There was still dew on the windshields of the cars parked on the shady side of Ten Broeck in front of Lisa's house. I angled across Ten Broeck to the corner and crossed Clinton Avenue in warm sunshine, dodging the morning traffic. A block and a half up Clinton I turned left on Swan and walked downhill into the Hollow, back into cool morning air but with the upper half of the long stair in front of me lit by the bright morning sun. At the corner of Orange Street I turned right and made my way up the length of Orange with the sun again on my back.

By the time I passed my own house behind the Salvation Army, I was thoroughly warmed up. It was going to be a hot day after all. At the end of the street I turned left on Robin, then in two blocks turned back to the right on Sherman and continued west. Janet Rowley's house was in the last block on Sherman, just before the street ended behind the Central Avenue McDonald's.

Like a lot of houses in the neighborhood, it was originally a very small under-built wood frame house, but a succession of working class occupants had added a series of rooms, porches, and porches-converted-to-rooms, straggling back through the narrow lot. At the front of the house, what had once been the main entrance was all but lost behind an undisciplined lilac hedge. The blossoms were gone, but there was still a lingering scent of decaying lilac bloom. A cracked concrete walkway ran back through the alley tight to the side of the house. Turning down the walk, I was suddenly aware of a racket of bird sounds.

The walk ended at a doorway into one of the rear additions. Hanging over the door was a two-foot weathered plywood cut-out of a parrot, most of its painted plumage having flaked away over what must have been many years. Beyond the door the bird sounds intensified in a clamor of shrieking and squawking like a burst of raucous almost human laughter. I knocked but could barely hear the sound above the shrieking. I then pounded with my fist, and the clamor abruptly ended.

In the silence, a voice from within said, "Wait a minute." I waited, and eventually, from just behind the door, the voice — a surprisingly quiet woman's voice — asked, "Who is it?"

"My name is Warren Crow. I..."

"Oh, yeah," she said. "Well come in quick when I open the door. Birds are loose."

The door opened just wide enough for me to slip into a warm, dimly lit room. The smell reminded me of the hen house I had to clean periodically as a boy — the smell of feathers and bird shit. Beside me, almost under my elbow, the door was closed by a short stout woman with graying shoulder-length hair. "Have a seat if you want," she said.

Around the walls of the room were tiers of bird cages, large and small, some containing birds, some empty with their doors open. In the middle of the room there was an old enamel-topped kitchen table with three chairs around it. Perched on the back of each chair was a large parrot. I didn't particularly want to sit down with the beak of a large bird poised at the back of my neck. But one of the birds now sidled to the edge of its perch, hopped to the table, peered back at me and said, "Aye sweetheart. Ave a seat."

The woman moved to the table and offered her arm to the bird, which stepped onto it. As far as I could tell, the vacated chair was free of bird lime, so I sat. She sat across the table from me, stroking the bird's neck and back.

"I'm here to talk with Janet Rowley," I said. "I assume that's you."

She shrugged, her eyes on the parrot. "Last time I checked."

"I talked with your son Buddy."

"That's not my problem."

"We talked about the offers you've had to sell the Gander Bay property."

"You should have talked to me."

"That's why I'm here. To see if you're still open to other offers, or if you've signed something with Breston."

"I don't think you know what you're talking about."

However wacky, she seemed to be playing a hand held very tight to her chest.

"There are some things I don't know," I said. "For instance, I don't really know if you know why I'm here and who I'm representing — although you sounded just now like you were expecting me. Maybe you heard from Buddy. Or maybe you heard from McFadden, or maybe Duber..." I paused, trying to remember the name that was out there on the margin. "Or maybe Ms. Green. Or I suppose Breston might have told you."

Her brow twitched, as though she might be surprised or puzzled by one of the names. Then she said flatly, "I talk with everyone."

"Including Breston. It looks like we're all talking to each other. So..." I could see nothing else to do but to play what I thought was the one middling-strong card I held. "As you know, Eddie McFadden optioned his properties, even if it wasn't what he was supposed to do, to the Neighborhood Housing Association — which I represent and which intends to exercise its option. Which will mean Breston's project will be blocked. In which case he'll have no reason to buy the Gander Bay Bar. The only possible buyer for the bar will then be the NHA, which will be prepared to go ahead with its project if you will accept a reasonable market price for your property."

Her eyes flicked up to meet mine for the first time — blue-green eyes, intense, focused and comprehending. "No," she said. "The project isn't dead. Eddie's dead. And you're an idiot." She shifted her arm on the table, repositioning the parrot, which turned its head and fixed me with one bright eye.

"Why am I an idiot?" I asked, knowing I wouldn't get any sort of useful response. She was in control.

"You don't know what you're doing," she said.

"I don't think you do either. But we'll see." I had no idea what she knew or what her plan was, or whether she had a plan. For all I knew she might be as desperate to sell as Buddy, or as frightened as Eddie. For all I knew she was insane. I gazed at the birds perched inside and on top of the cages along the wall in front of me — parrots, parakeets, cockatiels, others I didn't recognize. "This is quite an aviary," I said. "How many birds do you have?"

"A hundred and thirteen."

"You buy and sell? And raise some yourself?"

"You didn't come here to ask about birds."

"You're right," I said, standing up. "Thanks for your time. This has been useful. I'll be in touch."

Once outside I crossed Sherman Street, walked across the parking lot and went into McDonald's, where I bought a small coffee and sat down with it in the near-empty mid-morning quiet of the place. The only other people present were a disheveled homeless man who hadn't been kicked out yet and several other more socially acceptable senior citizens. I felt as though I had just half-awakened from a strange dream and needed to retrace its outlines before it faded away.

I had made a point of not calling ahead to arrange to see Janet Rowley. I had wanted to get an unrehearsed response to what I would tell her — especially what I would say about Eddie McFadden and Breston. But she had seemed completely unfazed by my arrival and by what I had said. Probably Buddy had told her to expect me — or maybe she was always that way. Was she shrewd, or crazy, or both?

And what had she meant by *Eddie's dead*? What did she know about Eddie? Did she know anything?

I put the top back on my half-full cup of coffee, carried it outside, and started home by way of Central Avenue. I wanted to go after the questions. I wanted to go talk to the other people on my list. But I also needed to finish some of the work I'd promised to others. I really had to spend the rest of the day at my desk.

15

It was a new experience to be lying in Lisa's bed on the edge of sleep with no Lisa present. It was past midnight and she still wasn't home.

I was tired. After more than eight hours of staring at a computer screen I had locked up my house and walked to Lisa's, picking up some West Indian takeout and then a bottle of Jack Daniel's on my way. When I had eaten, I turned off the lights in Lisa's living room and sat by the windows, sipping bourbon and resting my eyes on the eastward nightscape beyond the shadowed rooftops. By eleven-thirty my eyelids were heavy, and, thinking she would have to be home soon, I'd gone to bed and tried to read the *Times Union*. But it was hard to focus on newsprint.

Now I wanted to give up and just let sleep flow around me. At the same time I was impatient to see her and eager to hear what she had learned. And in the back of my mind a shadowy worry had begun to gather, and behind that, I have to admit, was a shadow of jealousy. She had said she would be spending the "whole evening" with someone who she admitted was an "admirer." But I hadn't expected the "whole evening" to run past midnight.

Not that I had a right to be jealous, or even to worry. I was not Lisa's keeper, and didn't want to be. Her independence was a part of what I liked about her and about our relationship. On the nights when I slept at home, I didn't even think about what she was doing, where she was, who she was with. But here in her bed, where every turn of my own body stirred the fragrance of her absent body, it was impossible not to think of those things.

I had started to wonder whether there was a way I could find out who she was with, make a phone call, see if she was at least safe — and whether she would ever speak to me again if I did — when I heard her key in the lock.

When the outer door had opened and closed, I said, "Hey. You want a night cap or something? I'll get up."

"Stay where you are. I'll be right there."

I heard her go into the bathroom; then heard the shower running. It seemed to me it was late to be bothering with a shower, but I supposed it gave her a way to make the transition from one setting to another, one kind of company to another. I resisted the idea that it might be something more specific, that it might have to do with the transition from one bed to another. My need for sleep was completely gone. Waiting for her was strange and exciting. But not altogether comfortable.

The bathroom door opened and for a moment her naked body — small, trim and in my eyes perfect — was illuminated in the doorway before she turned out the bathroom light and the sound of her footsteps came toward me in the dark.

"I hope you had a pleasant and informative evening," I said.

Slipping under the covers, she said, "Later," and touched a fingertip to my lips. Then the finger was replaced by her insistent moist mouth as her body crowded toward me.

She was intensely aroused, and for a moment the question lingered: who had excited her this way — me or someone else — or the combination? Then I was too busy to think about it.

* * *

"I didn't exactly strike it rich," she said. "But I did find a certain vein of information." We were at the kitchen table, drinking coffee, she in a bathrobe, me in jeans, without shirt or shoes.

"Okay, I think I'm awake — ready to hear the details. Beginning — if it's not a secret — with *who*. Who's this vein of information?"

She wrinkled her nose. "Not a secret. I certainly intended to tell you. It is part of the story. Dick Frost."

"Richard Frost, the one-time developer?"

"Him. Dick Frost who not only made a ton of money on a couple of projects but was smart enough not to keep putting his profits into bigger and bigger projects until one crashed on him."

I had barely met the man, but I knew some of the stories about Frost's business successes. I also knew that, in addition to being quite wealthy, Frost was handsome, charming and recently divorced. "So...Frost knows Breston. Does that mean he's done business with him?"

"As a matter of fact he has — that is...in the way he *does* business now."

"Which is...?"

"Well, you know the kind of thing. He handles some commercial properties as a broker, just to stay connected he says, but what he really seriously does is he invests. And he's well enough capitalized now so he can put money into a property and afford to let it sit as long as necessary...until some developer will pay his price for it and take the risk of developing it. And sometimes he'll finance the deal for them, take back a mortgage on the land, so if the project fails he can take back the land itself. And sit on it again until the next guy comes along...because it's always land that you know is *going* to be developed, sooner or later, one way or another, and he can afford to wait and doesn't have to take any big risks at all."

"He did that kind of thing with Breston?"

"Exactly that kind of thing. Sold Breston a very expensive piece of land for a mall development in Dutchess County. Sold it to him and held the paper on it. Breston had been riding high and thought he had a sure-fire project and no one could stop him. A local group had tried to stop his last project, but he'd beaten them down and he was primed to do the same thing this time. But this time the local group was more sophisticated, and also luckier. The environmental review turned up an archaeological site. Some Native American groups took an interest. It turned out it didn't amount to much archeologically but of course it brought everything to a stop. The local group had time to organize and work the media. Resistance had time to build. Dick's loan for the land was more than ten million, and payments were coming due. Breston was able to hang on for a while, but he wasn't capitalized to ride it out all the way. Dick wound up taking the land back, and Breston lost just about everything else too — everything he'd put up to finance predevelopment costs, including his house."

"How long ago?"

"Two years ago."

"But he's back on his feet already? Enough to take on another project?"

"Apparently more than anyone thought should be possible — at least if his way of getting there was entirely above board. There are rumors. Dick says some of them are probably true."

"Rumors of what?"

"Rumors about underworld connections."

"And does Dick know a lot about that kind of thing?"

She put down her coffee cup and stared at me. "I thought you wanted the details."

"I'm sorry. I do."

"Then just shut up and listen, and no more snide comments about the person who was good enough to share some information." She pursed her lips, then smiled. "But just so you know, I don't actually *mind* the fact that you're acting a little bit jealous."

"Okay, I'm listening. And just so *you* know, your ability to dig up all this information so fast impresses the hell out of me."

"All right, what Dick said was, he had no way of knowing if any of the rumors are true but he could certainly believe that the only kind of person that would invest in a Breston project at this point would be someone who was either a complete fool or a crook. That was about as far as I could get him to go. I had a feeling he knew more, and I came back to it a few times and teased him about being so cautious, but he wouldn't even say exactly what the rumors were — just kept insisting they were *only* rumors."

"Did you say anything to him about Sheridan Hollow?"

"I'm getting to it. He of course wanted to know why I was asking about Breston. In fact he seemed *very* interested in the question. I gave him the obvious kind of vague answer — that Breston's name had come up in connection with some property turning over in Albany...but that it was just a rumor and I had no way of knowing if it was true, and anyway it was just small-time stuff in a depressed neighborhood — not Breston's kind of deal, and not Breston's territory. 'Then why are *you* so interested?' Dick wanted to know. And I said 'I'm just curious, why are you so interested?' And he of course said he was just curious too, and that's about as far as we got. But he knows more than he's saying."

"As did you."

"So it was pretty much a stand-off. But one surprising thing —
guess who he asked about."

'I have no idea."

"You. He said he had heard I was seeing 'this guy Crow,' as he
called you."

"We h a ve been seen in public together from time to time."

"Su re. But the intere sting thing was he said he'd heard you'd
been doing some wo rk for the NHA since Jonah's death and he
wondered how it was going."

"What did you say?"

"Said it was keeping you so busy I hardly saw you any more. So
it was another stand-off, but he really wanted to know more. I
don't think it was just idle curiosity."

"You think he might actually be invo lved with Bre ston
again?"

"No. I can't believe he would be. I mean why would he be? He
doesn't need that kind of thing. And the pro perties we're talking
about are not exactly Dick's kind of property. I think he's maybe
like us — just trying to figure it out. I think he's heard a few things
and is trying to put the pieces together. I think he can help. That is
if you'll let him."

"You're going to see him again?"

"He invited me to have dinner with him again Wednesday
night. I told him I would have to see if I could do some reschedul-
ing and would let him know. Really I needed to talk with you first.
I don't want to go off on my own and complicate things for you."

"What you're doing is very helpful. I wouldn't even know who
Breston is. He'd just be a mispronounced name if it wasn't for you.
But it is a new experience. I'm someone who's used to wo rking
alone. And sleeping alone..."

"And now there's this woman who won't leave you alone."

"And I don't want her to.... Anyway, it sounds like another
dinner with Frost would be useful, if you're up for it."

"You know I am. I'll call him."

"Are you up for any other research on this thing? Do you have
any time this week?"

"Maybe. What do you have in mind?"

"It feels like there's a lot that needs to be done right away. I did
talk with Janet Rowley yesterday. Remind me to tell you about that
experience. Anyway, I mentioned Breston's name and I told her —

as I told McFadden — that NHA was ready to exercise its options on McFadden's properties. Unlike Eddie, she didn't let on a thing, except it seemed pretty clear that she knew what I was talking about. Told me I didn't know what I was doing, as though she *d i d* know what I was doing — or at least knew what I was talking about.

"So I've tried to stir things up, make something happen. But I — we — don't really know enough about the overall situation. What you've dug up about Breston helps a lot, but now we need to know more about some other things, like the ownership situation for the other Sheridan Avenue properties that would be or could be involved in a Breston project. I'm going to try to talk today to the one other owner I know of who was on Jonah's list. But there are also other properties that were not on Jonah's list but that might be on *Breston's* list — if there is a Breston list. Jonah wouldn't have needed to go after every property Breston might have needed. All he had to do to stop Breston was take a good bite out of the middle of his project."

"Actually," Lisa said, "I need to do some title work today. While I'm at it I can check those other properties if you can give me a list of addresses."

"If you do I'll take you out to dinner."

"Good — if we can go home early."

"To whose home?"

"Oh!" She had started to get up from the table but stopped abruptly. "We've been going to my house, but we could go to your house."

I hadn't actually planned to suggest it, but since I'd let the question come up I said, "Yes, let's go to Orange Street for a change."

16

I stood on the sidewalk and studied the large run-down house at 1107 Sheridan, up the street and across from the Gander Bay. Before leaving Lisa's, I had checked my pocket calendar for the phone number I'd noted for Greta Green, the presumed owner of this address. I was going to call and try to arrange to talk with her. I still had no idea who she was; I only knew that her name and phone number had been in Jonah's "Possible Acquisition" file for 1107. I didn't even know if Jonah had actually contacted her.

But as I picked up the phone I realized that the number I had written down was not an Albany number. It was a 272 number, a Troy number. Apparently Greta Green, whoever she was, did not live in Sheridan Hollow. So I decided to walk past 1107 and see what I could see on my way home. I could still call the Troy number when I got home.

The house was one of those that someone had "rehabilitated" at one time by wrapping the decaying wooden structure in cheap vinyl siding, which had now bulged and begun to slough off in places like dead skin. From the street I couldn't tell whether the place was being lived in, but it was not boarded up, as its neighbor to the east was, and the narrow walkway between the two buildings was not overgrown.

I climbed the steps to the high front porch and pushed the doorbell. Since I didn't have much hope that the bell would actually work, I also knocked on the aluminum screen door, which caused the latch to spring loose, letting the metal frame sag partway open. Pulling it all the way open, I rapped hard on the wooden door behind it. I still had no real hope that anyone would answer my knock, and I was about to leave, when the door was opened by a tall, slender man with a jet black ponytail and Native American features. "I thought you might come by," he said.

Taken aback, I said, "I'm not sure why you thought that. And I'm afraid I don't know your name, even though we sat next to each other at Jonah's funeral."

"You can call me Raymond," he said. "You're Warren Crow. I was going to call you if you didn't show up. Come in." He led the way down a dark hallway to a large kitchen at the back of the house.

There was a smell of strong soap and fresh-brewed coffee. The worn linoleum on one side of the kitchen was wet. A mop stood in a bucket of dirty water near the sink. On the dry side of the room there was a coffee maker on a makeshift wooden table — a two-by-four frame with a plywood top. Against the wall beyond the table was a set of board-and-block shelves loaded with books. More books, magazines and papers were stacked beside the shelves. On the wall above were several black and white posters. The one closest to me proclaimed:

DON'T LET THEM DESTROY OUR LAND
FIGHT JAMES BAY II

Below the words was a picture of a drowned landscape, with the tops of spruce trees protruding from an expanse of water.

I had the same poster on the wall of my bedroom. Looking at it, I said. "The one project Hydro Quebec couldn't get done."

"Not yet anyhow," Raymond said. "I hear you like the northern country."

"I do. But where do you hear that?"

"Jonah told me." He turned away toward the homemade table. "Want some coffee?"

I accepted a cup and we sat at the table. Raymond settled into stillness, elbows on the stained plywood top, staring through the back window into the trash-filled yard. After a time, he said, "Don't really know much about you. Only what Jonah was saying, before — and now what I hear you're doing lately."

"You knew Jonah pretty well?" I asked.

"We used to talk." He looked at me but only for a moment. "We lived in the same house. Before he moved in with Zera."

"But it wasn't this house, was it? Wasn't he living with folks in that house around the corner on Dove?"

"Until it was sold. That was when Jonah moved in with Zera. The rest of us moved into this house of Greta's that her mother left her. But now Greta's with her new girlfriend in Troy, so it's just me, when I'm down here, and a couple of Mohawks when they're down here, and the two women on the second floor but they're going to move out too."

"But you still saw Jonah sometimes after he moved out?"

"He used to stop when he was in the neighborhood."

"In the neighborhood trying to put his Sheridan Hollow project together — did he talk about the project?"

"Sometimes."

"And that's why you thought we should talk.... But why did you think I would know that and come find you? I mean I *did* come and find you, but I didn't know I was going to."

Raymond shook his head. "Just a guess. Thought you might find out Jonah was talking with Greta about this house, and you'd call her and she'd say you should talk with me. Or it would happen some other way. Didn't really know, so I was going to call you if you didn't come."

"You seem to be at least a step ahead of me. I don't know much of anything about this house, except that Jonah had a file on it and the only thing in the file was Greta Green's phone number. I was going to call her, but I decided to come by the place first. Anyway, it sounds like you can maybe tell me things I want to know."

Raymond continued to gaze through the window into the backyard. "I don't know what you already do know," he said.

I was ready to trust this man, though I wasn't sure why. Maybe it was just that we had sat together at the funeral and that we had the same poster on our walls. "I don't know a lot," I said. "It's no problem to tell you the extent of it. I know Jonah was trying to put together a project here on Sheridan. I've read his project description in the application he put in to the state. I know he bought a couple of buildings across and down the street here — bought them from Arnold Duber — and it appears he bought purchase options from Eddie McFadden on the properties down the other side of the Gander Bay. And in between, he was dickering with Janet Rowley for the Gander Bay property itself."

Raymond looked at me again briefly and nodded.

So I continued. "I know that a developer named Thomas Breston was also trying to buy the Gander Bay, and probably the other properties. I know that Jonah's board was not very enthusiastic about the project, and that it was not the kind of project he himself would normally want to do, so I assume he had a very special reason for doing what he was doing, and I can only guess what the reason was."

Raymond looked at me and raised his eyebrows.

"I have to figure Breston had a plan that Jonah was determined to block. The only thing that I can think of that would make sense in that location for someone like Breston is something that would actually serve Capitol Hill right above it. So I'm thinking something like a parking garage. I can imagine that Jonah would have seen it as an invasion and exploitation of the neighborhood and one more wedge between the neighborhood and Capitol Hill."

Raymond nodded.

"But there's a whole lot that I can't make sense of. Jonah was talking with you during that time?"

"Only when things got to him. Most of the time he was doing his regular thing with other people."

"But he wasn't talking about this project with other people — not even very much with his board."

"He didn't like it that he couldn't talk about it with his own people. But he said he couldn't tell them the project was really about stopping Breston."

"I don't really know why he couldn't tell them. If he had, they might have wanted to support it."

"Or might not have wanted to. But he didn't want to ask. Didn't want to ask them to fight Breston. And the more he got himself in to fighting Breston the more it got to be like a private war, and he didn't want to ask other people to join."

"Do you think it was that private war that got him killed?"

"Yeah. But I don't know how anyone can prove it. Unless maybe by doing what you're doing until they come after you too."

"I'd rather get it done some other way," I said. "Maybe you can tell me some things that will help get it done." I was still thinking about what he had just said. I had known that if Jonah had been killed because of his Sheridan Avenue project, I'd begun turning myself into a problem in the eyes of whoever caused his death, but I hadn't really got to the point of worrying about it. It had all seemed so improbable that I hadn't associated any real danger with it — until hearing Raymond's terse assessment.

He was sipping at his coffee, still gazing through the window.

"Did Jonah talk about Breston?"

"Some. He hated him."

"How did he find out about Breston's project?"

"I don't know where he first heard, but he was talking to the Rowleys and he knew they were dealing with Breston. Or Breston's guy McFadden."

"A couple of things I don't understand," I said. "If McFadden was buying property for Breston, why did he sell options on that property to Jonah? Is he really that stupid?"

Raymond shrugged. "Maybe he just figured Breston was going to push Jonah out of the picture one way or another, so it looked like easy money to him. He likes easy money."

"Certainly seems to," I said. "Though he works so hard scraping it up that it doesn't wind up being easy. Anyway, you could be right. He's used to dealing with people he can take advantage of. Another question then. Eddie McFadden had already bought those properties across from here before Jonah bought Duber's properties up the street. Why hadn't Eddie bought Duber's properties too? How did Jonah get in there ahead of him?"

"McFadden did try to buy them. But Duber hates that guy's guts. I guess they'd had run-ins. He didn't want anything to do with McFadden, and he was doing that deal with Jonah on Clinton Avenue, so I guess he offered these buildings down here to Jonah. Or maybe the two deals were really the same deal from the start. I'll take this off your hands and you take those off my hands. Could even be he told Jonah what was going on down here and gave him the chance to get into it. Could be that's how Jonah found out."

"So Duber sold Jonah the pieces that got him on the board — into something like a chess game with Breston. But how did he think he could win that game? Do you know if he actually got in touch with Breston then? Was he actually talking with him?"

"They killed him before he could. He'd started trying to get McFadden to set up a meeting for him, or at least give him the phone number of the guy, but Eddie was doing everything he could to keep him away from Breston. Then Jonah did get Breston's number — maybe from Duber, maybe the Rowleys, I don't know — so he called Breston and was going to meet him somewhere the Monday after the weekend he was killed.

"Meet him here in Albany — do you know?"

"In Albany. Downtown someplace is all I know."

"When did you see him last?"

"Night before he was killed he stopped in. That Friday night. He'd just talked to Breston on the phone and set up the meeting and was wound up pretty tight. He was going to offer to buy out everything Breston owned in the neighborhood. He was sure Breston would refuse. He was counting on him refusing. Because it was going to take a good long time to rake up the bucks for the NHA to buy that much property. But he said he was going to put the offer on the table and tell him he was going to hang onto the properties he already had and wait it out, as long as it took."

"I wonder if he gave Breston an idea on the phone of what he was up to."

Raymond shook his head. "Don't know. Don't think Breston would've thought it was going to be a social call. He had his people in the neighborhood. Had to know more or less what Jonah was doing. Certainly knew NHA got the Duber buildings."

"And you think he just got rid of Jonah?"

"Yeah."

"How? How would he get it done? What did you mean by him having his people in the neighborhood?"

"Besides McFadden and whatever's going on with the Rowleys — there's two guys Jonah had his eye on. Guys that hang out at the Bay. One is a black guy called Bax, but not very black. Actually about my color but looks African." Raymond wiped a hand quickly across his own face. "Little guy. Got one of those little pointy beards. The other one is a big white guy. One of the bikers. Big gut in a leather jacket."

His description of the first guy sounded like the man who had watched me so persistently the first time I stopped at the Gander Bay. I didn't know about the other one. "I've seen a couple of bikers in leather jackets around the bar..."

"This one is big. They call him Bear. At least six three or four. And heavy — two-fifty, two-sixty, maybe more. Not too old, maybe thirty, but his hair's gone gray. Long gray hair in a ponytail."

"I guess maybe I haven't seen him."

"You'll know him when you do. Jonah started noticing both these guys a while after he got wind of Breston's project. According to him they started sort of turning up whenever he was in the Hollow, and making it real obvious they were watching him, like they wanted to scare him off."

"And he assumed they were working for Breston?"

"Yeah. He assumed."

We sat in silence for a while. I couldn't think of any more questions and Raymond wasn't volunteering any more answers. But I hadn't finished my coffee and didn't want to rush off. Finally I said, "This has been helpful."

Raymond nodded.

"You've told me a lot about what was going on with Jonah," I said, "but nothing about yourself, which is of course none of my business..." But I was curious about him.

A smile flickered across his face. "You mean what's an Indian doing down here? What I do right now, I work nights for the state running a fork lift and daytimes I'm doing some research and some writing."

"And at other times...?" I asked. "I mean I'm just curious where you're from."

"I go back and forth to Canada. But not like you. I have family up there."

It felt like he had said all he wanted to say. I put my cup down. "I'd better get back to work," I said. "Thanks for the information."

"Right," Raymond said, and stood up. "Keep in touch. I'm mostly here daytimes till four-thirty."

17

Back in front of my computer by mid-morning, I set to work on a cash flow projection for NHA. In one of the folders on my hard drive I found a spreadsheet file that I'd developed for the same pur-

---

pose when I was working with NHA the year before. The nature of routine receipts and disbursements would not have changed too much. It would not be hard to update the numbers for such things as monthly rent receipts and regular reimbursements from the CD Agency and regular expenses such as office rent, phone, electricity.... The big question was, of course, payroll expense. For the present, with Jonah gone, it was a very large zero. What the NHA board needed to know — at least one of the things they needed to know — was how much money would be available to pay a replacement. I was going to start by doing a short-term projection with zero payroll and see how much cash could be accumulated.

But it was a strange kind of projection to be doing. Jonah reduced to $0.00 payroll expense. I found myself thinking again about the circumstances behind the numbers on my computer screen. Jonah's last days and his plans for a meeting with Breston. The two threatening characters that Jonah had been watching and that apparently had been watching Jonah, and might have killed him. And that I had to assume were now watching me.

What should I do with the information that was beginning to accumulate? Should I call Reilly again, and if so how much should I tell him? Would Reilly just think I was spooked to the point that I imagined danger in every shadow?

The phone rang beside the computer. I answered it and a woman's voice said "Warren Crow," not questioning but flatly identifying me.

"Yes?"

"Judith Rosen. We've met, if you remember."

"Of course," I said. "Hello, Judith." I knew Judith Rosen as a smart, aggressive attorney who, in her work, pursued hopeless causes, including cases she took from the Public Defender's office.

"I believe I need to talk with you," she said. "I am defense counsel for Ronald Burns. I think you know who he is."

It took me a moment to remember that Ronald Burns was "Loosh," accused of killing Jonah and still in jail. "Yes, I know who he is."

"I understand you've been helping the Neighborhood Housing Association after Jonah Lee's death. I am hoping you have information that would help my client's defense."

"I'm glad you called. I'm not sure I know anything useful, but I'd like to help. I don't think he's the killer."

"That's a start," she said. "Everyone else has got him convicted already."

"Where are you?" I asked.

"In my office on Central, between Robin and Quail."

"Close by. If you want to talk, I'll walk over."

"Second floor, over the Chinese take-out. Door to the stairs on the right."

"I'll be there in five minutes."

I could have just stayed on the phone with her, but I was curious and wanted to talk face-to-face. And of course I welcomed the chance to escape my desk again.

Judith Rosen's office was small, drab and under-furnished. Judith herself was tall and sternly elegant in a high-necked black dress. "They don't really care," she said, "whether he did it or not. He's young, black and mouthy. A piece of shit in their eyes. If they can convict him of this they figure good riddance whether he did it or not." Her anger apparently had more to do with the presumed motivation of the accusers than with any notion that the accused might actually be innocent.

"But what have they got?" I asked "Besides a fingerprint on a taped-up hundred dollar bill that's been from hand to hand to hand?"

"Then you don't know the latest — they're saying they found the gun, the murder weapon, in the place they claim he was staying."

"No I didn't know that. His own place? His own gun?"

"A girlfriend's place. Though *girlfriend* may not be the right term. The relationship is not entirely clear. But they say he was staying with her at least some of the time. At least visiting. I don't have enough information yet about how they found her, but the gun turned up in a bureau drawer under her underwear. But no fingerprints. Nothing to say it's actually his gun."

"But they've established it's the gun Jonah was killed with?"

"They say they have."

"They've still got problems with the case they're trying to make," I said. "They must know that."

"They think they've got it nailed shut. Fingerprints from the scene. Murder weapon found in a place he admits having been."

"One fingerprint on a bill that could have got there any number of ways. But no prints anywhere else — not on the file cabinet, not on either of the doors. And not on the gun. What's wrong with this picture?"

"Exactly," she said. "But I need more. I need to know anything and everything you can tell me about who might have had a reason to kill Jonah Lee. Because unless I can make a jury believe someone had a good reason to frame my client, it is going to be next to fucking impossible. Ronald Burns is not the kind of kid that encourages a presumption of innocence."

I wasn't sure that Judith Rosen was the best person to persuade a jury that *anyone* was truly innocent, but I thought she might be quite good at portraying another person as guilty, which was probably what was called for. "Okay," I said. "I don't have the complete story at this point, but in fact there is someone who seems to have had a reason to want to get rid of Jonah. And a couple of characters who seem to have been working for this guy are regulars at the Gander Bay Bar, where your boy Loosh also hung out, which I suppose could implicate him further, but which could also make it easy for them to frame him."

Judith picked up reading glasses and a pen from the top of her desk and pulled a legal pad toward her. "I want it all," she said. "Every goddamned detail."

It took a while. She asked many questions. She wanted more details than I could imagine mattered, but by the time we were through, I was coming to believe that Loosh was fortunate in having this woman as his attorney. I was also a step closer to believing that Thomas Breston was in fact behind Jonah's death.

Before I left, we agreed it would be useful if we went together to talk with Ronald Burns. She would arrange a time tomorrow and let me know.

* * *

When I got home I cooked myself a substantial brunch of bacon, eggs and potatoes. Then, after washing the few dishes, I went back to my desk, where I checked my phone messages.

There was a call from Lisa saying she had a five o'clock meeting in Troy and proposing that we meet at six at the brew pub on River Street. Also, to my surprise, there was a message from Eddie McFadden. "Crow, this is McFadden. I need to talk to you. Soon. Call me."

I dialed Eddie's number, got his answering machine and left a message. "McFadden, this is Crow. Yes, you do need to talk to me. Call me back."

While I was at it, I dialed the Troy number for Greta Green, reaching her answering machine as well. I explained as briefly as I could that I was calling to see if it was still possible that she might sell 1107 Sheridan Avenue to NHA, if it turned out NHA was able to go ahead with Jonah's project.

Next I awakened my computer from where it drowsed behind a darkened screen and got online to check my e-mail. There were half a dozen messages that I knew related to pieces of work that were not moving ahead as fast as I had promised they would. I put off reading them and instead opened a message from Erica Schmidt, which turned out to be as enigmatic as it was brief. "What's happening with NHA re. Sheridan project? Deep silence here except for some weird echoes. Let's talk."

I tried to decide whether to wait until after the NHA board meeting to call her, or whether it would be useful to check with her right away. What kind of weird echoes?

In the meantime I opened a message from Dave Potter. "Hey, my set of maps came yesterday and I'm having a blast looking at the route, but also wondering. So many long rapids where you can only guess how much is runable and how hard the carries will be. I know you've been over your maps pretty carefully and projected day-by-day progress, but I can't help wondering if we can make it for sure to Kujjuack in 26 days, as we need to if we're going to make arrangements with someone to fly us back to Schefferville for the train on day 28. Should we talk about it?"

It bothered me that Dave was worrying about whether we could complete the trip in the time available. I was pretty sure we could do whatever was necessary to finish the trip in time to get to Schefferville for the once-a-week train, and part of the pleasure was not knowing exactly what *would* be necessary. But I knew why he was concerned. He works for a small publisher in Saranac Lake, and it was a real stretch for him to take as much as a full month of vacation all at once. He was also married. He didn't have my flexi-bility. An extra week seemed out of the question to him. To me it would have been a bonus.

If I could find the time I would go over the route again and do a fresh estimate of daily progress so that I could possibly offer Dave some reassurance. There was no way he was going to back out now, but that didn't mean he wouldn't worry — and I didn't want to spend a month alone in the wilderness with a worried man. In less than two weeks we would be getting on the train in Sept Isle for the all-day ride north to Schefferville, and then it would just be a matter of doing the trip. I didn't want to have to think about anything other than what the river did around the next bend and what weather lay over the horizon...and the bugs and how tired we were and how hungry, and when and where we would camp.

Everything in the here and now. No questions about the further future, or the past.

But I wasn't there yet.

I worked more or less diligently through the afternoon. At quarter-to-five I wrapped up a development pro forma for a mobile home park tenant buy-out near Plattsburgh, and shut down the computer. Then I pulled into my lap the spiral notebook that I use for day-to-day phone numbers, addresses, reminders, lists of must-do items. I keep one of these notebooks open on my desk from day to day until it fills up and joins a row of others on the shelf to my right. For everything else I use the equipment linked by the tangle of wires in front of me — computer, monitor, keyboard, mouse, modem and combination scanner-fax-printer. But I've never liked digital calendar/organizers. To organize my days I still need to pick up a pencil, scribble notes, make doodling lists and sketch relationships with elaborate arrowing lines. Among other things, I like the physical sensation of carving question marks on paper.

Toward the bottom of today's page, I started a new list.

Ronald Burns/Loosh — ask about Bax and Bear? Who gave him $100?

McFadden — ??

Reilly — when to talk?

Erica — how/when to resubmit application?

NHA board — restart project? Modify project? Smaller scale possible?

Duber — call??

Greta Green?

Raymond — Follow up. Actual nature of Breston's project?

Breston — when/how contact?

Gander Bay — Bax & Bear? Buddy?

The last item involved a thought that had been taking shape since my talk with Raymond in the morning — the thought that I ought to spend more time at the Gander Bay, or at least stop in more frequently. It was no longer any sort of secret that I had taken an interest in Jonah's Sheridan Avenue project. If that meant that certain people were watching me, then I ought not to turn my back. I ought to be watching *them*. Also, though Janet Rowley had told me nothing, her son Buddy had told me quite a lot and it wouldn't hurt to chat with him more often.

I looked at my watch. I still had an hour before meeting Lisa in Troy.

* * *

In the vacant lot beside the Gander Bay there was a motorcycle, a ten-year-old Cadillac, an even older Oldsmobile and a new Jeep. I parked the Mazda pickup beside the Cadillac, walked around the corner and went into the building.

There were not yet a lot of people at the bar. The identity of the one biker was obvious. In spite of his black leather jacket he looked downright frail — definitely not the one Raymond had described as Bear. Nor was the young man Raymond described as Bax among the handful of black patrons, most of whose faces were familiar. The one white man in addition to the biker was a wiry middle-aged Mediterranean type. He sat dead still, staring into space. I had never seen him before.

Behind the bar was yet another provocatively dressed bleached blond, somewhat better looking than Aileen and her apparent sister Margie. When she came down the bar toward me, the eyes of the patrons followed the movements of her exposed midriff — except the wiry Mediterranean type, whose eyes looked straight ahead without a flicker of interest.

I ordered a pint of Killian's and carried it back to where Buddy sat in one of the booths, looking just as he had the last time I had seen him, large beard, leather vest, bulging belly. He squinted at me but said nothing.

"Hello, Buddy. I paid a visit to your mother."

"Yeah and I wish the fuck you didn't."

"It's not like we did any kind of business. Not like she even told me anything. I did meet a lot of colorful birds though."

"Yeah well, just you going there screwed it for me."

"What do you mean?" I sat down facing him across the booth's scarred wooden table.

"She *sold* the friggin place," Buddy hissed. "And if you say it out loud in here I'll kill you."

"That's not what *I* wanted to happen. But I thought it's what you wanted."

"Yeah, well she didn't sell it for cash. She sold it with friggin seller financing. All the money that guy's got and she had to finance it for him — take a mortgage. Says he give her some stock in his friggin corporation too. Says it's a good deal — which I wouldn't know. Meantime I'm looking at no job, no cash. Nothin. So thanks a lot Crow."

"Why do you think it was me going to see her that made her

sell? How did that change anything?"

"Because you're making people nervous around here, Crow. You're making *m e* nervous."

"But maybe I can still help you out," I said.

"How the fuck you going to do that? The deal went down. That's it. End of game."

No matter how antagonistic Buddy got he didn't stop talking. I didn't actually know how I could help him — if I wanted to help him — but I thought there were various ways we might go on talking. "Maybe," I said, "if your mother is throwing in with Breston that way, you should throw in with me."

"What — you gonna give me stock in *your* corporation or something?"

"NHA is a nonprofit corporation — no stock — but it can still do business like any other corporation. And it's doing business in this neighborhood. Things are not going to work out the way Breston thinks. Your mother joined the wrong team, but that doesn't mean you have to."

"Bullshit — the game's over, Crow — and I wish you'd get your friggin ass out of here."

I stood up. "I'm not going to hassle you Buddy, but think about where things are at. The game's not over. NHA still owns property here. It has resources. It has friends. It can go to City Hall. It can go to the press. Breston has a problem. And it seems to me you have a problem too, unless you figure out who can help you out and who can't." I set the mostly full glass of beer on the table. "Think about it. Maybe I'll stop by again tomorrow."

18

Having arrived in Troy ahead of schedule, I sat alone at a table on the second floor of the brew pub, nursing a pint of lager that was a good deal better than what I had left behind at the Gander Bay. Only a few other tables were occupied on this floor, though the downstairs was crowded with college students from RPI and Russell Sage and a mix of young professionals. I liked the lofty spaciousness of the upper level of the building, a minimally remodeled old industrial structure built more than a century ago when there actually was industry along the banks of the Hudson. In spite of the historic connection with the world of grit and sweat, the place was as different from the Gander Bay as one bar could possibly be from another. No one in the place, other than the busy waiters and waitresses, looked as though they had spent their day in any sort of manual labor. Everyone in the place looked middle class and of course almost everyone was white.

Sipping my beer, I was trying to think of something tangible that I could offer to Buddy Rowley to hold his interest and encourage him to be helpful — in particular to encourage him to share what he saw and heard during his long vigils in the back of his establishment. My thoughts were interrupted by Lisa's voice from behind me. "So, you sneaked in and got a head start on me." She placed a hand on the back of my neck, then stepped briskly to the table and lifted the glass from my hand and took a sip. "What is it?"

"It's called Lansingburgh Lager."

"I think I want something with more character." She sat down, tucking her briefcase against the side of her chair, and picked up the beer menu. "I have a lot to tell you."

"I'm all ears," I said.

"There's a lot going on out there...but I have to order something here. In the meantime, tell me what you've been up to all day."

"As you say, there's a lot going on out there. I started out the day by meeting someone I should have met sooner. Or should have talked to when I did meet him — when I sat next to him at Jonah's funeral." I gave her a quick account of my meeting with Raymond.

"A real live Indian," she said.

"Like you're real live Albany Irish among the other things. Yes, he seems to have some Indian in him."

"Did you know that my mother claimed to be one thirty-second Micmac?"

"We're all mongrels. But really? Micmac?"

She had easily caught the eye of a waiter who hurried to our table — a pale young man with extremely short hair and a ring in his nose. She ordered a pint of oatmeal stout and turned back to me. "So he knew Jonah Lee? Jonah actually confided in him?"

"They were both part of a group household on Dove Street before Jonah moved in with Zera, and Jonah would apparently drop in to see him on Sheridan sometimes when he was in the neighborhood. It's not hard to imagine they shared some kinds of things. I don't begin to know who Raymond is but he's maybe a little like the kind of loner-activist that Jonah was. The kind of half-outsider activist that Jonah was. But with quite a lot more emphasis on the outsider side. Anyway it seems Raymond was someone Jonah could talk to about his loner project."

"So did you learn anything important about the project?"

"He confirmed a lot that we'd only begun to suspect. That Breston's plan was — and no doubt still is — to build some kind of parking garage there south of Sheridan, and that Jonah was in fact trying to block it."

"Raymond actually confirmed that the project is a parking garage?"

"He's a man of not too many words, but I understood him to confirm my suggestion that the project is some kind of parking garage."

"It's just too far-fetched. It would be easy to get to the place from I-90 or I-787, but once they were there...People that parked there would still have to climb up the long stairway to Capitol Hill."

"Suppose the garage was set deeply into the hillside, so the top story was actually on ground level on the south. So you could park and take an elevator up to where you could walk out right on a level with Elk Street."

She stared at me. "You should be a developer. You might actually make money at it."

"I would lose my shirt."

"So how did Jonah know about all of this?"

"Raymond suggested it might actually have been Duber that told him what was going on, and that Duber might actually have shared Jonah's interest in blocking what Breston was up to, or what McFadden was up to. He said Arnold Duber hates Eddie McFadden. But it's not clear exactly what Jonah learned from who — from Duber, from McFadden, from Janet Rowley. Apparently he was talking to all of them."

"Which you already knew."

"But also...He had actually caught up with Breston and arranged to meet with him. According to Raymond, he was scheduled to meet with Breston the Monday following the weekend he was killed, and was going to offer to buy out Breston's Sheridan Hollow holdings — at least as a way of drawing a line in the sand, making it clear he was not going to sell his own holdings to Breston. And Raymond thinks it was why he was killed — thinks Breston already understood that Jonah intended to block his project."

The waiter arrived with Lisa's stout. Lisa ignored him and stared hard at me. "I don't like this at all," she said. "Is it also already obvious to Breston that you have exactly the same intention?"

"It probably is, but I'm not nearly as vulnerable as Jonah was. Breston can't just go on killing everyone who gets in the way. It's one thing to try to disguise Jonah's murder as armed robbery, but the death of someone who was following up on Jonah's project would start to look pretty suspicious. Besides, I have a fierce friend who packs a gun."

"Not funny."

"I'm sorry. But I do take this seriously, and I'm very seriously interested in protecting myself, and my fierce friend."

"Who doesn't pack a gun except once in a while. Or that's how it used to be." She picked up her glass of stout and studied me over the rim. "What *I* learned today...is that Breston is moving very fast right now."

"You checked those property titles?"

"Since Jonah died he's taken title to them *all*..." She drew out the word *all* emphatically, with her lips rounded above the rim of her glass so her breath dimpled the dark surface of the brew. "Every one on your list. That is, they are now owned by something called Alton, Inc. I had a few extra minutes so I stopped at the Secretary of State's office and looked up the corporation. Alton, Inc. was incorporated last month. Guess who the three initial board members are."

"Thomas Breston?"

"And your friend Janet Rowley, and someone named Elizabeth Michaels."

"Janet Rowley? Just an hour ago, I learned from her son Buddy that she's sold the Gander Bay to Breston's corporation — and took a mortgage on it, and also received some stock. So apparently she's a director and a stakeholder of sorts."

"And here's something else," Lisa said. In spite of her declaration that she didn't like the situation at all, there was at least a part of it that excited her. "I checked the ownership of the McFadden and Rowley properties and found no record that they'd transferred them, but then I asked Billy Seymour, the clerk, if they'd received any new deeds from Alton that hadn't been recorded yet. He said, 'Funny you should ask.' Sure enough — Alton deeds for the Gander Bay and the lot next to it *and* the McFadden properties were sitting right there on his damn counter."

"Buddy seemed to blame me — my visit to his mother's house yesterday — for somehow stampeding her into selling. But it sounds like she'd probably already done it."

"Maybe not. I got Billy to show me the deeds. They were all signed and notarized just yesterday."

"You do awfully good work," I said. "If I had asked Billy Seymour to show me those deeds — if I had asked him practically anything — he would have told me to go screw myself."

"You're probably not very nice to him. He's really just an old sweetie."

"If you say so, but I don't think the old sweetie is particularly interested in me being nice to him. I expect your niceness is different."

"I should hope so."

I turned over the menu on the table in front of me and stared at it blindly. "Do you suppose my visit to Mother Rowley actually did stampede her into selling to Breston as soon as I walked out the door?"

"Or maybe she just picks up the phone and tells Breston you came to visit and it stampedes *him* into action."

"Or not exactly *stampedes*, but makes him think it's time to get the deal done."

"Both deals. McFadden's too."

"McFadden tried to reach me this morning. Left a message saying we had to talk. Whereas, until now, he's been insisting there's nothing to talk about. I am really curious about what's going on with Eddie McFadden."

"Of course both those closings could already have been scheduled for yesterday," she said. "That would have been the more obvious scenario. Especially considering Alton, Inc. had closed on eleven other Sheridan Avenue properties within the last month with three other owners. It's obviously been consolidation time."

"Did you recognize any of the other three sellers?"

"One was Elizabeth Michaels, the third director. The others I didn't recognize, but it seems a safe assumption that they were all straws, holding the properties until he was ready to take title. Until Alton, Inc. was set up and could legally own property."

"And this Elizabeth Michaels? You've never heard of her?"

"No, but she seems to be quite busy. She was also the notary on the Rowley and McFadden deeds. Probably an employee. Someone he brought with him and set up in some kind of an office in Albany." Lisa picked up a menu. "Are we going to eat here, or move on?"

"Here is fine with me."

"Then let's. I'm starving."

We both ordered fish and chips. I ordered another Lansing-burgh Lager. When the food came she looked at it and said, "I'm not sure it's enough, but it's a start."

"If you'll come home with me afterwards, I'll make peanut butter and jelly sandwiches."

"Deal," she said.

As we ate, I told her about my talk with Judith Rosen and the interview we had scheduled with Loosh for the next day.

"So you think Judith might actually be able to get him off?" she asked.

"I don't know. Now that I've thought about it I'm less opti-mistic than when I first talked with her. The connection with the murder weapon isn't exactly direct, but it's still a connection. The finger print on the hundred-dollar bill is odd. It's the *only* print and it's hard to explain the bill to begin with, but it apparently is his print and it *was* at the scene. As Judith said, unless she can show someone had a reason to frame him..."

"As Breston did."

"As Breston had if he arranged to have Jonah killed by some-one else. We of course have no real evidence that he did."

"Why do you assume it wasn't this kid Loosh himself that Bre-ston manipulated into doing the dirty work?"

"I suppose that's possible."

"If I wanted to get rid of someone and make sure no one con-nected me with it, I think I'd look for someone else who had their own reason to do the thing, and then I'd maybe help them focus on it and get it done."

"It's something to think about. But there are still problems with it. It's not like Loosh shared an interest in getting rid of Jonah. If he was actually at the scene his motive would have been just what the police assume. He would have been looking for cash, not look-ing to kill someone. And from the sound of it he's an impetuous screw-up. He'd be hard to manipulate in any predictable sort of way. There'd be no way to know what would happen with him in Jonah's office. I think if I was Breston and wanted to get rid of Jonah, I'd hire a dependable professional to do the job and then try to make it *look* like it was just some kid like Loosh off the street."

"From what Dick told me about Breston, he might have the sort of contacts you'd need if you were looking to hire that kind of professional."

"Or he might not have had to do any actual hiring. From what you've said, he might have the kind of investors who would just quietly make the necessary arrangements once he told them about this guy who was trying to block the project."

"I don't like thinking about it." She put down her fork and stared into space. Clearly she *was* thinking about it. "Of course there was no very big investment, and there still isn't. It's not like one of those mall deals where it takes millions just to buy the land. All those Sheridan Avenue properties put together wouldn't be worth more than a couple hundred thousand. And apparently he didn't even pay cash for the Gander Bay. So how much would your so-called investors really have at stake? Would it really be enough to kill for?"

"Maybe if they were people with a lot of dirty money that they needed to put someplace, then what they had at stake wasn't just whatever they might have already put in. It was the future opportunity to put millions more into Breston's project so they'd wind up with a supposedly legitimate asset that would generate legitimate income."

"It's so..." She was frowning at the remains of her meal. "I hadn't thought of it quite that way. I'd thought of it as Breston's project, with maybe some shady investors making it possible, but not with the whole thing driven by people off in the shadows somewhere. The way you're describing it, it's so hard to put your finger on. The money could be coming from anywhere. The actual killer could have come from anywhere. The whole thing could be controlled by people who could be anywhere."

"The global economy comes to Sheridan Hollow," I said.

"I don't like it," she said. "I don't like deals where you can't know who you're dealing with."

"In some ways it doesn't really matter where the capital comes from. It comes from anywhere and everywhere. We're still dealing with Breston and the local situation. The way Jonah was. He wasn't fighting a big-time crime syndicate; he was fighting a local land use that he thought was bad for his community."

"Well yes, but whatever he thought he was fighting, you're saying he was killed by something coming from outside."

"I'm just saying we can only work from what we know, from what's in front of us. It's all I know how to do."

"But I wish we knew more," she said.

19

She had in fact eaten a peanut butter and jelly sandwich. Now, licking her fingers, she was studying my bachelor kitchen with interest. "It feels different being here with you," she said.

"It's a different kind of place."

"It's actually quieter than my place, and probably safer, but it feels…"

I thought I knew what she was feeling. "Threadbare? A little dreary?"

"I was going to say *old-fashioned.*"

"Your building is older."

"I know, but it doesn't feel that way. My kitchen isn't old. This is an old-fashioned kind of kitchen. It makes me realize you're an old-fashioned kind of guy, in some ways."

"You don't really know a guy until you've eaten a peanut butter and jelly sandwich in his kitchen."

"And it was excellent. You do make a fine peanut butter and jelly sandwich. Now can I have a drink?"

I got ice from the refrigerator and Jack Daniel's from under the sink and poured us each a drink. "It does feel different," I said. "It's different to think of you spending the night in my bed rather than vice versa."

"Yes," she said. "Though I don't know why it should. With the lights out and you in my arms, what *i s* the difference?"

"I guess we'll find out."

"I guess part of it is I'm still feeling unsettled by what we were talking about over supper. The idea of something going on — something threatening going on — that you can't pin down and deal with directly."

"It's not the most comfortable feeling."

"One thing I need to ask you," she said. "When you talk about what's going on, you're obviously involved in it up to your ears — and maybe I am too — but I'm not exactly sure what the goal is. I mean in a general way, yes, to figure it out. But then what? If the next thing is to somehow fix what went wrong, what does that mean? Seeing that the bad guys are punished? Or accomplishing what Jonah was trying to accomplish? And does that mean actually doing his crazy project?"

"I don't know. I guess a part of figuring out the whole thing is figuring out what's possible, where it's possible to go with it."

"So you're still just wading into it without a plan. Ad-libbing. I guess I'll have to do the same thing with Dick Frost tomorrow night."

I wasn't sure I liked the idea. I assumed Frost's goal in meeting with Lisa was clear enough — Lisa herself being the goal — so I wanted her to be guided by a plan of her own. I said, "Let's see if we can at least define the questions he might help answer."

"My big question is just what does he really know. I need to find a way to tease it out of him — to get him to say more than he would say last time."

"You could also just trade information for information."

"What information for what information?"

"What we know about Jonah's project for what he knows about Breston's project."

"We also know some very recent stuff about Breston. The deeds that came in today..."

"And we have some very specific questions about Breston that Frost might or might not be able to answer."

"Those being..."

"One being...has Breston been talking with someone at the city, or the county? And what kind of deal have they talked about? He can't move beyond the property acquisition stage without dealing with the city. He wouldn't even start acquiring property unless someone gave him reason to think he *could* have a deal with the city. Or the county. Or both."

"Okay. Dick can probably find out if he doesn't already know."

"Another thing we need to find out is how to contact Breston. There've got to be other ways to get that information, but if Frost happens to know..."

"You're going to contact Breston? Then you do have a plan you're not telling me about."

"I don't. Not yet. But there is definitely going to *be* some contact soon. If he's assembled all the property he needs except for what the NHA has, he's got to contact the NHA. I wouldn't mind making the first move."

"But you're not the NHA."

"Neither was Jonah."

"Exactly. The NHA itself he can probably deal with, but you... like Jonah you're an obstacle that Breston either needs to get around or remove. It's what scares me."

"But it's now too risky for him to just remove someone as an obstacle..."

"I wish I was sure of that." She was hunched forward with her elbows on the kitchen table and chin supported in her hands. She looked tired, lacking her usual positive energy.

I had got to my feet and started around the table toward her when the phone rang. In passing I plucked the receiver from the wall and said hello. A weary voice said, "Crow, this is Reilly."

I let myself be reined in by the phone cord. "Yeah... Hello...What's up?"

"I'm over here at your friend McFadden's house. You left a message on his machine this morning."

"That's right."

"Which was either just before or just after he died."

I felt as though I had just walked into a wall in the dark. "Died?"

"Killed," Reilly said.

I couldn't think of a way to respond.

"I need to ask you some questions. It would help if you came over here. I guess you know the place?"

"It'll take me a few minutes. How long will you be there?"

"Too long," Reilly said. "You come now maybe it'll speed things up."

"Quick as I can," I said, hanging up. When I turned away from the phone, Lisa lifted her gaze from the table. "That did not sound good."

"It was Reilly — the cop. Eddie McFadden's dead — was killed."

"My God. How...Why?"

"I don't know. Reilly is there now, at McFadden's house. He wants me to come over. I guess I have to go."

"McFadden wasn't even an obstacle. He'd already signed over his property."

"Yes... unless..." I stopped, not quite believing the momentary thought and not wanting to give Lisa more reason to worry.

She stood up from the table. "Why does Reilly want to talk to you? I mean I'm glad he does, and I think it's time you told him everything."

"I don't think he wants to hear everything I might tell him. He wants to know why I left a message on Eddie's machine this morning. Anyway, we'll talk and maybe I'll learn something...And while I'm gone, you know you don't have to stay here if it doesn't feel comfortable. I'll understand if you want to go back to your own place."

"Thank you. I'll go if you'll come there too. Afterwards."

I would have liked it if she had insisted on staying — if I could have come home to find her warming my own little under-furnished, under-decorated house — but I knew the place felt exposed and unsafe to her. "Sure," I said. "I'll come to your place afterwards."

* * *

For the second time in ten days I presented myself to a uniformed policeman at the front door of a building in which someone had just been killed. After waiting outside for several minutes in the calm June evening, I was led into the house, then through a hallway to a living room where Reilly was slumped on a sofa, writing in a small notebook, as when we had first met.

"So what was it you and Eddie needed to talk about?" he asked without looking up.

"He called me earlier in the morning and left a message saying we needed to talk. I called back as soon as I got the message. I'd been trying to get *him* to talk about a deal he made with Jonah Lee before Jonah was killed."

Reilly raised his eyes and stared at me. "What kind of deal?"

I sat down in an armchair facing him. "Eddie owned some buildings on Sheridan Avenue next to the Gander Bay. It seems he bought them for a developer named Thomas Breston who's been assembling property on Sheridan for a project. That is, he either bought them *for* Breston or he bought them because he knew Breston *wanted* them and would pay good money for them. But apparently he got greedy — extra greedy — because he also sold options on those properties to Jonah, who wanted them for a project *h e* was putting together. I've been following up on that project for the NHA and I'd told McFadden I wanted to talk about exercising those options."

Reilly continued to stare. "What are you suggesting?"

"I'm not suggesting anything. I'm giving you some background that seems relevant."

"Relevant because you think McFadden's death is linked to Jonah Lee's death?"

"I have no evidence, but I know they were both problems, or potential problems, for someone with a possibly very profitable project in Sheridan Hollow. I also know that McFadden deeded his properties to that person — or that person's new corporation — and that those deeds were brought in to be recorded this morning. The deeds themselves were signed and notarized yesterday." As I said it, I wondered if yesterday was really when they were signed. If the person who notarized the signatures was one of Breston's own people...But why would there be a reason to falsify the date?

"Wait a minute," Reilly said. "Back up. None of this makes sense. The guy doing this project is who?"

"His name is Thomas Breston. He's a developer from Dutchess county. The name of the new corporation — apparently set up for the Albany project — is Alton, Inc."

Reilly wrote briefly in his notebook before looking up again. "So explain to me...what's a guy like that doing in a place like Sheridan Hollow? The only project anyone ever did in that neighborhood bigger than a shade tree car-fix-it was the state's bright idea of heating their buildings by building a plant to burn garbage — until the neighbors started to complain."

"Okay, you're right, it needs explaining." I liked Reilly's very accurate response. It was true that the only thing that could be called a Sheridan Hollow project to date was the trash-burning plant built by the state to generate steam to heat government office buildings. "This project is pretty much like the trash burning plant," I said. "Capitol Hill would get the benefits. The Hollow would get the fumes. Breston's project is a parking garage. Access from Sheridan Avenue but serving the area right above to the south."

"And how come no one knows about this? It sure as hell hasn't been in the news."

"I assume because Breston doesn't want it in the news before it's a done deal."

"Okay. But now you gotta explain why someone like your big developer can't push aside the guys like Jonah Lee and Eddie McFadden without getting his hands dirty. No way he had to kill two people just to build some parking garage in a neighborhood that's been taking everyone else's garbage ever since I can remember."

"I don't know if he did get his hands dirty," I said. "His own hands. But the reason he couldn't push Jonah aside was that Jonah was smart and stubborn and couldn't be bought. He couldn't push Eddie McFadden aside because Eddie was greedy and was used to having his own way in places like Sheridan Hollow."

"You better come look at something," Reilly said, standing up.

I followed him to the doorway of a dining room dominated by a large, incongruously formal table made of what appeared to be mahogany. In a chair pushed close to the table, his back to me, a small balding man that had to be Eddie McFadden was slumped as far forward as was allowed by the clothesline that was wrapped several times around his middle and tied behind the chair. In front of him half the table-top was covered with a dark mess that appeared to be partially congealed blood. Reilly walked to the edge of the table and pointed at it. "Look at this."

I stayed in the doorway. I thought I had the general idea and preferred not to look more closely.

"No," Reilly said, "you have to come over here and read this."

Reluctantly I went to the table, where I couldn't help seeing the blood-soaked front of Eddie, whose throat had been laid open from ear to ear.

My eyes leapt away from the sight. I found myself staring blindly at two people in white coveralls who were on their hands and knees on the floor beyond the table. Reilly was still pointing. "This here," he said doggedly.

Where he pointed, someone had written with a finger in the blood.

SELL ME SHITTY HOUSE

NOW YOU PAY FOR IT

I made sure it said what I thought it said before I looked away. "I don't believe it," I said.

"Don't believe *what* for christsake? This sure as hell *h a p p e n e d.*"

"The message. Eddie McFadden sold shitty houses to quite a few people. But I don't believe it was one of those people that did this."

Reilly stepped away from the table and motioned with his chin in the direction of the door to the living room. I followed him.

"So you don't think that message says what it looks like it says?" Reilly asked, moving toward the front of the house. "Let's get out of here. My car's out front, we can talk there."

Following him, I said, "I think the message looks like someone wanted it to look."

We left by the front door. It was a huge relief to get out of the house into the summer evening. Reilly didn't say anything until we were both seated in the front of the car. Then he said, "Explain to me what you meant by that — the message looking like someone wanted it to look."

"It just seems like an easy way for someone to make it look like Eddie'd been killed by a homebuyer who thought he'd been cheated. But I don't really know, of course. The whole thing is too bizarre."

"Grant you that," Reilly said. "But tell me what you're thinking. Why not a pissed-off homebuyer?"

"I don't know, but most of the people who buy houses from the likes of McFadden don't even know they've been screwed. They move in smelling the fresh paint and they think he's done them a favor fixing the place up and helping them get a mortgage to buy it. A couple of years later when the real problems start showing up, they blame the contractor who tells them it'll cost thirty or forty thousand dollars to fix the foundation, replace the sills, redo the bathroom floor...I don't know that it even occurs to them that McFadden took advantage of them."

"It must occur to at least a few of them, and when it does...one of them could get real mad, don't you think?"

"But what's that person going to do? He might come over here and give Eddie a hard time...and Eddie would tell him to fuck off, so the guy might take a swing at him, and maybe even wind up beating the shit out of him...but this?" I pointed toward the house, where all the windows were brightly lit.

Reilly shrugged. "This is what we've got. So tell me who did do it. If you're still thinking about this developer guy...isn't this a little more than he would've needed? If we're just talking about persuading McFadden to sell some property?"

"I don't know what to make of it. I did see Eddie a couple of days ago and he seemed really uptight, in fact frightened, about what he'd got himself into, but he refused to deal with me, insisted there was nothing to talk about. Then this morning he called and left a message saying we needed to talk."

"Okay, wait a minute. Deal with you why? Because you're representing Jonah's organization?"

"Unofficially. Pulling together information for them."

"And when and where did you see him?" Reilly's notebook had reappeared from a jacket pocket.

"Late Sunday afternoon. For a few minutes, in his backyard. He was barbecuing. With Linda Bettleman."

"Then he called you this morning...at what time?"

"He left a message sometime between ten and noon, but I can't say exactly. My machine gives the time that a message comes in, but it's screwed up, so the times are way off."

"You erased the message yet?"

"Actually I don't think I did."

"Let's go to your house then."

I gave him the Orange Street address, got into my pickup and drove home. When I got to the house, Reilly was already parked at the curb.

In the kitchen, the bottle of Jack Daniel's still stood on the counter. Reilly eyed it. I said, "I'd offer you a drink, but I don't suppose you do that when you're working."

"I don't do it at all anymore. Though times like this it's not easy. Let's hear the message."

I pushed the button on the machine and we listened to Eddie's voice. "Crow, this is McFadden. I need to talk to you. Soon. Call me." The robo-voice then articulated the date and time. "Tuesday. June thirteenth. Three twenty-one p.m."

Reilly scribbled in his notebook; then picked up the phone and dialed a number. "Reilly," he said. "I need a call-back to check the answering machine here. Leave a quick message, doesn't matter what." He gave my number and hung up.

The phone rang four times. The machine picked up and we waited through my greeting followed by a female voice saying, "Quick message, Dave. Bye." Then the robo-voice said, "Wednesday. June fourteenth. Three forty-seven a.m."

We both looked at our watches. Reilly sat down at the kitchen table and did the arithmetic in his notebook. "I make it ten forty-three a.m. when he called. M.E.'s preliminary estimate puts the time of death between ten and two. Play that thing again, would you."

I played Eddie's message again. "Crow, this is McFadden. I need to talk to you. Soon. Call me."

"Does sound kind of urgent," Reilly said. "Any idea why?"

"Only what I've already suggested. I think he was feeling some pressure because he'd sold Jonah those options on property he was supposed to be holding for Breston, and I was telling him NHA wanted to exercise those options. Except that it now seems he'd already deeded those properties to Breston's corporation — yesterday. So I don't really know why he was calling me this morning. Either he thought he was going to have to deal with NHA on the fact that he couldn't deliver on the options, or..."

"Or what?" Reilly asked.

"I guess that's all. The only reason I can think of is that he must have thought he still had to deal with the options question."

I didn't mention the possibility that the deeds might not have been signed when the dates indicated. They had been notarized by the woman named Elizabeth Michaels who was working for Breston and who therefore might not be the trustworthy witness a notary public is supposed to be. It was something I wanted to think about privately. But there were also other things that I perhaps should tell Reilly, including the fact that I hadn't actually been able to find the option documents themselves. And the possibility that the documents had been taken from the NHA office by whoever killed Jonah.

"You mentioned a woman's name," Reilly said. "Who was with McFadden when you saw him on Sunday. Who was that?"

"Linda Bettleman. She works for him. Did work for him. They seemed pretty familiar. I think she probably lived with him...but maybe you've already talked with her. This has got to be pretty terrifying for her."

"Never heard of her," Reilly said. "Unless she's who called it in."

"About Eddie? You mean someone found him and called and you don't know who it was?"

"A woman called and said there was a dead person at McFadden's address. She wouldn't say any more than that and wouldn't give her name. Really upset. Call was from a pay phone down the street." Reilly turned to a fresh page in his notebook. "Spell Bettleman for me."

"Okay, but wait a minute." I lifted the phone from its hook again. "The message on his machine from me...When I made that call, the greeting on the machine was Linda Bettleman's voice." I handed the phone to Reilly. "You might want to hear the voice."

Reilly checked his notebook and dialed. After a minute he said, "Does sound like her." Then, "If you guys are still there at the scene, pick up. It's Reilly." Then, "Yeah, get the greeting on the answering machine and check the voice against the one that called this in."

He hung up. "So, yeah, Bettleman...the spelling?"

I gave him what I assumed was the spelling.

"Any idea how to reach her?"

"No idea, but I might be able to get you a name or two to start with — people who might know her."

When Reilly nodded, I dialed Lisa's number. She picked up almost immediately.

"It's me," I said. "I'm back at home and Detective Reilly is here with me, checking the message Eddie left on my machine this morning. He has a question you might be able to help with." To Reilly I said, "My friend Lisa. She was here when you called." Then to Lisa again: "They're trying to locate Linda Bettleman, the young woman who worked for Eddie. Who may or may not know he's dead. It's possible she walked in on a really terrible scene and took off in a panic. I thought you might know of people in the real estate business who might know her, or at least know something about her."

There was a deep silence at Lisa's end of the line. Finally she said, "God...I'm trying to remember...I do know who you mean, and there was someone she hung around with...Oh...Janice Eliot. She's an agent now — at O'Casey and Smith. I don't know if they're still in touch, but it's easy enough to check. She ought to be reachable through her office."

"Good. Janice Eliot. O'Casey and Smith."

"Are you still coming over?" Lisa asked.

"I don't know what I'm doing. I'll give you a call when Detective Reilly leaves."

* * *

By the time Reilly had left it was almost midnight. I called Lisa and filled her in, with as little detail as possible. To my relief she did not ask questions and did not object when I said I thought I would just have a drink and go to bed where I was.

I poured a drink and carried it to the old easy chair in the darkened living room, where I could look out on the quiet emptiness of Orange Street at midnight.

McFadden's murder made no sense. I was sure the note written in blood was like the hundred dollar bill found at the scene of Jonah's murder. Another attempt — so far another successful attempt — to suggest the wrong motive and implicate the wrong person for a killing that I had to believe Thomas Breston was somehow behind. But I couldn't understand why Breston needed to kill McFadden. It would be one thing to tie him up and scare him — possibly even with a blade against his throat — in order to make him sign the deeds. But once he had signed, why go ahead and cut his throat? The only possible explanation, other than sheer bloodthirstiness, was that the motive was to make a bloody example of him. And the only person I could imagine such an example being intended to impress was myself. It seemed far-fetched. Especially since neither I nor the NHA had yet heard a word from Breston.

I sat looking into the street, listening to the hum and rustle that took the place of deep nighttime silence in the city. After a while I became aware that I was hearing a throbbing rhythm in the sound, barely perceptible at first but gradually growing stronger, until I realized it was an approaching boom box. Eventually I could hear the militant human voice rapping over the bass beat, louder and louder until finally I saw the top of someone's head pass under my window. I couldn't make out the words, but the feeling of compressed anger hammered through the neighborhood. It was a long time before the sound faded completely into the background hum and rustle.

Later, in bed, I became entangled in a long, repetitive, confusing dream in which I was trying to meet Breston, who was supposed to be somewhere on Capitol Hill. But I couldn't find my way onto the hill. Every place I tried I found a massive vertical wall. On one side there was the high east wall of the South Mall, where the highway entered the mouth of the parking garage. I knew that if I could get onto the highway I could get into the fortress, but the only way to get onto the highway was to get onto the Interstate — one of the Interstates — and I couldn't seem to remember where the entrance ramps were. I knew that there were also other ways to get onto the hill, streets that actually made their way up the hill, but every street I tried ended against another wall or an impenetrable row of buildings, or set of cliffs. After a while getting onto the hill became an end in itself. Breston was still on my mind, but not as someone I had to meet on the hill. He was some sort of adversary who confused the landscape in a way that had something to do with the fact that he had no real location in it. At some point I remembered having learned that Breston was not a person at all — he was a corporation.

By the time I began to wake up, the dream had shifted and I was no longer in Albany. I was trying to find my way to the railroad station in Sept Isles, Quebec, a gateway to freedom impossibly far away in another country.

20

I got up at five-thirty, feeling unrested but unable to ignore all the things I needed to do. After two cups of coffee and a bowl of generic wheat flakes I sat down at the computer and worked until ten. Then I walked the few blocks to Central Avenue to meet Judith Rosen, with whom I had agreed to drive out to the jail on Shaker Road to talk with Loosh.

Judith had read in the morning paper about Eddie's murder, and she knew from what I had told her that Eddie was connected with Breston's project, so she was full of questions inspired by the hope that this second murder would point to a killer other than her client.

I didn't give her a lot of encouragement. "Right now they're going to be busy looking for some poor homeowner who might have been angry enough about what Eddie McFadden sold him to do something horrendous to him."

Judith, at the wheel of her car, shook her head. "Jesus."

"Let's hope we can learn something useful from Loosh. It seems more likely that you can get him acquitted than that Breston will ever be convicted of anything. You have a plan for this interview?"

"I'll go over the story with him again for your benefit, and we'll see if anything strikes you. And I want to focus on his relationship with the woman who found the gun in her bureau drawer. Questions are coming up about her and his relationship to her. And you can ask about those Gander Bay associations you were telling me about."

When we eventually sat facing Loosh through metal grillework, I was impressed by how small he was, and how defiant, and how young. He obviously saw Judith and me not as allies or protectors but as just another couple of white people pursuing him with accusations clothed as questions. "What you mean? Why should I have to stay the same place every night?"

"You don't," she said. "No one's telling you where you have to stay."

"They sure the fuck is. Lock me the fuck up."

She started over. "No, we're talking about where you were staying, on the outside, because the prosecution will say you were staying with your friend Jacquelyn so the gun that turned up in her drawer must be your gun. That's what they'll say. The gun that someone used to kill Jonah Lee. So it's important for us to be able to show you *didn't* stay there, you just visited her once in a while, and you didn't go there right after Jonah Lee was killed."

"Go there most every day. Jacquelyn she page me, tell me she need it, tell me I the only one can do it for her."

"Jacquelyn would page you and you would call her and she would invite you to her apartment for sex, and you would go and have sex with her and then leave, and as I understand it this was usually in the daytime."

"She say she don't get enough with nobody else."

"But she is not your regular girlfriend. You didn't live with her.

You didn't regularly spend the night with her, or even visit her at night. In fact you usually stayed with your brother in North Albany or with your sister in Troy."

"Stay where I fucking want. No bitch tell me where I got to stay."

"So this Jacquelyn...who was she seeing besides you?"

"She hang out with different guys. But when she really need it she call this here Loosh, who got what she want."

"Does she ever hang out at the Gander Bay?" I asked.

Loosh stared at me. "What you thinkin man? She don't go for no fucking white dudes."

"I thought maybe she might know some guys I know that hang out there."

Loosh shook his head, as though the idea was preposterous.

"I was just wondering. Guys named Bax and Bear. You probably know them and I thought possibly they could help with your problem."

"What about'm? How the fuck they going to help?"

"Are they friends of Jacquelyn's?"

"No way. She use to be Bax's bitch, but she too much for the dude."

"Up until *when* was she Bax's bitch?" I asked.

"Why you give a fuck?"

"We give a fuck," Judith said, "because a gun was found in Jacquelyn's bureau drawer under her underwear. If it starts to look like it might have been Bax that put it there, or that gave it to Jacquelyn to put there — and that told her to report it to the police — then maybe we can get your ass out of jail sometime before your hair turns gray. So...it's very important that we know everything there is to know about the relationship between Jacquelyn and this Bax — including when it ended — *if* it ended. Up until *when* was she Bax's girlfriend?"

Loosh dragged the back of his hand across his nose, snuffed loudly, and said "Dunno."

"Did she tell you she had stopped seeing him?" Judith asked.

"Say she need a man can give her what she need."

"Beginning when? When did you start seeing her?"

"Dunno — couple weeks."

"So it was maybe a week before they arrested you?"

Loosh shrugged and snuffed again and said nothing.

"And was it just that one week, more or less, that Jacquelyn was calling you and you were going to see her?"

"She beep me, tell me she need it."

"So you went to her apartment from time to time during that week. Can you say how many times, altogether, you went there?"

"Most every day."

"But she never actually said she stopped seeing Bax?"

"With me she don't need no fucking Bax."

"Ronald, do you think there is any chance she was setting you up?"

"What for? Why the fuck she gonna do that?"

Judith raised her eyebrows, shook her head. "That is what we're trying to figure out here. Jacquelyn called the police and said she'd found a gun in her bureau drawer and she didn't know how it got there. She did not do the careful thing, put it in a bag and toss it in a dumpster somewhere so she wouldn't have to answer a bunch of questions from the cops. No, she did the girl scout thing; she called the cops, let them ask all their questions. When they asked how long it could have been there, she was most helpful — told them she goes to the laundromat Saturday mornings. The Saturday Jonah Lee was shot she washed her undies and brought them home and put them in the drawer, and there was no gun there. A week later she does the same thing, brings the laundry home and goes to put away the clean underwear and there's the gun. They of course ask her who had been in her bedroom during that week and she gives them one name, yours. By this time you were of course in jail, charged with killing Jonah Lee with a handgun that first Saturday night, so she knows she is not exactly doing you a favor. So, yes, the question is why would she do what she did. One answer to that question is that she was doing it for Bax. That she set you up for Bax. What do you think?"

Loosh stared at her in sullen silence. What she had just said ought to have given him some reason to hope, but he didn't look at all hopeful. What he had heard was a belittling lecture from someone who sounded like a school teacher.

I said, "Loosh, this is probably a dumb question, but you didn't ever give Jacquelyn any hundred dollar bills for any reason, did you?"

"Motherfuck, you saying I had to pay for it?"

"No, no, but you know how it is sometimes. Like if she was short a couple hundred for the rent and you might have offered to help out. Something like that."

"I give the bitch what she need and it wasn't no fucking hundred-dollar bills."

"How about other people you might remember giving a hundred to?" I asked. "That is, back before Jonah was killed and they found a hundred with your fingerprint where it happened? How about Bax, or his buddy Bear...you ever give either of them a hundred-dollar bill for any reason?"

It was a long shot, and I only expected to hear more uncooperative bluster from Loosh, but the boy suddenly smiled. "Never give them nothin, but Bear he give *me* a hundred once. Sitting at the bar he says to me, 'Buy me a drink, dude.' I says 'Why should I buy a drink for a fucker like you?' He says 'Cause I a *generous* fucker and I gonna make it easy for you.' And he sticks this hundred in my hand. Beat up old thing with tape on it."

"This was at the Gander Bay Bar?"

"Yeah, at the Bay. So I say why the fuck not. I buy a round for the house and keep the change and Bear he don't give me no shit about it."

"Who was the bartender you gave the hundred to?"

"The skinny blond."

"Aileen, or her sister Margie?"

"The skinny one, Aileen."

"And she just put the money in the register?"

"Except most of it goin in my pocket."

"But the hundred-dollar bill went in the register. Do you have any idea after that how it might have got to the place on Second Street where Jonah Lee was killed?"

"You still sayin I killed the fucker. Get off my back, motherfuck."

"Wait a minute," Judith said. "I told you this man is trying to help. He's working with me, and I'm your attorney, and *I'm* trying to help you get your ass out of here."

"Yeah, right," Loosh said. "Both just likes to see dudes get their black asses out of jail."

"Ronald," she said, "you need to pay attention. You need to think real hard about what's happening here. Someone — whoever killed Jonah Lee — has arranged certain things so your ass is in jail and not theirs. You have been framed. We need to prove you've been framed. We need your cooperation if we're going to prove it."

Loosh stared at her, uncertainty struggling with the habitual defiance in his face.

She stood up. "We have to go. I'll be in touch with you soon. In the meantime, do some thinking. See what you can remember...anything that might help show how someone did this to you. And I don't mean the cops, I mean whoever made those certain arrangements to make you look guilty."

In the car, heading back into town she said, "So that was useful."

"But it still *c o u l d* be Loosh who hid the gun in that drawer. It seems he did have the opportunity."

"If he was the one that did it, I could see him stashing it in a vacant lot — someplace where he could get it again if he decided he needed it. I can't see him hiding it where it was found. It wasn't where he lived. He didn't have a key. And he doesn't trust her. Beyond the sexual braggadocio he has never said anything to suggest there was any kind of trust with her, or with any woman — or with any person at all — except his sister. Except for his sister, he is about as alone as anyone can be. I'm more and more certain of what we've got here — though not of how to handle it."

She was keyed up, drumming her fingers rapidly on the steering wheel. "That was very helpful about Bax and Bear, and the thing about the hundred-dollar bill actually rings true. With some guys you would have to figure it was just a convenient story, but this kid hasn't been coming *up* with stories. He hasn't been coming up with *anything* to help himself. Until that. The question is how to pursue it. Because by itself it isn't exactly a clincher."

"I need to pay a visit to the Gander Bay today. Maybe I can learn something. If the bartender Aileen is there maybe I can see if she remembers Bear giving the hundred to Loosh — and possibly what happened to it after that."

"That would be...But it sounds like you better be careful in that place if it's where these guys hang out."

"It's the public place where they hang out. I'm not so worried about meeting them in a public place."

21

Back at home I made a salami and lettuce sandwich and started a fresh pot of coffee. By the time the coffee was done, I had eaten the sandwich. I made a second sandwich, poured a cup of coffee, and carried them up to my office to eat in front of my computer as I read my e-mail.

The first message was from Lisa. "Weird time. Would like to hear your voice. Can you call me at the office this afternoon."

Then a message from Erica Schmidt. "New info. I'll be in Cafeteria A at 12:30 if you get this in time and can make it. Or call me at home after 6:00."

The current time, as reported on my Windows screen, was 12:14 p.m. The last time I had noticed, the computer's clock had been almost ten minutes slow, but I could still get to the cafeteria before Erica left if I just drove down Sheridan and went up the stairs. As usual I welcomed the opportunity to escape from my office.

I drove around the block onto Sheridan, then the few blocks to the foot of Swan where the stairs went up. There were many cars parked along the street but I was still able to find a place to park without great difficulty — as would not have been the case if I had driven over to Capitol Hill and looked for a parking place there.

I jogged up the stairs, drumming my way up a dozen or more steps between each landing. There were twelve landings. By the time I reached the top there was just enough pain in my legs to give me a sense of accomplishment. I walked the one block south, then jogged the block and a half down Washington and went into the Capitol through the north entrance. Continuing straight through the Capitol, I went down the stairs to the great subterranean corridor that crosses under State Street and extends more than a quarter mile beneath the full length of the Plaza. Cafeteria A was on the left part-way down the corridor.

Erica was sitting at a table along the west wall, in more or less the same location as when I had last seen her here.

"Guess you got my e-mail," she said as I sat down across from her.

"Just a few minutes ago," I said.

"Fast. You double park, or what?"

"I parked down on Sheridan and came up the stairs. The Jonah Lee Memorial Stairway."

"Better than the McFadden Memorial Stairway," she said. "What do you know about that one — the McFadden murder?"

"More than I want to know. I got called to his house by the police because I'd left a message on his machine around the time he was killed. It was a godawful gory scene. But beyond what it *looked* like I don't know any more than anyone else."

"You think it has anything to do with what you were telling me about?" She had both elbows on the table, with a sandwich held firmly in both hands. Her gray eyes gazed directly at me. "If I understood what you were telling me, McFadden was sort of in between Jonah Lee and this guy who wants to build the garage. Did that have anything to do with what happened to him?"

"Possibly. He did transfer his Sheridan Avenue properties to the corporation that Thomas Breston has set up for the project.

Very shortly before he was killed he signed the deeds, which should have removed any motive Breston might have had for having him killed. Of course I don't really have any idea what Breston is capable of — no idea of what he might be willing or able to do, or get done, even if he has, or had, the motive." I realized that I was still revved up from the exercise I'd just had, and was saying more than I needed to. "I certainly don't want to be quoted on any of this," I said.

She finished chewing a substantial bite of sandwich, then said, "I think we both agree that the conversation we're having is one we will never have had."

"Absolutely."

"Okay then. Here is what I learned just this morning. And what is interesting is that as far as I can tell I was *supposed* to learn it." She put the sandwich down, then reestablished her elbows on the table and rested her chin on her folded hands. "This comes from the top and was passed along to me by someone who would normally be very tight-lipped with any such information. It seems the Commissioner is upset about Jonah's application disappearing."

"The Commissioner? He knows about it?"

"Knows and is upset. That is the word that was used — *u p s e t.* And of course within the Division, an upset Commissioner is very upsetting to us all. Anyway, I was given to understand that the disappearance of the application was the result of an intervention by the office of a downstate legislator. The Commissioner does in fact tend to be upset by that kind of intervention in his tidy little Division, especially when it's an intervention on behalf of someone he considers undeserving, *by* a legislator he feels he cannot afford to challenge, which is of course most legislators."

"So the Commissioner either swallows his upset," I suggested, "or he reacts through some sort of back channel. Are you saying that you're the back channel in this case?"

"I believe I am, at least part of it. I believe we are actually supposed to be having this conversation which we are of course not having."

"I don't think I ever properly appreciated this cloak and dagger aspect of life within DHCR."

"Let me tell you, it's an exciting life."

"So the significance of the Commissioner being upset and perhaps wanting certain others to know he's upset is...?"

"That he would like to see NHA resubmit the application, or a follow-up, possibly modified, application, but would rather not go out on a limb and proactively invite it."

"Are we then to understand that if NHA does resubmit an application, it would be considered, even though the application deadline passed some weeks ago?"

"I think that is what we are to understand. If NHA takes the initiative and explains the very unusual circumstances, the Commissioner could, in his great mercy, agree to let it be considered."

"This is very timely," I said. "The NHA board meets tonight and I'll be reporting to them on the status of various things, including the Sheridan Avenue Project. They know they will have to do something, one way or the other, about the Sheridan Avenue properties that Jonah bought from Arnold Duber."

"Would the application have to be changed much to square it with the present circumstances?" she asked. "With Jonah gone it can't really look the same, can it? I mean if the Division is actually going to consider funding it."

"It's intriguing to think that, with the old version out of sight, it can be modified. The trouble is, what has changed is not just that Jonah is gone. Breston has consolidated his holdings. He now has deeds to McFadden's properties and to the Gander Bay property — both of which were included in Jonah's proposal. If the application is resubmitted, it's going to have to make the claim that those properties are still somehow available to NHA."

"And if the owner says they're not..." She had started to pick up her sandwich, but put it down again. "But *would* he say that? Would he come out in the open and let himself be seen as blocking a righteous community development project in order to build a parking garage? Blocking a project that the martyred Jonah Lee presented as the exact opposite of the parking garage — linking a low-income neighborhood to Capitol Hill instead of sealing it off."

"He has to come out in the open at some point," I said. "He knows there's going to be controversy when he does, and you'd have to figure he'd rather not start the public fight until he knows he can win it. So the question is, where does he stand politically right now? Does he have the support he needs to get it locked up before there's enough negative publicity so the political winds shift and he starts to *lose* support? He's had that happen to him before."

Erica gazed at me thoughtfully. "You know, that crazy half-baked proposal of Jonah's is making more and more sense to me. He *did* know what he was doing. And he must have somehow let what's-his-name — the garage guy — know what he was doing with that proposal."

"I think so. I think he must have found a way of letting Breston know about the proposal — and what could spin out from it, what could happen even if the proposal wasn't funded, even if DHCR buried it. Jonah could give a copy to the press. Breston had to have known that, and known what the press could do with the story."

"And you think Breston killed him because of that?"

"It makes a lot more sense that he would take the risk of killing him to head off that kind of publicity than that he would do it just to shake a couple of properties loose from NHA. There had to be easier ways to get the properties. He could have offered the organization ten times what they were worth, or more — whatever it took."

She had gone back to work on her sandwich, which she again held in both hands as she chewed methodically. Eventually she said, "Interesting strategy, using the state to get that kind of publicity."

"I'm sure a lot of state *workers* would actually be on Breston's side — would prefer to see the parking garage built."

"But the people who make the decisions already have parking."

"A lot of their secretaries don't."

"They also don't have much influence in this paper-pushing world. Anyway, I think what's important is that the Division doesn't want to be seen as running interference for some outsider who comes in and does a development that flies in the face of what a low-income neighborhood is trying to do for itself. DHCR is still supposed to stand for the Division of Housing and Community Renewal, not the Division of Downtown Development."

"I hope you're right," I said. "Now tell me...the person who leaked the information to you about the Commissioner...is it possible for you to tell that person that you've just happened to hear that NHA is actively considering resubmitting the application?"

"Actively considering? What do I say when they ask what that means?"

"You can say you don't really know, but you think if they do it they'll do it next week."

"Okay, yes, I can say that. Next week. So, when do you go north?"

"Toward the end of next week."

She squinted at me. "What I want to know is, are you actually making a living, in between this stuff with the NHA and your great northern adventures?"

"Not this month. Or next month either, of course. Although next month I'll at least catch some fish, pick some berries."

* * *

I came down the stairs more slowly than I had gone up, savoring the view out over the rooftops and treetops of Sheridan Hollow. It was almost the summer solstice. The midday sun was high and hot in the southern sky behind me. In front of me to the northeast, the blue sky descended cloudless to the far hills of Rensselaer county. For a moment I felt as though I had been lifted out of the city altogether and had an urge to take the afternoon off and go climb a mountain or paddle a river — which was not at all what I was supposed to be thinking about. Too much needed to be done before I headed off far to the northeast to leave all cities behind for a month.

Reaching the bottom of the stairs, I turned left onto Sheridan Avenue, passing the church and my parked pickup and continuing up the street to where the Gander Bay sign hung over the sidewalk.

As I had hoped, I found the bar open but nearly empty. The blond bartender Aileen, wearing an unbuttoned faded plaid shirt over her usual cut-off tee-shirt, was mopping the floor. "Widja inaminute," she said over her shoulder.

I could see the bearded head of Buddy Rowley in the usual booth beyond the bar. He was watching me without acknowledgement. Beyond him there were two more people huddled in the furthermost booth. There was no one sitting at the bar. Aileen went on mopping. I slid onto a stool and waited.

Eventually Aileen leaned the mop against the wall, came behind the bar and said, "So whaddaya want?"

"I guess it will have to be Killian's," I said.

She drew the beer and set it on the bar in front of me, spilling some, which she more or less mopped up with the loose sleeve of the plaid shirt. The shirt hung open in front and I found myself gazing at the oversized ring dangling from her navel.

"Hey," I said, "I've got a question I wanted to ask you. A confidential question."

She eyed me suspiciously but didn't back away. "You can ask anything you want," she said.

"I don't know if you remember...this would have been a couple of weeks ago probably. You know the guy they call Bear..."

She frowned and made a motion with her thumb toward the back of the bar. "Back there. In the booth."

"Oh yeah, didn't realize it was him," I said. I was sure I couldn't be heard from the back booth, but I lowered my voice anyway. "Well a couple of weeks ago he was in here sitting at the bar next to the guy th ey call Loosh, Ronald Burns, who's in jail now."

"Sure, those guys're always in here. Bear and Bax and Loosh, 'cept for Loosh being in jail now."

"So Loosh used to hang out with Bax and Bear?"

"Not like *together*. Not like Bax and Bear." She tossed her head in the direction of the back booth. "But Loosh, he was always in here, same as those guys."

"Okay, so there was one night when Bear was sitting next to Loosh at the bar, and the way I heard it Bear says to Loosh, Buy me a drink. And Loosh says something like, 'Why should I?' And Bear says, 'Because I'm a generous guy,' and he gives Loosh a hundred-dollar bill. So then Loosh buys a round of drinks."

I looked at her questioningly. She stared back at me. "So what?"

"You remember it happening that way?"

"It happened. Like I say, so what?"

"Loosh paid for the drinks with the hundred-dollar bill. You gave him change. I guess the hundred wound up in the till."

"What else am I gonna do with it, stick it in my drawers?"

"Probably not. Do you remember anything in particular about that particular bill?"

"There was this number one with these two zeros after it."

"Fresh new bill? Old bill?"

"Old crudded up thing."

"Torn?"

"What are you some kind of antique money collector? Could h ave been to rn, sure, and taped back together. Still wo rth the same."

"Okay, my last question is, do you happen to remember if the hundred came back out of the till?"

"You mean like someone comes in and pays for a Bud Light with a thousand-dollar bill, so I give him change in hundreds?"

"I thought maybe someone might have had a bunch of smaller bills and they might have wanted to change them for a hundred. Or something. But I guess that didn't happen."

"It was late. Closing time, Buddy takes the money downstairs, counts it up."

"And some of it is change for the next day, and some of it goes to the bank. Am I right that hundreds wouldn't be kept for change? The guy with the thousand-dollar bill doesn't come in that often."

"You already had your last question."

"You're very sharp. I think I'll go bother Buddy now."

She stepped close to the bar and pointed toward the door. "If you was smart mister, you'd turn around and walk *o u t a* here."

"I'll only bother him for a minute. Then I'll take your advice."

I left my glass, still full, on the bar and went back in the direction of Buddy's booth. Slouched in his usual position in the corner of the booth, Buddy watched me approach. "You're not welcome here," he said.

"Okay. Just wanted to check in — see if you'd figured out whose team you're on yet." In the back booth, the very large man named Bear was staring at me through small eyes surrounded by a great deal of graying hair. Across from him in the booth, the small light-skinned African American man named Bax who had challenged my presence on his first visit to the Bay had half-turned in his seat and also stared.

"Ain't on *n o* friggin team," Buddy said. "Sure the fuck ain't on yours."

Standing at the end of the booth, I said, "Buddy, you need a team. Alone you're just going to be used by everybody that comes along."

Bear stood up and started toward us, followed by Bax. "People like these guys here ," I said. Bear was approaching with arrogant slowness. "Them and their employer Thomas Breston. They've used you, and they'll use you some more and then they'll dump you. If you're lucky maybe you won't actually get your throat slashed like Eddie McFadden."

Buddy said, "You're an asshole, Crow."

Bear was at my left shoulder. With a large hand he took hold of the back of my shirt at the collar and lifted. I drove my left elbow backwards into the big man's solar plexus. There was an explosive grunt and I was released.

Buddy had drawn the gun from his shoulder holster. He pointed it at me, then toward the front of the bar. "Get out," he said.

"Gladly," I said.

As I passed Aileen on my way to the door, she said, "Toldja." She looked almost happy. I had at least enlivened her afternoon.

By the time I reached my pickup, the adrenaline was sizzling in my veins and I felt a need I had no way to meet. It was not exactly that I had walked away from an unfinished fight. The situation had played out more or less as I would have chosen if there had been any real choice involved, and I was glad to have been able to walk out at all. But the brief physical contact with Bear left me with an itch. It would be a kind of relief to just throw my full weight and strength against a large body like Bear's, and let the whole thing be just a wrestling match. Instead I had to go back to my desk and deal with the details of a situation that seemed to have more details by the hour.

22

I had to call Judith Rosen and fill her in on my conversation with Aileen. I had to reread Jonah's proposal and think about how it should be modified if it was going to be resubmitted. I had to finish the cash flow projection that I had started for the NHA board, and think about how to present its implications to them. And I wanted to find out — if I could — whether the police had had any success in finding Linda Bettleman and whether there was any new information about Eddie McFadden's murder. And I had to figure out what else I had to do.

And of course I needed to call Lisa. But before calling her I wanted to think about why the abortive evening with her at my house was so unsettling. How would that evening have played out if Reilly hadn't called me away to the scene of Eddie's murder? And how would the upcoming evening play out — after the NHA meeting and after Lisa's second dinner with Dick Frost? If she was late, was I going to wait for her at her house again?

I decided to do the easy thing first. I checked my e-mail. In the two hours since I had last checked, four messages had come in.

There was a message from Dave Potter, which I would open later. There was something from the group in Rochester, to whom I still owed some work. I would open it later too. There was something from a group in Trenton, which I knew also related to promised work not yet done.

I moved on and opened the last message, which was from Harry Cooper at his state office address.

"Warren, I just got a call from Thomas Breston here at work. Says he wants to talk about buying the Sheridan Avenue properties from us. Told him the board's meeting tonight and we'd get back to him. He gave me an Albany number and asked me to call him tomorrow. See you this evening. —Harry."

I got up, went downstairs, poured a cup of coffee from the pot I had made earlier, and put it in the microwave to reheat. The press of new info rmation was beginning to excite me — a feeling like being at the head of a rapid with the current picking up speed, things happening more quickly, options narrowing and becoming clearer.

Back upstairs I called Lisa's office and was told she was on another line. I let the receptionist put me on hold and used the time to sort th rough the piles of paper on my desk until I found the copy of Jonah's proposal. With the phone on my shoulder and the proposal on my lap, I began to read once again, this time as an editor, thinking about how to moderate the style without losing the impact of Jonah's challenge.

"Where is the Sheridan Hollow neighborhood? It is very close at hand. Standing on the steps of the Capitol you would be looking right into it, just a block away, if it weren't for the fact that it lies conveniently at the bottom of a ravine where the City and State have been content to leave it to deteriorate, out of sight and isolated. So you will have to walk five minutes north and look down the slope to see what poverty looks like. What you will see is real, the reality of the problems faced by residents of real low-income neighborhoods everywhere. It is also symbolic, a dramatic symbol of what is wrong with a society that isolates and turns away from those it has come to call the underclass, even when they live just a block from the state capitol."

I would have to make some changes. It sounded as though Jonah was actually blaming the state for not somehow hauling the Sheridan Hollow neighborhood up out of Sheridan Hollow. But I didn't want to lose the impact of the last sentence. The issue — d rawn between Jonah's plan and Bre sto n's plan — was whether the neighborhood would be more isolated, or less isolated.

"Warren," Lisa said.

"Hey," I said. "Busy day. How are you?"

"Yeah busy, but it's good to hear your voice. I've been worrying, actually, which is probably silly, but there's just too much stuff going on."

"Yes, a lot of stuff. A lot of new information today, too. Including information suggesting how the kid Loosh could have been set up by Breston's people for Jonah's murder. Also interesting scuttlebutt from DHCR about Jonah's application. And I just heard from Harry Cooper that Bre ston called him and wants to talk about buying the NHA property on Sheridan. Breston gave him a phone number, by the way, so that's one piece of information you don't need to worry about tonight."

There was a brief silence. Then she said, "You seem to be working at this thing full-time."

"More than I bargained for."

"But you seem to be bargaining for more and more. Anyway — speaking of tonight — I wonder if there's time for us to get together someplace for a drink, five-thirty or sixish, before your NHA meeting and before my dinner date with Dick. So you could fill me in on things, and we could talk about how Dick might be able to help."

I wanted to see her but was beginning to feel desperate about my schedule. "I'm going to be flat out getting ready for that meeting," I said. "Maybe you could stop by *here* for a drink."

There was another silence. "I was thinking more in terms of someplace public and cheerful. Maybe the Pump Station."

"More cheerful than my old-fashioned kitchen."

"No, it's not that," she said firmly. "It would just be nice to be out of the shadow of all this stuff for a little bit."

"I know. But things are coming to a head and we'll be completely out of it soon, one way or another."

"That's not very reassuring, the one-way-or-another part."

"It'll work out just fine. The big thing right now — the thing I need to really work on before the meeting — is to figure out what's workable for NHA — what's best for the organization."

"What's best for the organization, or is it really about the best way to restart Jonah's project whether NHA wants it or not?"

"Okay," I said. "Yes, that's something I need to think about some more."

Lisa sighed in a way obviously intended to be audible over the phone. "Well tell me what you want me to try to get from Dick."

I was beginning to regret that I hadn't simply agreed to meet her someplace public and cheerful, where the conversation might have gone more easily. But I pushed ahead. "We have the contact information we need and I assume we'll be talking with Breston soon. So any information that Dick Frost can give us that would increase our leverage in dealing directly with Breston..."

"Any information. That means basically telling Dick exactly where you're at and what you're doing, and inviting him to say what he knows that might help."

"I guess that's right. At least generally where we're at and what we're doing."

"The less general I am the less general he's going to be."

"Okay, you're right. There's no point in going halfway with him — at least if he seems to be interested. And the other specific thing we talked about asking him is...who might Breston be talking within the public sector. The word from DHCR is that some down-state legislator intervened to make Jonah's application disappear."

"Can I tell Dick that?"

"I suppose so, if it feeds his interest. It's not like it's the first time a legislator ever weighed in for or against someone's application — though they aren't usually able to make the application just disappear the way Jonah's did."

"Okay," she said. "Anything else I need to know?" She was speaking now in her professionally upbeat realtor's voice.

"One thing I'm wondering about now...I don't know if Frost would have any way to know anything about it, but I'm wondering what Breston has actually got for working capital at this stage of things. We're assuming that he's got investors waiting in the wings with tons of money, but what does he have right now for working capital? Is he really so short of cash that he had to get Janet Rowley to take back a mortgage on the Gander Bay property — or did that have to do with keeping her loyal to the firm?"

"I'm not sure I understand what you're getting at."

"How liquid is he — or how liquid is Alton, Inc. How big a check could he sit down and write right now."

"You mean how big a check could he write to NHA for those properties? But he wouldn't have to write that check today. The money could still come from the investors through whatever arrangement they have."

"Sure, but I'd still like to know how much he's got in his pocket, as it were."

"What it sounds like," she said, "is you want to know, if you could corner him and squeeze him, how much money could you squeeze out."

I laughed. "That's not quite the way I'd put it."

"Well I wasn't trying to be funny. I think it's a dangerous idea, and I'm not particularly interested in helping get you killed."

"I certainly don't want you to press for anything with Dick Frost that you're not comfortable with."

"I'm not sure you understood what I just said. It's not my comfort that's the issue here."

"Okay. I guess there's a lot we need to talk about. Can we talk tonight? At your house when you get home, if I come over there after the NHA meeting?"

"If we can't talk sooner, then yes, I'd like you to come over, but only if you don't...Only if you feel okay about it. I've got to run. Client just walked in."

I was left feeling an unsorted mixture of frustration and worry and, in spite of it all, eager anticipation of the evening with her when the rest of the day's tasks had been taken care of.

* * *

After calling Judith Rosen I went back to Jonah's proposal — determined this time not to be drawn into editing Jonah's prose but to focus on the property-by-property facts of the proposal and think about the nuts and bolts adjustments that would need to be made. I did think some adjustments were possible, and the possibilities excited me.

But after I had re-read the whole application, my excitement had ebbed. The bare facts didn't offer many possibilities. There was no longer a way to suggest, as Jonah had, that the NHA controlled or was close to controlling the properties that had belonged to McFadden and the Rowleys. I could claim only the two properties purchased from Arnold Duber, with the possible addition of the Greta Green property on the other side of the street. It didn't add up to a project on anything like the scale that Jonah had proposed — or anything like the scale that DHCR's request for proposals had invited. It couldn't even *pretend* to be "a project designed to launch and anchor the renewal of a neighborhood."

The best I could do now was to say that NHA was actively negotiating with the new owner of the McFadden and Rowley properties, even though selling those properties was the last thing Breston wanted to do. I also wondered if I could continue to claim that NHA held options on the McFadden properties. I still hadn't actually seen those options and didn't know when they expired. And I had no idea what it would mean legally to hold options from someone who had turned around and sold the properties to someone else. Presumably the person who sold them would be liable for breach of contract, but that person was no longer alive. The question that remained was whether a court would hold that Breston bought the properties subject to the options and would therefore be bound to honor the options. If NHA *had* the options, it would certainly be worth proceeding on the assumption that they were still binding. But NHA didn't have them, or at least couldn't find them.

The one thing that NHA did have was the two Duber properties right in the middle of Breston's project. I stared at the segment of a tax map that Jonah had attached to his proposal. On the map the Duber properties had been darkened with heavy cross-hatching. Those two properties still gave me the basic leverage with Breston that Jonah had. But if I was going to make good use of that leverage I needed Breston to know that the state was once again considering a credible application from NHA. And if the application was really going to be credible, it needed to be bigger. It needed to include more properties. I pulled the tax map onto my lap and looked at the properties across the street from the Duber properties. I hadn't paid much attention to them because Breston didn't need them and hadn't acquired them. Jonah — with his focus on defending the steep south slope of the Hollow against Breston's plans — hadn't bothered with those across-the-street properties either. But quite possibly they could be included in a housing project to bring it up to scale. I would need to go and look at what was there — and find out who owned it.

But not this afternoon. Right now I had to do the work that would let me address the most immediate concerns of the NHA board, so that — I hoped — they would agree not to sell out to Breston right away and would give me some time to restructure a proposal for Sheridan Avenue.

After returning Jonah's proposal to the pile of active work that accumulates to the left of my keyboard, I woke up the computer and located the spreadsheet file in which I'd been developing the NHA cash flow projection. Finishing it would mean catching up with some pieces of information that I had put off looking for. I also had to rough out a proposed operating budget for the next year.

After several hours of work, my stomach had begun to rumble, and I checked the time. It was five-thirty. I still wasn't finished, but I would need to eat sometime and I decided it might as well be now. I would take a quick walk out to Central Avenue and bring back some Chinese take-out.

Just before I reached Central, I was joined by Jesse astride his bicycle. "My man," Jesse said. "Ain't been seeing you."

"I know. I've been working hard on stuff. Haven't been out and about as much, except when you're in school."

Jesse looped ahead on the bicycle, swung back and stopped, facing me. "Come on, man," he said. "I know what you doing. Ain't working hard on stuff. New girlfriend is what it is."

"How do you know that?"

"Seen her last night, getting out of her car out front of your house. So I ask her, you a friend of Mr. Crow's, and she say yes she is. So I ask, you his girl friend? And she say, whadda you think — I look like a boy or something?"

"She's kind of a smart-ass."

"Nice *l o o k i n'* though. So don't give me that stuff about working hard. What's her name?"

"Okay, Jesse, I guess you got me. Her name's Lisa."

"Only one a them I know is my teacher. Mrs. Lisa Johnson. She kind of old though, not so nice lookin'. Where you going, anyway?"

"Just around the corner for some Chinese take-out."

"Man, I could use some of that."

"Come on then," I said.

On the window of the tiny restaurant was a sign done in black crayon on an 8 1/2 x 11 sheet of paper.

SPECIAL

CHICKEN

2 PIECE $1.00

It had been there for months. I had never been sure whether it meant that the chicken was special or that the everyday house special was chicken. Not that it mattered. The family that ran the place had adapted their menu to neighborhood taste by adding something that, although cooked in a wok, looked and tasted very much like Kentucky Fried Chicken.

"Want some chicken?" I asked.

"Oh man."

"The regular fried kind?"

"What I really like...that General kind."

"Good choice. And the general outranks the colonel anyway."

"What colonel?"

"Colonel Sanders."

"Oh man."

We bought some General Tso's chicken and a Szechwan vegetable dish that I knew was fiery hot. When we got back to Orange Street with the food, I said, "I'm going to eat in my office while I finish some work. You can eat down by the TV or take some chicken home if you want, or you can eat up in the office with me but it could be pretty boring."

"Can I use your laptop?"

"If you don't get chicken grease on the keys. I'll get us a roll of paper towels. We'll both need them."

I gathered paper towels, plates and forks from the kitchen and led the way upstairs. When we entered the office Jesse went straight to the desktop computer and nudged the mouse with a finger to clear the screen saver, then gazed at the monitor. "Excel spreadsheet," he said. "What you doin' with it?"

In recent months I had been teaching him how to set up and use some basic spreadsheets. Though he seemed to be bored by elementary school math classes, Jesse was quick to see relationships and he liked the building-block architecture of electronic spreadsheets, especially when he got to use the laptop.

"It's called a cash flow projection," I said "I'm doing it for the housing organization on Second Street."

"Where the guy got shot?"

"Yes, where the guy Jonah Lee was killed. They're having a meeting tonight and I'm supposed to have this spreadsheet ready for them to look at."

"So what's it do?"

"Okay." I sat down and, with Jesse beside me, pointed at the screen. "The columns go by month — June, July, August and so on. Then the first line shows how much money you have at the beginning of the month, and the lines under that show how much money you expect to have coming in for different things — rent that people pay them, and so on. And down here it gets totaled up so you know how much is supposed to come in altogether during the month. Then these lines down below show how much money they're going to have to pay out for different things — like the phone bill, the electric bill — and all t h a t gets totaled up down here. Then the spreadsheet calculates how much you'll have at the end of the month, by taking the amount you had at the *beginning* of the month and adding what comes in and subtracting what goes out. And it puts that ending balance up here as the beginning balance for the next month. It just rolls along like that from month to month."

At my shoulder Jesse was motionless, completely focused.

"You want to try one for yourself?" I asked. "Do your own cash flow projection?"

"Got no cash to flow."

"I thought you got an allowance."

"Yeah but it don't *fl o w*, man — don't last the week."

"Well, suppose you decided to save up for a new bicycle. So you make some money mowing lawns, and in the winter you shovel snow, and maybe you get some money for Christmas, and then there's the allowance coming in every week, and you decide you're going to spend less money, just buy the stuff you really need. So then you want to know how long it's going to take to save up enough for the bicycle, so you do a cash flow projection. I'll make a copy of this one, and you can take the laptop and change the names on the lines for the money coming in and going out, and put in your own numbers and see what you get."

I copied the NHA spreadsheet onto a diskette and got Jesse started with the laptop before going back to my own desk, where financial reports were spread out on either side of the computer. I still had to figure out how much to project as monthly rent receipts. I knew how much was supposed to come in from 31 occupied apartments. I knew the vacancy rate for past years and how much uncollectable rent had been written off. But it was hard to decide what to project as actual receipts for the coming months, especially with Jonah no longer there to make sure rent was collected.

With a plate of rice and Szechwan vegetables on my lap I once again sorted through the reports on my desk. To my right Jesse studied the laptop resting on his knees. He had one hand on the keyboard, one hand holding a piece of chicken.

"Man," he said, "never mind that lawn mowin' bullshit, I gonna be a landlord. These guys getting more'n *'leven thousand* a month from folks just paying their rent."

"That's how much they're *supposed* to get. I'm trying to figure out how much we should figure they'll *really* get. Because some people might not pay on time, or might not be able to pay at all."

"Evict 'em. That's what they do."

"You really want to be putting families out on the street?"

"My mama says you got to pay the rent before anything else."

"She's right. Anyway, landlords don't necessarily get rich, at least if they do everything they're supposed to do. Look at that amount every month for maintenance, and the amount for mortgage payments, and then in August the big insurance bill, and in September the big tax bill. You sure you want to be a landlord?"

"Maybe not. Sure hate to give up that big 'leven thousand a month though."

"Yeah well the idea here is to figure out what you're really going to have coming in and going out, and then figure out whether you can build up some cash or whether you're going to end up in the hole. So put in those numbers for allowance and lawn mowing..."

"Okay, where you gonna find lawns to mow on this block?"

"Not on this block. You might have to range out a little. Look for grass and knock on doors."

"Got no lawn mower neither."

"We could talk about a loan so you could buy one. Have to

make loan payments every month then. Or you can go look for people who have their own mower and just want someone to do the job for them."

"Man, what you trying to get me *into,*" Jesse said, but the light sound of keystrokes began to come from the laptop.

I decided the projection for NHA rent receipts should be on the optimistic side. The board needed to think positively and do what needed to be done to see that collections didn't falter, and I thought Helen Hamilton could be counted on to stay on top of the rent roll.

But even with healthy rent collections, the projection was not reassuring. There was still not really enough money to pay a capable full-time replacement for Jonah. I made another copy of the worksheet and started another version of the projection with a major fund drive projected for the fall — a Jonah Lee Memorial Fund Drive.

"I got it made," Jesse said.

"How much is it showing you can save?"

"Three hundred dollars by New Year's."

"Must have found a lot of lawns to mow."

"Couldn't find no lawns, but somebody give me three hundred dollars for Christmas."

"Who? Who's the big giver?"

"Gonna have to work on it," Jesse said.

"Let me know if you find one. I know some other folks can use a big giver."

23

We left the house at five minutes before seven. Jesse provided a bicycle escort down Robin, across Clinton and along Judson to the corner of Second Street, just as he had done the evening Jonah was killed. On the corner, he rode one full loop around me, then coasted on down Judson toward Livingston and the entrance to Tivoli Park. I turned and walked the half block down Second to the NHA office.

I had not expected that the meeting would actually start at the theoretical hour of seven o'clock, so I'd hoped I would have a chance to hear from Harry about his call from Breston before others gathered. But, to my surprise, the little meeting room was almost full when I got there.

"Most everybody's here," Harry said. "We're just waiting for Zera."

As far as I knew, Zera Kay was not a member of the NHA board of directors, but apparently she was seen as a stakeholder who should have as much say in matters now before the board as the nine board members already gathered around the table.

Of these nine people, seven were African American residents of the neighborhood. Of the seven, five, including Helen Hamilton, lived in NHA housing and were officially designated "resident representatives," one was Sarah Williams, a young woman currently enrolled at Albany Law School, and one was Harry Cooper. The two non-African-Americans were a young man who was on the staff of another nonprofit housing organization, and an ex-nun, Barbara Randolph, who was the one member of the board whose politics were probably as radical as Jonah's had been.

Tonight the group was unusually quiet, hushed by the absence of the man who had brought them together in the first place and had energized and guided their meetings. His absence was especially hard for Harry Cooper, who shuffled papers, checked his watch, reshuffled papers, rechecked his watch. To Harry's left, Helen Hamilton was as quietly composed as ever. I leaned toward her and said, "I put together some handouts. I wonder if we could make copies."

Helen rose and came around the table and took the sheets from me and disappeared down the hall toward the office.

Harry seemed even more agitated with Helen out of the room. I caught his eye and said, "So Breston called you..."

"Yes, today, at work. I guess you got my e-mail."

"He didn't actually make an offer — didn't mention a price?"

"No. Wanted to know *our* price. Said he wanted to talk and was sure we could do business. I told him he couldn't just do business with me, it was going to be up to the whole board."

"Are you thinking the board should set a price and authorize the sale?"

Harry studied his hands, checked his watch, then turned troubled eyes on me. "I need to ask you something. Could we step into the hall for just a minute?"

We rose and made our way awkwardly to the door, sidestepping between the wall and the backs of seated board members. In the hall, Harry said, "Uh...I wish we'd had a chance to talk before this, but I want to know what you think. I mean, would we be doing business with the Devil? Do you think Breston *did* have something to do with Jonah's murder?"

"Sorry I didn't call you right after work," I said. "Yes, that is what I think. It looks more and more like he, his people, were behind it. But as for doing business with the Devil, I wouldn't necessarily say you shouldn't take his money if the deal is what's best for the organization. I'm not convinced that it is the best thing, but I think that's the question for you as a board — how good is the deal, not how good is the guy you're dealing with." I didn't like the sound of what I was saying. It sounded glib.

Harry stared at me. "But to just do business with the man who maybe killed Jonah as though..."

"I know. It's more complicated than what I just said. Jonah himself wouldn't sell those properties to Breston, because of what Breston wanted to do with them, which is part of what got him killed. I guess, if it's okay, I'd like to have a few minutes to fill the board in on what I've learned about that whole Sheridan Avenue situation."

"Definitely," Harry said. "We need to know." He edged back toward the meeting room. "Good. But I wonder where Zera is."

We had barely reseated ourselves at the table when I heard the door opened at the other end of the hall, then Zera's clear bright voice greeting Helen.

Shortly the two women came into the room. Helen handed me the photocopies she had made and moved quietly around the table. Behind her Zera looked at me and said, "Oh, good. I have something for you too."

She followed Helen around the table and took the one remaining empty seat. She put her purse on the table, removed a plain white business envelope and slid it across the table toward me. "Some papers of Jonah's that I found. I don't know if they're important. I thought you might know what to do with them."

I was aware that everyone was watching me. I could have set the envelope aside and let the meeting begin, but I opened it, as much as anything to keep myself busy in the presence of this vivid woman whom I hadn't seen since her voice had affected me so unexpectedly at the funeral.

There were three sheets of paper in the envelope. The first sheet was headed "OPTION TO PURCHASE." The other two had the same heading, the same format. I read all three as carefully as I could under the circumstances.

"What is it?" Harry asked finally.

"Purchase options. From Eddie McFadden, for his Sheridan

A venue properties." I looked carefully at the signatures. "Signed
originals. They run until August — not expired yet."

Each of the sheets had been notarized by McFadden's friend
Linda Bettleman. I looked up from the papers and met Zera's eyes.
"They were in a folder stuck in a pile of books," she said.

"Thank you for bringing them. They could be important. The
board will need to talk about it."

"Maybe we should get right to it then," Harry said. "This is a
special meeting. We don't have to do the regular routine. Our
agenda just says 'discuss how to deal with the situation that faces
us after our loss.' And Sheridan Avenue is a big part of that situation."

"It's one part," Helen said, "and I agree we need to talk about
it, but, Harry, I think we need to deal with first things first, and I
really think the first question is who's going to do whatever needs
to be done — whether it's on Sheridan Avenue or Second Street.
And we're not even sure yet whether we can afford to hire someone."

"Thank you, you're right," Harry said.

"Warren did some figuring on that," Helen said. "Maybe we
could start by looking at what he's got for us."

"Good idea," Harry said.

I passed around the financial material I'd prepared — a statement of current assets and liabilities as of June 15, with two versions of the cash flow projection; then a report comparing actual
and budgeted income and expense for the first ten months of the
current fiscal year, together with two roughed out versions of a
budget for the fiscal year that would begin on August first.

"I can go over all of this if you want," I said, "but let me start
with what it adds up to, as I see it."

"Yeah, just give us the bottom line," said one of the resident
representatives, a large, sweet faced woman with a hoarse voice.

"The bottom line is going to depend on what you decide. Right
now you have almost twenty thousand in cash in your operating
fund, but you're going to need just about that much to pay the
insurance bill in August and the tax bill in September. It will be
hard to scrape up enough cash in the next few months to pay someone a half decent salary unless you borrow it from the reserve
account. There's now about nine thousand dollars in that account.
For the long run you want it to be there for when you need it, but
you could borrow it for a few months to cover a cash flow problem.
So the real problem isn't just how to scrape up enough cash to get

th rough the summer. It's how to find enough income for the next year — and beyond — so you can hire someone permanent to run the organization."

"And we're not going to be able to find someone who'll do like Jonah," Harry said. "Someone who wo rks sixty, seventy hours a week for a salary that's half what he deserves, and then doesn't even pay himself as much as he's supposed to half the time. We're going to have to treat it like a real job with a real salary."

"There are other dedicated people out there," Barbara Randolph said, a little too crisply. As one of those dedicated people, she herself held a combination of social justice jobs that added up to many hours per week at probably less pay than Jonah had received.

"Not like Jonah," several voices said at once.

"Not who can do what he did," Harry said. "He was one of a kind."

Zera stood up. Moving around the table she whispered, "I'll be back in a little bit," and left the room.

Helen started to get up to follow her, but then shook her head and sat down again. Picking up the papers in front of her, she looked at me. "You gave us two budgets. One of them has a director's salary of twenty-five thousand. In the other it's thirty thousand. Where does the extra five thousand come from?" She was way ahead of everyone else. She had probably studied the budgets while doing the copying.

"It's in the donations line," I said. "The smaller budget has just five hundred dollars in donations. The larger one has fifty-five hundred. It would take a real push. Maybe a fund drive in Jonah's memory. Or something. Maybe you can come up with some other fundraising ideas."

In fact th ey proceeded to come up with many ideas — from bake sales, dinner-dances and raffles, to benefit performances by various local musical groups, to an appeal to a famous athlete that somebody's cousin used to know. After a half hour there was at least the beginning of a consensus around the idea of a fund drive that would be launched with a gala memorial evening with food, live music and dancing. Enough optimism swelled up around this idea so that the group briefly considered offering a salary of thirty-five thousand for a new executive director. But the cautious perspective of Helen and Harry prevailed. A budget was finally approved that included a thirty thousand dollar annual salary but that assumed that a new director would not be hired until at least one month into the new fiscal year, so only $27,500 was budgeted for salary in that year.

"In the meantime," Harry said, "I was wondering...but, well, maybe this is premature. Maybe, Warren, if you would fill us in on the Sheridan Avenue situation."

"Okay," I said. "It's kind of a complicated story and I still don't know the *whole* story. But there's one more handout I want to pass around. It's an excerpt from the narrative Jonah wrote for the application to the state. Most of you haven't seen it, so I wanted you to read at least a bit of it."

When the sheet had been distributed, I read aloud the excerpt — the introductory description of Sheridan Hollow as seen — or not seen — from the steps of the Capitol. I then summarized the major features of the proposal itself. "Anyway," I said, "you already know more or less what kind of project he was proposing. But I don't think you know the real reason he was pushing it."

I told them what I knew as succinctly as I could. Breston's plan to build a parking garage. Raymond's confirmation that Jonah knew about the plan, was trying to block it, and had been scheduled to meet with Breston the Monday after the weekend he was killed. My own search for the McFadden purchase options that Zera had just brought to the meeting. The transfer of the McFadden properties — in spite of the options — to the newly created Alton, Inc. just before McFadden's death. The transfer, as well, of the Gander Bay properties. The disappearance of the proposal from DHCR, and what I had learned today about the Commissioner's interest in having it resubmitted.

I paused, trying to decide what else I needed to say. It was a lot of pieces of information for people to absorb all at once. The faces around the table looked stunned. There was dead silence.

"Of course your NHA properties on Sheridan are right in the middle of the land Breston needs. He can't do a thing without that property. So, well, Harry heard from him today. He can fill you in."

"He called," Harry said. "He wanted to know what we would sell for. Wants to meet right away. Said he would pay a good price. I told him the board needs to talk about it. We surely do need to talk about it."

"What properties on Sheridan?" asked the large woman with the hoarse voice.

"It was about the time you came on the board," Helen said. "Jonah bought — that is we bought — two shells right next to the vacant lot next to that bar, the Gander Bay. Now I guess we know why we bought them."

"And maybe we also know now why Jonah was killed," Harry said. "Anyway it's possible..."

"But they arrested that kid," Sarah Williams, the law student, said. "It sounded like pretty much open and shut armed robbery."

I told them I had talked with Loosh and his attorney. I said, "I don't think the case against him is as open and shut as they've made out. We need more answers but I think there's something in what Harry suggested. It's quite possible that Thomas Breston had something to do with Jonah's murder, and had something to do with setting up the kid Ronald Burns to take the rap. Then there is the coincidental killing of Eddie McFadden. I think we, all of us, need to be very careful."

The large woman said, "Sweet Jesus!" in her hoarse voice. No one else said anything.

"What I hope..." I said, "is that you'll consider not selling to Breston — at least not right away, now that we have the options..." I was looking at Helen, who had brought her hands together in a praying position in front of her face. Now she began to nod slowly, and I went on. "I would like your permission to try to put something together for you to consider as a board. I can't even say yet what it might look like — but a response to Breston that would *not* just give him what he wants so he can go ahead and do what Jonah was trying to stop."

Everyone was nodding now.

"It would take a few days. I'd like to meet with Breston. Maybe Harry and I together, or maybe just one of us."

Harry was leaning forward, forearms on the table. "Could be either way, but I've been thinking...Warren's been putting a lot of time into this whole thing. He knows our business like nobody else right now. I've been thinking maybe we should appoint him acting executive director, so folks will know he's our man — will know he represents us. And we should try to pay him something for what he's doing. He's doing what Jonah would have done. What Jonah *was* doing."

There was more nodding.

At one point it had occurred to me to ask them to do what Harry was suggesting, but I had backed away from the idea when I thought about how much responsibility would come with the title. But now that it was being offered.... "If you wanted me to," I said, "I would consider doing it for a short time. You wouldn't need to pay me, but you should know that I'm planning to be away — completely out of touch — starting the end of next week and then for all of July."

No one was looking at me. Everyone was looking toward the doorway, where Zera had reappeared, her face puffy. She sat down quietly and lowered her head.

Harry took off his glasses and pressed his fingers against his eyelids. "I think we know what we have to do," he said.

* * *

I walked east on Second Street, which would take me the length of Arbor Hill to Ten Broeck just above Lisa's building. It was past nine. The light was fading. The sky had clouded and the air was warm and moist and rich with a summer mix of city smells — new-mowed grass, food, garbage, smoke. As I crossed Henry Johnson Boulevard there was a spicy smell of Caribbean cooking, giving way to the smell of diesel exhaust. I felt immersed in the neighborhood. For the present I wanted to be immersed in it. It was another one of those times when I felt like I belonged here.

24

Lisa wasn't home yet. I mixed martinis and put the shaker in the freezer compartment at the top of the refrigerator, then sat down at her kitchen table and removed the envelope with the purchase options from inside my shirt.

I looked at the documents carefully to make sure I knew exactly what I had. They were signed and notarized on May 16, which would have been just before Jonah submitted the application to DHCR. The options ran for three months, until August 16. They gave NHA a right to buy the properties, during that time, for $50,000 per property, which was way more than they were worth. Probably McFadden had counted on the option price being unworkable for NHA when it came right down to it. DHCR would certainly have had problems with NHA paying so much for a vacant lot and two buildings that needed total gut rehab. DHCR would *still* have those problems. But for now — as was true for Jonah when he submitted the original application — the actual price was a down-the-road technicality. Breston might not take much comfort from the fact that the option price was as high as it was. As far as I could determine, the options still encumbered, or at least clouded, Breston's title to the properties.

Having them in my possession was important. After putting them back in the envelope, I stood up and rummaged in Lisa's kitchen cabinets until I found a zip-lock plastic bag. I put the envelope in the bag, then re-opened the door of the freezer compartment where I had put the martini shaker. There was an ice-maker with a storage container for ice cubes on the left side of the compartment. Between the container and the side of the compartment was a narrow slot. I slid the plastic-encased envelope far enough into the slot so that it was no longer visible. It seemed a little silly, but now that I finally had the elusive options I didn't want them slipping away.

Returning to the kitchen table, I took my laptop from my daypack, opened it and turned it on. My last task before leaving home for the board meeting had been to scan my copy of Jonah's proposal and then copy the file onto a diskette for use in the laptop. Now I opened this file and went to work.

By the time Lisa got home, an hour had passed quickly.

She was wearing a short, high-necked black dress and black high-heeled pumps. Inside the door she quickly removed the high heels. I stood up and she came straight into my arms and held on for a long time. When she finally stepped back, she said, "Working away, are you?"

"I was. Before someone distracted me."

"I like finding you in my kitchen."

"Want a martini?" I got the shaker out of the freezer.

"One more. How did you know this was a martini evening?"

"I didn't think it would be another bourbon evening like last night."

She hunched her shoulders as though shivering, and shook her head. "Definitely not."

I poured two drinks and carried them into the living room. Lisa followed and curled herself into her corner of the sofa. I gave her one of the drinks and sat in the other corner, with my feet propped on the magazine-covered coffee table. I was eager to know about her dinner with Dick Frost, but I was not going to ask. She would have to be the one to bring it up.

"So how was the board meeting?" she asked.

"Dry. They didn't serve martinis."

"Pity. But seriously..."

"Actually very interesting. A useful meeting, but also something very interesting fell out of the blue. Zera Kay brought in some papers she'd found at home, which turned out to be signed original purchase options from Eddie McFadden for his three Sheridan Avenue properties. All of them unexpired."

"Who in the world is Zera Kay?"

"Maybe I never told you. She and Jonah lived together — in an NHA apartment. I went to see her shortly after Jonah was killed, because of the question about whether he was accumulating the rent for the apartment as an off-the-record pool of cash that might be used for things like buying those purchase options. I didn't learn much at the time, but it now looks like he did in fact buy the options and must have used that cash to do it."

"I guess that's not a surprise at this point."

"But there was no proof. Now I have proof. Notarized documentation. Notarized by Linda Bettleman."

"Oh — Linda Bettleman — what was that all about? Have they located her?"

"I haven't heard that they've found her. I'm hoping she's someplace safe with someone she knows. It sounds like she's the one who called the police about Eddie. She was living with him I think, and either she came home and found him or possibly she was in the house when whoever it was came in. They say she was pretty thoroughly freaked-out when she made the call and they don't know exactly what she might have seen."

"God, I don't blame her for being freaked-out — whatever she saw. And it was her that notarized the options?"

"It was her. So she may know all sorts of things. Which could be even more reason for her to be hiding now."

Lisa was gazing at me over the rim of her glass. "What are you going to do?"

"About what? I mean there's a lot to think about."

"About the options. About the whole thing. Does having the options really change things, or not?"

"It changes what the new version of Jonah's old DHCR application is going to say."

"You said something about the application this morning. What's that about? What does it change?"

I told her about DHCR's interest in seeing the application reappear.

"So you'll revise and resubmit it?"

"And attach copies of the McFadden options. Which were probably attached to the original that disappeared."

"And you're assuming the options are still binding now that the properties have been transferred — binding on the new owner, on Breston?"

"I'm assuming that if you've optioned a property you could only transfer it to someone else subject to the option. The option wouldn't just go away. What would you assume?"

"I've never seen it come up. In a normal transaction there would be title insurance and the title company would have the seller sign something saying they were not aware of any encumbrances, recorded or unrecorded."

"I suppose Breston might have made Eddie sign something like that, but even if he did, it wouldn't make the options go away."

She looked at me hard. "I guess you'll make sure Breston knows you've got the options and are resubmitting the application."

"It's important that he know."

She was silent, apparently intent on rotating the olive in her glass with a finger nail. The level of the clear liquid in the glass had already receded to the top of the olive, and her eyes had a kind of brightness that I had seen only once or twice before when she had gone beyond two martinis. Finally she said, "And you'll resubmit the application why? Because it's the best thing for NHA to do? Because it's a way to vindicate Jonah? Because you've got sucked into the game and Breston is the opposition and you want to beat him?"

"Yes."

"Yes what?"

"I can't say no to any of those things."

"But you can't do all those things together."

"I don't know what's doable."

"If you beat Breston — kill his project — then the NHA is left holding over-priced properties in a down-and-out neighborhood."

"It's possible the project could be pulled off."

"But even with funding from DHCR it would be a pointless struggle. Why not do the obvious thing — sell out to Breston while they have the chance. They must need the money badly."

"And let Breston build his parking garage while Jonah's murder is written off as just one of those things that happens in that kind of neighborhood."

"You could still go on and do everything possible to help the police get the right person, or people, for the murder — for both murders. What would you lose by letting the organization opt out?"

"You would lose the opportunity to pressure Breston to the point where he makes a mistake."

She met my eyes briefly, then returned her attention to the olive. "So you're going to do *e x a c t l y* the same thing that got Jonah killed."

"I'm going to try to pressure Breston in the same way Jonah tried to pressure Breston — but in different circumstances."

"Not *t h a t* different."

"A lot has happened. Breston's situation is not at all the same as it was. He has to be much more careful than before."

She placed her glass on the floor beside the sofa, then stood up abruptly and moved to the windows. "It's hot in here."

Two of the three windows were open at both the top and bottom. The middle window was open only at the top. She took hold of the lower sash with both hands and lifted with the full force of her compact, purposeful body, going up on her toes at the end of the movement to push the window fully open. Still facing the window, she reached behind her neck and loosened the zipper at the back of her dress; then reached down and pulled the dress over her head.

Turning, she sat back against the window sill, wearing pantyhose and bra. "I think we've talked enough about this for tonight."

"I don't mean to drag you into it," I said, "but I'm still interested in anything you might have learned about Breston from Dick Frost."

"You're not dragging me. We'll talk in the morning. Right now I'm going to take a shower. Then I'm going to take you to bed. And you're not going to even think about Thomas Breston or NHA or DHCR or any of the rest of it until the coffee's brewed in the morning."

* * *

When I brought coffee into the bedroom at six-thirty, she was motionless, still deeply asleep. She had rolled away from me when I got up and she now lay with an arm across her eyes, her torso bare, the sheet twisted tight over the lifted curve of one hip. I set the coffee on the night table and sat on the edge of the bed and admired her. I'm not sure about the future of our relationship, but I'm sure I'll never get tired of looking at her, awake or asleep. After a time I lay back down on the bed and wrapped an arm around her. She rolled against me, mumbled something incoherent into my ear, and pressed her hips against mine.

It was seven-fifteen when we finally disentangled ourselves from the sheet and got out of bed.

By seven-thirty, we were at the kitchen table, she in her bathrobe, with her face rosy and her hair still damp from the shower. I poured more coffee into both mugs. My thoughts were already pulling away toward the day ahead. I needed to make copies of the options and make sure that the originals were safe. I could either take them around the corner to copy them right away and bring the originals back here, or I could take them to the NHA office to copy them and then leave the originals there, or I could take them home to copy and keep the originals at my house.

My house seemed like the least secure place for them. As far as I knew, no one was actively looking for the options any more, but if I told Breston I had them, someone might then come looking, and my house would be an obvious place to look. I didn't want my house searched, and I wanted even less to have someone come looking for them at Lisa's house. But hiding them elsewhere would not necessarily change where someone would look for them. So I decided I should put them in a safe deposit box and then just tell Breston that's where they were.

"So," Lisa said. "I owe you a report."

"You don't owe me anything. But I'm interested."

"Actually there isn't any earthshaking new information to report. But Dick seems pretty worried about what's going on."

"Why? What is there for him to worry about?"

"There's *you* to worry about."

"He doesn't even know me."

"So he isn't supposed to care if he helps get you killed?"

"Does he think that just by passing along a few bits of information to you over dinner he's endangering me?"

"Come on," she said evenly, "give him credit. He understands that he helped you figure out what was going on with Jonah Lee and Thomas Breston and that you want to do something about it. And he is aware that Breston's associates, or investors, or whatever, are potentially very dangerous."

"Okay, but most of what I know about what was going on with Jonah and Breston comes from Buddy Rowley and Jonah's friend Raymond, not from Dick Frost."

She placed her hands flat on the table on either side of her coffee mug. "Look...I don't know what we're talking about here, but never mind Dick Frost. *I'm* worried. Can you stand to have someone worry about you?"

I put my coffee down. "Yes, I can stand to have *you* worry, though I'd rather you didn't."

"All right then. On with the report. As we agreed, I did fill Dick in generally on what we've learned, and he did express a concern that we were dealing with a dangerous situation."

"And I share that concern about getting you into that situation."

"But you're the big strong man and it's okay for you to do dangerous things."

I started to respond, but she cut me off. "Never mind. I take it back. One thing Dick said...He said if Breston's associates wanted to kill someone they wouldn't give the job to a couple of punks who spend all their time hanging out at a local bar. He said he hoped you didn't think those guys are all you have to worry about."

"I think I have a pretty good idea what those guys are and are not capable of. At least in the case of the one called Bear. I'm not so sure about Bax. But I wasn't particularly looking for advice from Mr. Frost. I was hoping for some information."

"I'm getting there. I did ask the questions you wanted me to ask. I asked him what he might know about any connection between Breston and the city or county. He acted like he might have heard something, but all he would say was that he knew a couple of people he thought he could ask, and he said he *would* ask. He also said he would see what he can find out about how much cash Breston or Alton, Inc. have direct access to — which you were also wondering about."

I wanted to comment on the Dick Frost strategy of creating yet another excuse to have yet another dinner with Lisa to pass on still more bits of information, but her next words stopped me.

"He'll call you," she said. "I think soon. He said he would call and arrange to meet with you as soon as he had some information. I asked if I could come too, and he said no, he wanted to talk with you alone. Which pissed me off."

"I don't know why he thinks he has to talk to me directly — except that he is being very protective of you."

"He's being another pig-headed male person."

I stood up and opened the top door of the refrigerator and with two fingers pulled the plastic bag that held the options out from behind the ice maker. I fished my daypack out from under the table, unzipped the large compartment and placed the plastic bag inside.

Watching me, Lisa said, "What in the world...? The options?"

"Silly to be hiding them, but you see how careful I am."

"About some things."

"I need to make copies. Then I'm going to see if NHA has a safe deposit box, and if they don't I'm going to get one for them."

"In your new capacity as Jonah's successor."

"Actually — I didn't tell you — that is sort of my new capacity. They appointed me acting executive director. Very temporary — just till I go north."

"I can't believe I was actually worrying about that canoe trip of yours — like you wouldn't be safe up there in the wilderness. Now it seems like a pretty good way for you to *be* safe." She stood up. "But in the meantime — I want you to put my thirty-eight in your backpack."

"Have laptop and gun. Will travel."

"I'm serious."

"I still don't have a permit."

"You think the police are going to search your backpack? Just tell them your girlfriend must have hidden it there." She left the room and came back shortly, carrying the revolver. The daypack sat on a chair by the table. She unzipped it, put the gun in and rezipped it.

"My girlfriend seems to have hidden a gun in my daypack," I said.

"Please leave it there. It's loaded — cylinder's full except for under the hammer. I'd like to think at least when you're alone on Orange Street you have some protection."

"We disagree about the danger, but if it will make you worry less..."

"You know, danger — I mean physical danger — is one of the things that women are more sensitive to. I know it's supposed to be a man thing, but men seem to have to desensitize themselves — convince themselves there's nothing to be scared of. So pay attention. We're *useful* — like the canary in the coal mine. If we say we're scared, it means there's something to be scared of."

"I don't think of you as being scared of very much."

"I'm not saying I'm *t i m i d,* but that doesn't mean I don't recognize risk."

"You're smart about risk. Also excited by it."

"Some kinds of risk, yes. But challenging someone who deals with challenges by hiring professional killers is a kind of excitement that I would prefer to avoid."

"Well I would too. And I'm scared enough now to be very careful."

"I hope so." She studied me, frowning. "One thing you've got to understand though. Don't you dare push me out of this thing with the idea of protecting me. I would really hate that. We've got to stay in touch. I especially need to know if and when you're going to see Breston."

"I promise." I lifted the daypack off the chair. "Good Lord. Laptop and gun. I'm not traveling light anymore."

25

I walked the six blocks up Second Street to the NHA office, where I found Helen Hamilton on the phone. I made two sets of copies of the options, and when Helen got off the phone I asked whether the organization had a safe deposit box where the originals could be kept.

"It's one of those things he was going to do," she said.

I thought about the process of obtaining a safe deposit box for a corporation that I would formally represent for only a week. "We should get it done," I said. "We should set it up so you and Harry have access to it. But for right now, I have a box of my own at Capital Bank on Central. I'm going to walk these options over there right now and stick them in my box until we get something else set up. I made copies for the office and a set for myself."

"All right." She turned in her chair away from the desk and looked at me. "I'm making a list of things I need to check with you about. I don't know how much you really have time for, but I thought we should go over the list."

"Good. How about I come back this afternoon. Maybe one-thirty if that works for you."

"It works. Thank you, Warren."

On my way to Central Avenue I stopped at Orange Street. After removing the options and placing them inside my shirt, I left the heavy daypack under my desk.

Within a half hour I was back at the desk, checking my e-mail. There were half a dozen messages, but I read only the one from Harry Cooper.

"Warren, I tried to call Thomas Breston at the work number he gave me. The woman said he was out until Monday. Also have a cell phone number which I will try from home tonight. — Harry."

So there was nothing I could do on that front for the time being. I then tried to reach Reilly by phone and was told he was not available. I left my number with a request that he call me. I had no new information for him, but Reilly didn't know that, so maybe he would call back and maybe there would be news of Linda Bettleman. I then called Erica Schmidt at DHCR and reached her at her desk.

"So are you going to resubmit the thing?" she asked.

"Yes. How much time do I have?"

"Zero time. People would like the application to be unlost as of back when."

"Can you tell them it is already unlost and will be on their desk by the end of the day tomorrow?"

"I think so. It would be especially nice if you could get it to me and I could just walk down the hall and say, 'Oh, it turned up. Here it is.'"

"Okay. Tomorrow. How do I get it to you? Should I bring it to your office?"

"I have to be at the Capitol again in the morning. Can you meet me?"

"Cafeteria A?"

"No, not that place again. Weather forecast is sunny. I'll just meet you on the Capitol steps. East side. Around quarter of one."

"Okay, see you on the steps."

"Look for the bureaucrat in the trench coat."

I worked on the application for the rest of the morning. By noon it was, in most respects, ready to go, but there was still a strategic question that bothered me. I still hadn't looked at the properties on the north side of Sheridan, next to the Greta Green property where Raymond lived. I wasn't excited about adding more properties to the proposed project, but if those properties could be added, along with the Greta Green property, it would mean there was an alternative version of the project that Breston might not be able to block. I decided that after I finished at the NHA office I would walk down there and take a look, and maybe see if Raymond was home.

I was about to go out to get some lunch before keeping my appointment with Helen Hamilton when I got a call from Dick Frost, suggesting that we meet for a drink at McGeary's at five o'clock. My day was filling up. I decided that I should call Lisa and make arrangements to meet someplace for dinner — and tell her

I'd have to go home afterward and spend the evening working.

* * *

I went down the block to the Bridge Diner for a bowl of clam chowder, then wa l ked north on Lexington to Second Stre et and west to the NHA office.

Helen's list was long, detailed and practical. There were mortgage payments that had to be made. There was a voucher that had to go to the city, and I would need to talk to Bock Calloway at the Community Development Agency to make sure there was no problem in drawing the vouchered funds, which would reimburse the organization for a portion of Jonah's salary for the month of May. There were several over-due reports to other funders — who would understand the delay under the circumstances but should at least receive notes assuring them that the organization was still functioning. There were several residents who had missed monthly payments and ought to be contacted. There were several apartments needing maintenance wo rk of one sort or another. At the end of the list, Helen had written *Z e ra.*

"How is she?" I asked.

"She's getting along. But I thought we should maybe talk about the rent. I don't know if she ought to be paying rent. I mean not right away of course, but for the long run there's going to be rent due, and of course there's expenses on the building."

We got out the file for the two-family building on Third Street. The numbers we re very tight, as they were for all of NHA's buildings. With each apartment rented for $420, the income would just bare ly cover operating expenses and debt service on the building. If Zera didn't pay rent, the cost would have to be subsidized somehow.

"We owe her," Helen said.

"In a sense."

"For right now we owe her at least free rent — out of what would have been paid to Jonah if he was alive — but as the months go by it would be like a permanent vacancy. The re st of us would have to cover it somehow."

It would be about five thousand dollars a year that would have to be made up — a significant amount for this organization. "You all will have to decide," I said, "but in the meantime I'll work on it. M aybe there's a way we can get the cost down. Maybe refinance. Maybe there's some wealthy who-knows-who that would like to help out with the rent while Zera's in college."

"Oh my," Helen said. "And we already have one fund drive..."

I spent an hour at Jonah's computer writing letters to funders and NHA resident-members. I wrote checks for Harry and Helen to sign. I prepared the voucher for the CD agency. I called Bock Calloway and arranged to see him when I took the voucher in. Calloway thought the Agency would need a resolution documenting the board's appointment of me as Executive Director. Helen wrote up the motion that the board had passed, and signed it as Secretary.

"This is the last money we get from the city," she said, "until we start paying someone in Jonah's place. So maybe you ought to let us pay for some of your time after all. We can voucher the city for it."

"It's not worth putting me on the payroll for just a week and having to deal with all their paperwork just to get that little bit of money out of them. But what about you? You're going to keep on doing what you do here, and you aren't getting paid for any of it."

"I have the time. And I have my social security."

"But you could be on the payroll and still draw your social security. You're the person who's really keeping this organization running. We should pay you and voucher the city for *that*."

"I don't know." She frowned and shook her head. "They'd probably want to know why I wouldn't do it for free anymore."

"Well I think I'll talk with Bock Calloway about it. The city ought to do *something* to support the real work this organization does. But we'll need to give you a title. How about Property Manager?"

"I think I'd rather we called it *Housing* Manager."

"Okay, that would be more Jonah's style."

It was a five minute walk to the CD office on Henry Johnson Boulevard, where I then spent another five minutes with Bock Calloway. I told Calloway that I knew the city would be glad to hear that I was hiring Helen Hamilton as Housing Manager to cover the part of Jonah's job description that the city had been funding — so the funding could now continue. Calloway said he would have to check on the details but yes he was glad to hear that.

From the CD office, I walked south on Henry Johnson Boulevard as far as Sheridan Avenue. There I turned left and went down the long slope of Sheridan into the Hollow. It was the time of day when the state workers were appearing in the Hollow to get their cars. White men in ties, white women in dresses were making their way up Sheridan from the corner of Swan at the foot of the long stair — all of them intent on reaching their parked cars, unlocking them, getting in, re-locking them, getting out of this place as quickly as possible. The only exception was a red-haired man in a white shirt and tie who had pulled his car back to the curb and was making a purchase from a young black man who had stepped to the driver's side window. Both we re oblivious to me standing in front of a vacant lot just up the street.

B eyond the vacant lot we re two boarded-up buildings. The windows were cove red with sheets of plywood, painted red with black numbers stenciled on them, which meant they we re tax-foreclosed county-owned buildings. Beyond them was another vacant lot and beyond that the Greta Green property where Ray-mond lived. The county-owned buildings ought to be easy enough to acquire if the DHCR application was funded. The vacant lots ought to be easy, too, if it turned out that they we re owned by the county as well, but they might not be. I would have to check. And I really ought to arrange to get inside the buildings with one of the small contractors that did rehab work for NHA, so rehab costs could be estimated.

Moving on down the street I knocked on Raymond's front door. After a minute I knocked again, loudly, and then waited several minutes more before giving up. Either Raymond wasn't there or he was busy doing whatever Raymond did and was not going to answer the door. I would have to try to reach him by phone.

At Swan Street I turned left and went up the short block to Orange, where I turned right again and went along past the steam plant and finally crossed Chapel Street and emerged on Pearl. McGeary's was only a few doors to my left, but it was not quite five o'clock — a little early for my meeting with Dick Frost.

I was looking forward to having a drink alone while I waited. But before I reached the door I realized I was being watched by a bemused-looking bystander, a trimly handsome blond man whom I recognized as Dick Frost. He was wearing a neatly pressed oxford cloth shirt tucked into jeans. His belt was decorated with beadwork and an elaborate silver buckle. When I met his gaze, he raised an index finger, nodded and stepped toward the door.

We went in and took the last vacant booth. "All the times I've been past this place," I said, "this is the first time I've ever been in here."

"I get here now and then," he said. "What'll you have to drink?" A waitress who seemed to know him was poised over our booth.

I ordered bourbon.

Frost ordered scotch, a single malt with a name I couldn't have repeated. When the drinks came, he lifted his glass and said, "To your project." The bemused expression had never quite left his face.

"To Jonah Lee's project."

"Ah yes, the Jonah Lee memorial project."

I looked at the man and said nothing.

"It's *okay* for it to be a kind of memorial," Frost said. "I admire the concept."

"Actually it's not a memorial. It's..."

"I understand," Frost said. "I didn't mean that it's merely a memorial. I understand it's the very thing itself that Jonah Lee was trying to do."

"What Jonah was trying to do was to keep the Sheridan Hollow neighborhood from becoming the backside of a parking garage."

"Which I find fascinating — that he, and now you, would go to the lengths you've gone to on behalf of a place like that. You call it a neighborhood, and it used to be, but it isn't really that any more. I mean where the NHA is up on Second Street is a neighborhood, albeit a troubled one. Sheridan Hollow is vacant lots and abandoned buildings. And a parking garage on the side of it isn't going to have a big effect on very many people. So this is really about symbolism as far as I can figure."

I shrugged. "In any case, NHA has had to decide whether to just roll over and let the man who killed Jonah go ahead and do what Jonah was trying to stop him from doing — or whether to follow through with Jonah's project as best they can."

"Is it really NHA we're talking about, or you?"

"I can imagine Lisa raised that question in telling you about the situation. But the question doesn't matter. I'm working for NHA."

"This is no less interesting than I'd been thinking," Frost said. "But I do want to be sure you understand completely what you're dealing with. Because what you're dealing with is not really Breston. If it was just Breston, I'd say go for it, take the bastard down."

"I do understand," I said, "that the financing is coming from some investors who are not very nice people."

"*Not very nice* doesn't tell the story. *Breston* is not very nice. But these guys with the money, they're from a different world. They're lethal — businesslike and lethal. If they're doing business and it looks like someone might create a problem, they have him eliminated. End of problem. You've seen it. What happened to

Jonah Lee was business as usual for these guys."

"And what happened to Eddie McFadden was more business
as usual, would you say? It seems to me it was a little too messy to
be called businesslike?"

"From what I hear, yeah, kind of weird, that one, but it's got to
be these guys behind it."

"So what *do* you know about these guys — besides that they
kill people?"

"I made some more phone calls this morning. Quite a few
phone calls as it turned out. The parking garage deal is structured
as a limited partnership, and it's just one of a series of projects
structured more or less the same way for these guys to put money
into. More or less legitimate businesses that they can invest in up
front — and use down the road to launder cash. You can bet that
even if this garage is never more than half full it's going to report
very substantial cash receipts coming from somewhere."

"Breston involved in any of the others?"

"Just this one. But there are other Brestons. Plenty of Brestons
to go round."

"I assume in this case it's Breston's corporation, Alton, Inc.,
that will be the managing general partner?"

"If you want to call it Breston's corporation. In this case the so-
called managing partner is going to be managed by the so-called
limited partners. Breston is a pawn. Alton, Inc. is a shell, but no
doubt a well-made shell. There's nothing wrong with the legal
work these guys buy."

"It *is* Alton, Inc. that's holding the property," I said.

"Property with hardly any market value at present. Doesn't do
much for a balance sheet. But I did learn the corporation has a
moderately healthy bank account — here in Albany. Cash waiting
to pay *someone* for *something*."

"How healthy is moderately?"

"Until last week it was only a few thousand. Now it's a good
deal more." He put his drink down and leaned forward. "I don't
want you to think that I regularly pry into things this way. But this
morning, after I talked to some people who were somewhat familiar with these investors, I decided to ask around among my banker
friends — all of whom are honorable people so I wasn't exactly
asking for information outright. But I got lucky with an old friend
who is being squeezed out of Upstate Trust after the merger and no
longer feels a whole lot of loyalty to them. I told him enough of
what's going on to rouse his curiosity, and he was able to find the

account. The balance is now three hundred fifty thousand."

"And who can write checks on that? I don't suppose he told you who the signatories are?"

"Just one, and it's not Breston. A woman named Elizabeth Michaels."

"She's one of the three board members," I said. "Also she notarized the deeds from McFadden and some of the other deeds they collected last week — except for the ones that actually came from her. Apparently some of the property was first acquired in her name."

"Busy girl. I can check on her if you want."

"Sure, although I'm not sure what I need to know about her, other than that she's the one who can sign checks. But do you have any idea where that three hundred fifty thousand is headed? It's more than they would need to finish the property acquisition. Is someone going to be paid off?"

"I can't help you there. I did ask around a little with some city and county people, and I did get some confirmation that they know something is in the wind with Breston and company. But they're nervous. I don't think anyone has committed to anything at this point. I think everyone's waiting to see if the deal can go down without too much of a bad smell around it. Then they'll be happy to go along with it and they know there will be benefits for everyone involved."

"So the three hundred fifty thousand in up-front cash..."

"Petty cash. Pay off the local help. Whatever's needed. I don't know. It did cross my mind they might be planning to buy themselves a Warren Crow, but I'm afraid they're smart enough to know they'll have to deal with you some other way."

"The Neighborhood Housing Association could use a few hundred thousand dollars," I said.

"I'm sure it could. And I'm sure that kind of money would present something of a dilemma — for them and for you. Would you take the evil money and do some good with it?"

"I don't know what they'll do. Money is just money, and NHA can do some good with any money it can get. The real question is...do you let the people who murdered Jonah buy their way out of it?"

"The way I'm reading it, your goal is to get the money for the organization *and* take these guys down for what they did to Jonah Lee."

"That would be ideal. I don't know if it's doable."

"With the guys we're talking about it will be extremely difficult. You're liable to end up like Jonah."

I raised my glass to my lips and found only a remnant of ice water. I had drunk the bourbon without noticing.

Frost sipped at his scotch. Setting the glass down he made a slight motion with his hand in the direction of the bar, then wiggled a finger toward me.

I didn't particularly like having my consumption monitored this way, but when the fresh drink arrived, I said, "Thank you. And thank you for the information. This is very helpful."

"I'm afraid I'm not really doing you a favor — supplying ammunition to shoot yourself with. But I'd love to see you win this thing. If there's anything else I can do…"

"I'll keep in touch," I said.

"Good," Frost said. "And now you can tell me something I've always wanted to know."

"What's that?"

"About these trips you do. What it's like spending half a summer going down some river up north in the middle of nowhere? I don't think I get it. I mean, sure, the *idea* has a certain romantic appeal, but when I think about the reality of it…all day pinched into a very small boat, on a hard seat, in the rain, with the bugs. How can anyone really want to do that?"

"There are never any bugs when it's raining," I told him.

"Great. So you get to alternate from one torment to another."

"You sound like you've been there."

"As a kid. Summer camp. A week of pure hell."

"I can understand that. It's much better when you can do your own trip. When it's completely your own trip…"

"I don't imagine it makes the rain stop and the bugs go away."

"No it doesn't." I laughed. The talk of rain and bugs, of really being there, had given me a sudden lift.

* * *

I was sitting on my front steps. Above my right shoulder Jesse was sitting on the top step. It was after eight o'clock but the sun still hadn't dipped below the rooftops along Robin Street to my left. It shone down the length of Orange Street, turning the old brick pavement a warm rose color.

"How come you not at your girlfriend's?" Jesse asked.

"Had dinner with her, but I got work to do tonight."

"You work too much. Bad for you."

"I know. Vacation coming soon though."

"Your girlfriend going with you?"

"No. Not her kind of trip." I was thinking about our conversation at dinner. I had told her about Dick Frost's comments on the subject of rain and bugs and had tried to tell her how it had made me feel so suddenly happy. Not surprisingly she had seemed completely mystified. "I guess I'm more like Dick on that one," she had said. It was one of the points where I felt the distance between us. The whole dinner hour had been slightly strained. Friendly but not quite right.

"Guess she don't like sleeping on the ground," Jesse said. "Don't blame her."

A car was coming too fast up the street, rumbling over the bricks, accelerating, and I suddenly wished that Jesse was not there beside me. I swung my legs to the side and scrambled off the steps, moving several yards up the sidewalk until I was clear of Jesse. In front of me was the sunken entrance to the basement apartment of the house next door. I could dive into it. But Jesse still sat on the top step. I found myself standing still, feeling stupid and vulnerable.

A violent hammering of rap music erupted from the car, which continued to accelerate through the middle of the block, the teenager at the wheel oblivious to the man on the sidewalk and the boy on the steps. Approaching Robin Street, the car bucked and skidded, almost sideswiping a parked van before squealing around the corner toward Clinton Avenue.

"Whooee," Jesse said. "He make you jump some."

26

It was after nine a.m. and I had an impatient need to talk with someone in the county's *in rem* property office so I could wrap up the application that I had promised to deliver to Erica at 12:30. I had already called the county offices twice without reaching anyone who could help me. Now, having tried a third time, I was on hold while someone went to see if someone else had arrived at work yet. The current — and what I hoped would be the final — version of the application claimed that "county officials" had indicated that certain county-owned properties "were available." But I still hadn't talked to any such officials and still didn't even know for sure which properties were county-owned. And my

schedule for the middle part of the day had filled up about as full
as it could get.

Last night I had called Greta Green in Troy and learned that
she was the owner of the vacant lot between the building where
Raymond lived and the two boarded-up buildings that we both
assumed were owned by the county. She thought that the vacant
lot on the other side of the vacant buildings was also county-
owned, but she wasn't sure. In any case, she would be happy to
give the NHA an option on both her properties and would sign
something for me to attach to the DHCR application. She would
be coming over to Albany in the late morning and would meet me
at Raymond's. Then I would have just enough time to package the
application, deliver it to Erica Schmidt at the Capitol, and walk
down State Street to the meeting with Thomas Breston that Harry
Cooper had arranged for me.

Harry had called late in the evening with word that he had
reached Breston, who had said he could be in Albany around midday and was eager to talk. Breston had proposed a one o'clock
meeting in the Alton, Inc. office. Harry told me he could take
some time off and come downtown to "sit in" if I wanted him to,
but he thought I should be the one to handle it. I had said yes,
good, I'd do the meeting alone and then call him so we could talk
about how to follow up.

Finally, someone in the county office that dealt with *in rem*
properties picked up the phone. I asked about the two boarded-up
buildings and the vacant lot, giving the addresses of each. I was
then put back on hold and waited several more minutes before a
different person came on the line and asked, "What'd you want to
know about those places?"

"I just want to confirm that the county owns them and find
out what their status is."

"What do you mean *status*?"

"Are they committed to someone? Scheduled to be auctioned?"

"Scheduled to be auctioned. Again."

"Any chance of getting in to have a look at them?"

"Not today, Bud. Give us a call Monday and we'll try to set
something up for next week. You realize it's down in Sheridan
Hollow, right?"

I hadn't really expected to get into the buildings today. In fact
I'd already given up on the idea of doing a thorough inspection and
detailed cost estimate. On my hard drive I'd found pro formas for

roughly comparable gut rehab projects and a small single-family infill project. I'd updated and adapted the numbers as best I could for the county properties. The resulting dollar amount, I told myself, was no more speculative than a number of other features of this strange proposal I was reshaping for resubmission.

* * *

Greta Green was a small quick woman with an expressive face framed by dark curly hair. Sitting at Raymond's kitchen table, she said, "I'm so glad you're doing this. I just hope it's not a problem for Raymond."

Across the table from her, Raymond smiled. "It wouldn't be the first time an Indian had the real estate sold out from under him."

Greta looked stricken.

"No, just kidding," he said. "I'm glad he's doing it too. I'm glad you're helping. And even if he pulls it off I'll be out of here before they actually get to the point of doing anything with this building."

"It won't be next week," I said. I was sitting next to Greta at the table and now slid two sheets of paper in front of her. "We didn't talk about an option price, so I printed out two different versions of an option agreement. This one here has a space where we can fill in a price if you have one in mind. This other one just says if the NHA wants to exercise the option it will commission a market appraisal and will pay you the appraised value."

"I have no idea what it's worth, so that sounds like a good idea."

"You understand it's not going to appraise for very much in this neighborhood."

"Oh, I know. It will be a relief just to be able to do something appropriate with it finally. I mean...but maybe I should just give it to the NHA anyway. Do you think I should? It would be a sort of in-memory-of-Jonah kind of thing."

"Let's do the option for appraised value for now and see what happens. You can always decide to donate it later."

"Good. Can I sign it right now? But it looks like it has to be notarized. Do we have to go to a bank or something?"

"I can notarize it," I said.

She looked at me in surprise. Raymond said, "Greta, you didn't realize you were in the presence of a real live notary public."

She gave him a puzzled look.

He smiled and shrugged.

"Raymond," I said, "does this Indian ever paddle a canoe?"

"Me? What would I want to do that for?"

"I don't know. I was looking for some company on the river tomorrow. And I wanted to find a time to talk with you, but it doesn't have to be on the river."

"On this river?"

"The Hudson."

"Wouldn't mind seeing some of it from a boat. I've been working on the PCB stuff. On paper. I don't even know what this river smells like."

"Can I pick you up in the morning then?"

"You really use a paddle? You don't have a motor?"

"Very primitive."

"Oh well. For a few hours. I'll bring the beer."

* * *

I found Erica sitting on the Capitol steps in the sun and gave her the application. "Got to run," I said. "Got a meeting in five minutes with the man himself."

"What man?"

"Breston, the developer."

"So you can tell him DHCR has found the application."

"Yes. Thank you."

I walked down State Street a block and a half to the address Breston had given.

The building had once been filled by the expanding central offices of an Albany-based bank that had busily acquired other banks until it was large enough to attract the interest of a truly big bank, which acquired it and moved the merged executive offices to another state. Now the building housed the offices of a handful of local corporations and the regional offices of a number of larger corporations. The place felt transitory. The few people that I met in the foyer left me with the impression that no one knew, or expected to know, anyone else in the building. I rode the elevator alone to the seventh floor. The "suite" occupied by Alton, Inc. was identified only by the inscription "7G" on its door.

Entering, I found two people in the almost empty outer office. A slender blond woman was standing beside the only work surface in the room, a single desk on which a computer, monitor, printer, fax and phone were crowded together. Nothing was connected to anything else. Some file folders and loose papers had been stuffed in amongst the electronic equipment. There were no file cabinets in sight.

The woman held the telephone receiver almost hidden beneath long blond hair and murmured into the mouthpiece. To her left a lean, swarthy man was standing, his back to her, staring through the single window with his hands in his pockets — motionless. He had not even glanced over his shoulder when I entered.

Hanging up the phone, the woman gave me a sidelong glance and said, "Mr. Crow?" My first impression was that she was beautiful — with the finely chiseled, carefully composed beauty of a professional model.

"Yes."

"I'll tell Mr. Breston you're here." She picked up the phone and, turning away, spoke several words I couldn't hear. Then hanging up again, she moved to the door of the inner office, opened it, and, with a small movement of her fingers, motioned me to go in.

The room was only slightly less naked than the outer office. In one corner was a round table with four straight chairs around it. Otherwise there was just a desk with a telephone, a legal pad and a desk calendar. The man who came around the desk was large and fleshy, with a pale, freckled face capped by carefully arranged bangs. His handshake began aggressively, but when he found he couldn't overpower my hand he slapped me on the shoulder with his free hand and said, "So you're the guy!"

"Which guy are you thinking of?" I asked.

"Well I guess now you're the guy representing the Neighborhood Housing Association, which means you're the guy I want to talk to."

"For the time being I'm Acting Executive Director, and as you know I'm authorized by the board to discuss a deal with you."

"And I sure as hell am ready to discuss. Have a seat." He pulled one of the chairs away from the table and swung it around to face his desk, then seated himself behind the desk. He had one of those large padded desk chairs that swivel and tilt. He leaned forward, causing the chair to squeak, and rested meaty forearms on the desk. "I'm going to be completely honest with you. I want you to understand the whole situation before we talk about any kind of deal. So I'm going to put all my cards on the table up front and we'll go from there."

"That would be very helpful," I said.

"Okay, the first thing you got to understand is this thing is not a big deal. A small parking lot is what we're talking about. A small parking lot down there on Sheridan Avenue where parking is about the only damn use for those properties. Not worth a nickel for anything else. There's some demand for parking all right, but it isn't going to make anyone rich, so the whole thing is about nickels and dimes."

"So I guess you're saying the deal doesn't work for you unless you can get the land really cheap," I said.

"You're very sharp, Warren. That's going to make this much easier."

"I'm somewhat relieved myself," I said. "I was afraid this discussion might involve dollar amounts that would be out of our little organization's ball park, but it sounds like maybe we can do business after all."

Breston dropped his eyes to his desk, not quite quickly enough to hide his surprise. He picked up a pen and made a series of anxious little scribbles on the legal pad before looking up. "Glad to hear it. But I'm thinking maybe your guy Cooper didn't understand what I was saying, or maybe he didn't tell it like he should've. What I told him was...my company is interested in buying two properties that your organization owns on Sheridan Avenue."

"Yes, we understood that. But I think we jumped to a conclusion as to your intended use of the property. We were under the impression that the project you're working on involves more than a small parking lot. So we thought property on that part of Sheridan might be worth a great deal to you."

Breston leaned back and the chair squeaked. He stared at me. " 'Fraid you did jump to the wrong conclusion. Hope my offer isn't going to be too disappointing now — because I *am* ready to give you absolute top price for the properties your organization owns, considering where they are and what they're worth."

I shrugged. "Okay. We thought maybe your project increased the value of the properties to you well beyond what they're worth to others, which might have forced us to make a difficult decision."

" 'Fraid you lost me there."

"We thought your Sheridan property might cost more than we could pay — which would force us to reconsider our plans."

"Still don't follow you. But you were saying you thought we could do business after all, which I like the sound of."

"I do think we can do business, but a different sort of business from what you proposed. I think we — NHA — can offer *you* a better price for certain Sheridan Avenue properties that you own than you would be likely to offer *us* for the Sheridan Avenue properties that we own. Given the very limited economic potential of your project, as you've just emphasized, it seems it would be in your interest to reconsider your plans for that property."

"This does worry me. Seems you first jumped to one wrong conclusion and now you've gone and jumped way the hell off I don't know where. Or else...I got to say this...I got to think you're not being straight with me. If this is your idea of a negotiating strategy, you're way off base. It ain't going to fly."

I laughed. "Maybe you'd like to start over then. I know why you've been acquiring property on Sheridan Avenue, and you know why NHA has been acquiring properties on Sheridan Avenue. You've known for some time that NHA is putting together an affordable housing project aimed at improving the whole area as a residential neighborhood."

"Christ, they still talking about that? I thought they'd wised up. I thought for christsake they finally figured out it don't work. It's not practical, not financially feasible. And I thought you were the guy — if they didn't figure it out for themselves — you'd straighten 'em out."

"No, I'm the guy who's been helping put back together the pieces of Jonah's project."

"Pieces never went together in the first place. Numbers couldn't have worked."

"I don't think Jonah would have invited you to go over his numbers — but if you did..."

"Didn't have to see his damn numbers. I got friends who do housing. Started out in housing myself. All you got to do is look at that neighborhood and the people hanging out on the stoops and you know what kind of market you've got and what kind of rents you're going to get. Then look at those rotten buildings and figure what's the least you got to put into 'em to get a C.O. so you can rent 'em up. Plain as shit the numbers don't work." His heavy torso tilted forward again, the chair squeaking, until his arms were once more on the desk.

"Which is why the government subsidizes affordable housing projects," I said. "To make up the difference, so the numbers work. So you can cover the cost and still charge affordable rents. Which is why Jonah put in the application to DHCR."

"Don't know what you're talking about."

"But you do. Jonah might not have shared his numbers with you, but he certainly didn't keep it a secret that he was going to the state for money to do a project that was in direct competition with yours for the land we're talking about. He wasn't sneaking around behind anyone's back."

"Sure, I heard it. But like I said, I got friends and the word was...that application of his wasn't going anywhere. It was laughable. Like the state of New York is going to just throw money down the hill into that neighborhood..."

"But someone wasn't laughing. Someone took that application seriously enough to arrange for it to disappear."

Breston stared at me. "I got to say...I don't like how you're coming at this."

"I think I'm telling it like it is. And I'm still waiting for you to do the same."

His mouth opened, then closed again. He did more restless scribbling on the legal pad, then dropped the pen and heaved himself back in his desk chair. The chair squawked loudly. "This is a real pain in the ass, you know?"

"It's a pain in the ass for NHA too. You need some property the NHA has. The NHA needs some property you have. That's the pain-in-the-ass situation."

"How it really is...I got ten lots and I got the financing to develop them. Your two-bit nonprofit, it's got two lots, and shit for financing."

"Then you need to take a closer look. The NHA owns two properties, that's true. They also hold options on three of the properties you purchased — that Alton, Inc. purchased. And they hold options on some property on the other side of the street. To do its project, the NHA needs just two other properties that you're now holding — the two Rowley properties, the bar and the vacant lot. And the latest word from DHCR is that the Commissioner is now quite interested in seeing NHA's application funded. So here we are. What are we going to do with the situation?"

Color rose in Breston's face. The muscles at the corners of his fleshy jaw bulged. Finally he said, "This is not a goddamn poker game, Crow. You can't bluff your way through it."

"How could I be bluffing? I believe all the NHA cards are on the table now."

"I don't see any fucking *o p t i o n s* on the table."

"But you know they exist. Either you know it or the late Eddie McFadden played you for a bigger fool than I thought."

"McFadden sold the properties to Alton, Inc. That's it. End of game."

"Titles to the properties were encumbered by the options he sold to Jonah. He could only sell them to you subject to the options. The NHA holds the options and therefore has a right to buy the properties from you for fifty thousand each, which is of course way too much — no doubt way more than you paid Eddie for them — but the price is covered in the pro forma submitted to DHCR. You will be legally bound to sell those properties when the project is funded. Unless we agree on some other kind of deal here today."

"No options ever got recorded. If they ever existed they don't mean shit now. You're still bluffing."

I took the copies of the options out of my shirt pocket, unfolded them and slid them onto Breston's desk. "Not recorded by Jonah but recordable. Dated, signed, notarized, still in effect."

The chair squeaked forward and Breston picked up the papers and looked at them briefly and dropped them. Then he looked at the phone on his desk and said, "Come in here."

In a moment the door opened and the blond woman stepped through it and walked to the desk. She picked up the options, looked at them, and replaced them on the desk. She then walked to the table, got another straight chair and placed it to my left, off the corner of the desk. She sat down, crossed her legs, and, without looking at me, asked "And the originals?"

"In a safe deposit box."

"Of course," she said. Her lips did a brief imitation of a smile but there was no smile in the sidelong blue-eyed glance she gave me. When she had looked at the options, it had seemed that there was something not quite right about her left eye. As she was sitting now, facing a point halfway between me and Breston, I could see only the right side of her face.

"An interesting situation," she said. "As you say, what are we going to do with it?"

I assumed the speaker phone had been activated since I'd entered the office and that she'd heard the entire conversation with Breston. It appeared that Breston's job had been only to get things started and get me to reveal where I was coming from. Now she was apparently taking over.

"I'm afraid I don't know your name," I said, although I had a pretty good idea who she was. "Or exactly what your role is in this matter."

"My name is Elizabeth Michaels."

"Our attorney," Breston said.

She looked toward Breston. "I am not Alton, Inc.'s legal counsel," she said sharply. "I am a member of Alton, Inc.'s board of directors and an officer of the corporation, and I re present some investors on certain matters."

Breston looked annoyed but said nothing.

"I'm pleased to meet you," I said.

Again the sidelong glance flicked towa rd me, but she still hadn't turned her head and I still couldn't see her left eye. "Mr. McFadden of course assured us the options were a dead issue," she said.

I suddenly had a image of this woman sitting at the dining room table coolly interrogating Eddie McFadden, with Eddie tied to his chair and someone else, someone with a knife, hove ring behind him. I focused my gaze on Breston to avoid the image.

"For Eddie, it's certainly a dead issue," I said. "For Alton, Inc. it's not. For the prospective limited partners I would imagine it's potentially a serious issue."

"For the limited partners, I assure you a problem affecting our project is not a trifle. What did Jonah Lee pay for the options?"

"I believe the price is stated as one dollar and other good and valuable services."

"I didn't ask what the document says. I asked what Jonah Lee actually paid that stupid little man?"

"Much less than it will cost Alton, Inc. to buy them back."

"That could be the case, depending on what we decide to do with the situation." Her back was straight. Her hands we re motionless in her lap. She stared fixedly at that point halfway between me and Breston.

"If you don't buy the options," I said, "the alternative is clear enough. The NHA will exe rcise the options, pay you fifty thousand each for the McFadden properties and pay you a good price also for the Rowl ey properties next door. You'll have a tidy profit on those properties, and with the rest of what you own you can go ahead and do a small parking lot or whatever you want. You'll make out very well."

"As you suggested, we 're talking about a somewhat more ambitious project."

"A project that would have a substantial impact on the surrounding area and would therefore have substantial intere st for the public and the media."

"Perhaps."

"And in the eyes of the media and the public you would rather not look like you're just bulldozing a competing community-based project out of the way."

"Of course we would rather not," she said evenly. "Now, since we are all describing the situation so accurately, perhaps you could give us a little more information about the application to the state housing division. If the application disappeared as you indicated, how is it that you believe the Commissioner is interested in funding it? "

"I was informed that the Commissioner wanted to see it resubmitted."

"And you are obliging him by resubmitting it."

"In fact I did so on my way here."

"And the application states that your organization holds the options on the McFadden properties."

"It does."

"You are apparently assuming that the options survive the transfer and are still binding. I don't believe it is that simple."

"Perhaps not. But neither did they simply evaporate when the property transferred. If necessary we would take you to court."

"I believe your recourse would be to sue McFadden's estate — and you might well have a case. But it would not affect Alton, Inc.'s ownership of the properties."

"I'm not an attorney," I said, "but I assume NHA would want to sue Alton, Inc. as well — for taking title to properties that it knew were optioned to NHA, and perhaps for coercing Eddie McFadden to sell those properties to Alton, Inc. rather than to NHA. I may be missing some legal distinctions here, but you have to admit the story would have news value, given how Eddie died."

"Mr. Crow, it is true, yes, that we would prefer not to be seen as bulldozing your organization — or you personally — out of our way, but you mustn't think for a minute that we will not do whatever is necessary to get you out of our way. And I doubt very much if a bulldozer will be necessary."

"I recognize that it was not a bulldozer that pushed Jonah out of the way. Or that pushed Eddie out of the way."

Breston's chair squawked. Elizabeth frowned. I had the impression that it was not my words but Breston's squeaky chair that annoyed her. "I am not threatening you, Mr. Crow, but I think you understand the situation. In any case it remains true that we would prefer a quiet solution."

"So would NHA — a quiet solution that works for NHA."

"Very well, what is your price?"

"Fifty thousand each for the options. For two hundred and fifty thousand you can have title to all five properties — the options on the McFadden properties, and the Duber properties subject to existing mortgages."

Now, finally, she turned her head and looked at me. There was indeed something odd about her left eye. There was a scar and something not right about the lid.

"In other words," she said, looking away again, "approximately twenty-five times their market value. You know those properties wouldn't appraise for more than a few thousand each."

"Appraised value is not what we're talking about," I said.

"True, for the sake of a quiet solution, we might agree to pay twenty-five or maybe thirty thousand for everything that NHA owns on Sheridan Avenue — way more than its market value."

"But market value is the price agreed upon between a willing seller and a willing buyer. The price this seller is willing to agree upon is two hundred fifty thousand, net, for the five properties. You are going to have to decide whether you're willing to pay that."

"I'm afraid that is not a quiet solution."

"It can be quiet if you want it to be. And I'm sure your project budget can be adjusted to cover that amount, given the size of the project, and the resources of your investors."

"However, our investors would not be happy with such an adjustment. They are willing to pay a reasonable price, but they are not in the habit of being taken advantage of."

"Nor would they be happy to see NHA board members being interviewed for the evening news in front of 1098 Sheridan Avenue."

"I see." She sat still, gazing straight ahead — until finally she stood up. "We are very far apart, and in any case nothing can happen before Monday. I suggest you go back to your board of directors and try to persuade them to accept a reasonable price. I will consult the limited partner investors whom I represent. I'll call you on Monday."

I stood as well. "I'll do that."

She moved to the door.

I followed her. She opened the door for me and, as I passed to her right, there was the sidelong glance and an odd quick smile that suggested a kind of acknowledgement, but it was not a friendly smile. I went out and she closed the door behind me, remaining in the office with Breston.

The lean swarthy man had gone and the outer office was now empty. Passing the desk, I noticed a loose-leaf checkbook standing on edge between fax machine and printer. The opportunity was a surprise, and I surprised myself by seizing it. I slid the checkbook toward me, opened the black binder and tore out a sheet of checks from the back of the book, then slid the book back where it had been.

Heading for the outer door I folded the sheet and slipped it into my shirt.

27

We were having dinner in a new restaurant on the Central Avenue commercial strip in Colonie, less than a mile from the small suburban ranch house where I once lived. Lisa had said she wanted to go someplace out of the neighborhood, out of the city, someplace that didn't even *feel* like Albany. So we drove out Central Avenue without any particular destination and wound up in a restaurant that had recently been opened by a large chain with a western motif. We were waited on by a young woman wearing a plaid shirt, jeans and cowboy boots, who greeted us, "Howdy buckaroos, I'll be your server this evening." She was not yet quite able to say it without blushing.

It was not at all like Albany — definitely not like Sheridan Hollow. Nonetheless, our conversation stayed rooted in Albany, and there seemed to be no way to pull it free.

"So big bad Breston turned out to be not much," Lisa said. "Dick was right — it's the investors that are driving this thing."

This was something I wanted to think I'd understood without Frost's help. "It always is, isn't it?" I said, a little too argumentatively. "Isn't it investment — the money itself — that makes things happen?"

"The investment yes, the money itself, well no. Money is nothing, not a force at all."

"I'm glad you think so."

"It's the people trying to get ahead that are the force. Why are we talking about this?"

"Breston's trying to get ahead. His investors are not trying to get ahead. They're already way ahead. They're just looking for a place to park some money, and then a way to turn illegal income into legal income."

"Anyway, you decided you're willing to play their game, sort of?"

"I guess you can say that. Sort of."

"So how much did you ask for?"

"A quarter million net."

"But for *w h a t*? For getting out of their way?"

"For NHA's interests in five properties. That's including their options on the three McFadden properties."

"And for getting out of their way."

"Of course."

"But she — this Elizabeth person—she turned you down."

"We agreed we would consult with those we respectively represent. Over the weekend. She said she'd call on Monday."

"But I'm sure she didn't *like* having you walk in and try to hold them up like that. And they have other ways of getting you out of the way."

"She said as much."

"And you're just casually waiting for them to call up on Monday and say thank you for your offer but we've decided to just kill you and be done with it. But of course they won't call. They'll just do it."

Abruptly she put both hands over her face and bowed forward. Through her hands she said, "I'm sorry. I didn't mean to say that. But it's sitting right there. I can't help thinking about it."

I couldn't help arguing. "But they wouldn't be done with it that way," I said. "NHA would still hold property they need."

She straightened up and looked at me. Her face was flushed. "But you can't really think they'll pay that price."

"I think there's a chance. Frost says they have three hundred fifty thousand sitting in an Albany bank account. I have no idea what Elizabeth thinks, but I'm guessing the investors see a quarter million as petty cash and would have no interest in complicating things any further at this point."

"You're *guessing*."

"Okay, surmising."

"And if they accept that price, you'll sell — NHA will sell? And get out of Sheridan Hollow? That's the most hopeful thing I've heard in a long time. If they'd really meet your price — or come close enough to meeting it."

"Yes, we would sell," I said, "but it wouldn't necessarily mean getting out of Sheridan Hollow."

"But you'd *be* out of the Hollow. You'd have no more property there."

"NHA now has options on two adjacent properties across the street, and next to those are three county-owned properties. All five are included as available for development in the proposal to DHCR. There's some flexibility in the proposal. Or at any rate I tried to leave it so DHCR can be somewhat flexible in what they fund, if they want to be."

"Are you saying the NHA might sell its interest in the properties on the south side of Sheridan and still go ahead and do a project on the north side? A residential project facing the back side of a parking garage?"

"I don't imagine they would actually build it. But they would still have a base — a place to stand on to oppose the parking garage project. So they could still fight it out in public — through the media."

"Wouldn't they lose credibility if it was known they had sold most of their property in the Hollow to Breston's company and then turned around and tried to stop the people they'd sold it to? I mean what are they going to say — that they didn't know what he was going to do with it? That they thought Breston was buying the property so he could build a giant day-care center or something?"

"I don't know. It could be a problem. But I'm not sure Breston and company want to say too much about anyone's motivation — or where anyone's money came from."

"I'm sure *not*," she said, "but that's what worries me. What makes you think they aren't ready to just stomp on as many people as necessary to get rid of *all* opposition? So they won't have to fight it out in the media with *anyone*."

"We keep coming back to this point," I said. "I have a different take on it. What more can I say?"

"I don't want you to say any more. I want you to stop and think. I want you to take care of yourself."

"But I can't change course at this point. And I *a m* going to take care of myself."

"I *hate* this," she said.

"I know. I hate it too."

"Buckaroos shouldn't argue."

"Buckaroos are brave and cheerful," I said.

"I'm trying," she said. "The cheerful part is really hard."

It was a relief when our cowgirl waitress arrived with our meal. We ate quickly and didn't linger when we had finished.

* * *

I was sitting in my old over-stuffed chair in my living room, looking out on the midnight emptiness of Orange Street. The evening had passed slowly since Lisa had dropped me off after dinner, telling me sternly to lock my door, stay inside, be careful. I had done all of those things, but it hadn't made the time pass quickly.

Earlier, during the afternoon, I had tried again to reach Reilly — again without success — so there was no word on Linda Bettleman. I had then called Judith Rosen, who told me there was still no real change in Loosh's situation. "I'm hopeful," she said, "but, you know, there's still evidence against him, so it's basically guilty until proven innocent. But I think we'll get there."

At five o'clock I had reached Harry Cooper at home and had filled him in on my meeting with Breston and Elizabeth Michaels. He sounded astonished when I told him the terms I had offered, but he didn't object and I didn't really try to discuss the issue with him. I promised to let him know as soon as I heard from them on Monday. However, Monday morning felt a long way off. With no new information to think about, I felt stalled.

When Lisa had dropped me off, my plan had been to go over my canoe route one more time, carefully, from Schefferville to the Inuit community of Kujjuack, estimating progress from day to day, with allowances for a certain amount of slow carrying around rapids, a certain amount of time sitting windbound on larger lakes, and, hopefully, a certain amount of time to relax, to play with the big trout in the rivers, to hike to the crests of barren ridges and look down on country that went on for hundreds of miles uninhabited, undeveloped, affected only by natural forces. It wasn't that I thought I could really improve on my earlier estimate of the time needed for the trip, but I thought I could lose myself in the process of imagining future time on the rivers and lakes so the present evening at home would slip away. And for a while it had worked. I had closed the drapes, turned up the lights, and laid the maps out in order on the living room floor. Then, on hands and knees, with a string marked off to measure miles at a scale of 1:250,000, I had made my way slowly northward from Schefferville. I had traveled all the way to the Caniapiscau River when my little capsule of quiet future time was split open by a gunshot.

It was several blocks east and north, probably the other side of Clinton Avenue. Maybe on Lexington, or beyond Lexington. Whoever had been shot at was someone else, someone unknown. Someone in much greater danger than myself.

There was just the one shot, then silence, but it yanked me into the present. The maps had become mere paper, but I forced myself to finish the measuring task so I could reassure Dave Potter that we would have enough time. Then I picked up the maps, folded them and put them into the plastic map case, which I returned to the pile of gear I had begun to collect in the corner next to the front door. After that I went into the kitchen, poured myself a drink and returned to the living room to turn off the lights, open the drapes and sit looking into the street.

Midnight gunshots were always disturbing, but usually not because I felt personally threatened by them. It was not the people like me, the people that didn't quite belong here, who were killed by these eruptions of violence. It was people like Loosh and Bax who were killed when the accumulated troubles of the community erupted in them and through them. The gunshots were a chilling reminder of how deeply compressed the troubles were and how far beyond the ability of any one person to reach them and fix them. The gunshots seemed to rebuke the efforts of people like Jonah Lee.

I sat with my whiskey and tried to focus my attention out where the light from the streetlight shone on the red brick pavement of the empty street. I wanted to let everything flow out of me into the empty space. But I was only halfway there when the memory of Elizabeth Michaels floated up.

I still had no idea what to make of her. It was much easier to think about how to deal with someone like Breston, whose bluster and greed were things you could get hold of and potentially use against him. But Elizabeth Michaels had given away nothing. The beautiful averted face had been like a one-way mirror through which someone I couldn't see had observed me closely while carrying on a precisely managed conversation with me. I had tried to control what she was able to observe, but I wasn't sure how successful I'd been. I found myself wondering what she thought of me. What was behind the odd smile she gave me as I was leaving? Was it that, unlike Breston, she was actually enjoying the process in which we were engaged?

28

We sat on a log behind the gravel beach near the foot of the big island. Down river from us on the west shore was the chain link fence that enclosed the Waterford General Electric plant.

Gazing at the fence, Raymond said, "You can tell how much they love the river."

"The fence? It's to protect us from whatever they do over there."

"More likely it's to keep the guard dogs from going swimming. Those dogs get in the river, stir up the mud, release those PCBs, give people cancer."

"You think they really have guard dogs?" I asked. "Plain old-fashioned dogs?"

"Better'n people," Raymond said. "Work much better'n people. Better noses. More dependable. Teach them to bite the guy that climbs over the fence and they'll do it every time."

"And they're non-union. No strikes, no protests. No biting the hand that feeds them."

"I don't know. The hand that feeds them is just some *person's* hand. Dog bites it, well if the guy can't get along with the dogs, get rid of him."

"Or pack up your dogs and your machines and go set up in some other country where people would be *happy* to let the dogs bite them."

"And happy to let you pollute their rivers."

I opened a beer, handed it to Raymond, then opened another for myself. It was good to have someone with whom to drink beer and bullshit cynically about GE. "A person would almost think we're bitter," I said.

"Not me," Raymond said. "Big corporation like GE, it's just a big machine for making money. Big machine with no soul. You can't be bitter toward something that has no soul. It's just part of what is."

"But so is the river just part of what is. Only it's a natural force that flows, except where it's dammed — and supports life, except where it's polluted. The other thing is anti-natural — dam-builder, polluter."

"I don't know," Raymond said, "you leave me behind with those fancy ideas."

"Okay, I was starting to leave myself behind. Still, I have very different *feelings* about those different parts of what is. Don't you?"

"I'm not real good at talking about feelings," Raymond said. "Sure, I like the idea of saving the Great Whale and some other rivers I've worked on but never seen, and I don't have good feelings about Hydro Quebec that wants to dam every river in sight so they can turn river current into electric current and electric current into money. It's not an idea that feels good."

"And rivers do feel good. At least they feel good to me. Even this one, half polluted and half urbanized." I was watching a row of th ree cabin cruisers coming up river — the largest of them in the lead, followed by a medium-sized one, followed by a small one. They would have bunched up at the Troy dam and come through the lock together; soon th ey would go through the next lock together, and they would probably stay together that way, in that order, on up through the Champlain Canal into Lake Champlain.

"Never spent time on rivers ," Raymond said. "Didn't have a river growing up. Had..." He lapsed into silence, gazing out across the water.

"Where was it?" I asked. "That you grew up."

"Place by the tracks, in Quebec. Lac Gerard. Population zero to thirty, depending on who was home — in our family and a couple of others."

"So you had a railroad and a lake."

"Sort of. The lake was at the other end of the road. Two mile dirt road ran from the tracks to the lake. But, yeah, I spent a lot of time on the lake with my grandfather."

"You like it?"

Raymond took a swallow of beer, shrugged, and was silent for some time, until finally he said, "See, I was this ten-year-old kid sitting in a small boat with nothing to do all day while his grand-father fishes, or pretends to fish while he drinks, if he has any-thing to drink."

"Okay, I see."

"But actually I did like hanging out with my grandfather. And I liked outboard motors. I liked outboards a lot. Being on the lake when we were moving along, with the motor wound up and run-ning smooth, that was something else. And I got to be pretty good with motors. When we we re ten miles down the lake and it was g etting dark and the old Evinrude didn't want to sta rt, it was me that was either going to get it started or not. So I learned. The sound of an outboard running smooth is still one of the most soothing sounds I know — the sound of all's-right-with-the-wo rld. Whereas the sound of nothing but waves lapping on the shore and the wind in the trees, that's worrisome — the sound of oh-oh-might-not-get-home-tonight."

"Makes sense to me," I said. "I can remember times when I was a kid...if there was an ice storm and the power went off during milking. The radio would go off, the music would stop. The sound of the milking machines would drop off with a kind of sigh as the suction released, and you'd be there with no sound in the barn except the sound of the cows chewing and you'd realize that you had thirty cows that you might have to milk by hand...or maybe it's not quite the same..."

He laughed. "Maybe not that different. And not that different from how it is now when you're at the computer and the power goes out and your monitor goes blank and some piece of unsaved work dissolves into nothingness, or into some random arrangement of electrons, or whatever it is..."

"We were sounding bitter before. Now we're just sounding morose. I don't know which is worse."

"The fate of guys like us."

"Guys who work on computers and live in a funky neighborhood in Albany. Who aren't really with it and can't really get out of it."

"That littlest boat," Raymond said, gazing at the last of the three boats that were now coming opposite the foot of the island. "Got a nice big seventy-five horse motor. Open it up, hear it whine, feel the wind and spray in your face. Don't feel so morose."

"Well don't come too close to my little canoe... "

"My rule is...try not to upset anyone's little boat. If there's something makes a guy feel maybe everything is okay for a little while, don't take it away from him."

"Your grandfather..." I said. "I don't suppose he's still alive."

Raymond was silent. There was a vireo chatting away somewhere high in one of the cottonwoods behind us, going on and on, repeating the same loop of gossipy little exclamations and comments, over and over.

"I was just picturing your grandfather in his boat," I said. "A man in a small boat with his spinning rod and his beer. I was wondering if the world felt okay to him then."

"No spinning rod. He fished with nets. Very hard work for an old man to haul those nets. Especially on those days when he'd managed to get hold of enough alcohol to get drunk. Beer was mostly okay, but sometimes he'd get hold of a bottle of liquor from one of the railroad guys. That was how he died. Fell in, got tangled in the nets. Empty bottle left in the boat."

"I'm sorry."

"But you were right. When he was out there his world was all right. A little beer helped, but it had to be in the boat. Drinking at home he was not happy, and neither were the rest of us. Drinking at home he was a pain in the ass."

"But for you...it's not a small boat that makes your world okay.

I don't think it's really a seventy-five horse motor either..."

"Not quite."

The vireo continued to gossip about the weather in the top of the cottonwood. I drank my beer and thought about the vireo and the fact that I had never knowingly seen a vireo. Until recently I had not even known what bird it was that made that particular sound high in the summer foliage. It had just been one of the familiar but unidentified sounds that sometimes brought back the feeling of being a boy on a Rensselaer county farm in the summertime.

After a while Raymond said, "You actually had a meeting with this guy Breston. How'd it go?"

I told him about my talk with Breston, and the ensuing discussion with Elizabeth Michaels.

"She sounds kind of scary," Raymond said. "And here I thought all you had to worry about was big old Bear."

"Big old Bear is reassuringly big and dumb. This Elizabeth is not dumb, and not at all reassuring."

"Anyway you offered to sell them what they want — for a big price — and they're considering it, or something like that. Do you think they're really considering it?"

"I have no idea what to expect. They might just pay the price, which is not really a lot of money for the people financing this thing, and try to move ahead as quickly as possible. Or they might make a counter offer. Or they might try to do what they've done before — just get rid of the opposition."

"And you've got to sit on your ass until Monday to find out which it will be."

"If it takes them that long. Once they've decided, I don't think they'll necessarily wait until Monday."

A mid-day breeze was picking up out of the south, beginning to raise small waves against the current. Raymond reached behind his head, grasped the base of his ponytail with one hand, and with the other hand stripped the rubber band from his hair. He tucked the rubber band into his shirt pocket and shook his hair loose in the breeze. "It made more sense," he said, "when it was Jonah doing this stuff."

"It's true, I'm no Jonah. And it's not even my community that's affected. It's my neighbors but not my own community. But then Poste-de-la-Baleine wasn't your community when you got involved against Hydro Quebec."

"They were my people though. Same as people in Arbor Hill

were Jonah's people, even though he was coming from somewhere different."

"Then I guess I'm envious. I'm not even sure who my people
are. White suburbanites in Colonie who maybe grew up on dairy
farms thirty years ago?"

Raymond opened two more beers and handed one to me. "So
you're free," he said. "You can do any damn thing you want. And
here you are risking your life to stop a parking garage that isn't
even going to change anyone's life in the community that much."

"You trying to talk me out of it?"

"No. Just wondering what you'd say about why you're doing
it."

"It would be nice to think it's because I'm free to do any damn
thing I want. But more likely it's just the opposite. I got headed in
a certain direction and can't seem to turn around."

Raymond smiled. "Then let's figure out how I can help cover
your ass until things turn out one way or another. I got an old
twelve gauge double-barrel. Got a few old twelve gauge shells with
double-ought buckshot, came down from my grandfather."

29

The south wind had brought in the first really intense heat of the
summer. I'm of the opinion that air conditioning is an unneces-
sary waste of energy, and most of the time I don't mind the house
feeling warm and summery, but occasionally, at times like this,
the house does get downright hot — and stays hot, even well after
sundown, even with all the windows wide open.

The downstairs windows have sections of old chain link fence
stapled to the outside — not much of a barrier and not hard to pry
loose, but enough to prevent someone from just walking up and
climbing in through an open window. The upstairs windows have
nothing over them. The window over my desk, directly behind the
computer monitor, can easily be reached from the roof of Jesse's
family's garage next door. In fact, I've been startled several times by
the sudden appearance of Jesse's grinning face above the monitor.
Tonight I had pulled the drapes over the open window and was sitting at my desk trying to finish a couple of pieces of non-Albany
work. I wasn't making a lot of progress.

I hadn't been so hot since the previous summer. The air was
motionless and humid. I sat with a towel around my neck so I

could wipe my face from time to time to keep from dripping sweat on the papers I'd spread out on the desk.

Lisa was visiting a college friend in Boston. As far as I could tell, she had just recently arranged the overnight trip as a way of avoiding questions that neither of us really knew how to address. Like the question of whether we should have spent this night together.

Would it have put her in danger? Was there any real danger at all? Was the danger so real that I should have gone to Reilly and told him everything I knew immediately after my meeting with Breston and Elizabeth Michaels?

Or had she really gone to Boston to avoid more fundamental questions about our relationship — about whether we were after all just too different from each other to sustain the kind of relationship that had begun to seem possible?

I didn't know how to answer any of the questions. I tried to concentrate on a piece of work for the group in Trenton, but finally gave up and called Dave Potter in Saranac Lake. I told him I had rechecked the route and was still confident we'd have enough time. He said he was beyond worrying about that and just wanted to get going. I told him how hot it was in Albany, and we spent a pleasant few minutes speculating about northern weather conditions that would probably range from barely warm enough to downright cold. But when I hung up, the Albany night felt hotter and more oppressive than ever.

I thought about getting myself a drink, but drinking beer with Raymond and then paddling back in the afternoon sun with a warm wind in my face had left me feeling dehydrated and lethargic. I had drunk enough water since that time to rehydrate myself, but my body still felt like it had already had its alcohol for the day and the thought of whiskey was not appealing.

Finally I gave up, shut down the computer and retired to my bedroom. I didn't bother to turn on the lights — there was plenty of light from the windows that looked out on the street. I stripped off shorts and tee-shirt, stripped the one blanket and top sheet off the bed and lay down naked on the bottom sheet. Lying on my back I shut my eyes against the one streetlight that shone directly through the window, and immediately I felt sweat begin to trickle into my eye sockets. I turned on my side, away from the window, and tried to summon up a memory of what it was like to paddle into a cold northern wind. But I couldn't bring the memory close enough to make any difference.

When I finally slept, it was a shallow sleep filled with restless dreams from which I kept almost waking up. At one point in these dreams there was a blond woman who I thought was the woman I had met in Breston's office, but I couldn't see her face.

I felt I needed to see her face. There was something about it that I couldn't quite remember. She was talking to me as though she knew me, but with her head turned away, hidden behind her hair.

I didn't really sleep well until after dawn. Then I slept until midmorning and woke up feeling as though I'd spent the night drinking whiskey, which didn't seem fair.

I was in the kitchen, having barely started on my first cup of coffee, when Reilly called.

"Finally found her," Reilly said. "We need to talk."

"Who? Talk about what?"

"Linda Bettleman."

"Is she okay?"

"Yeah, scared but okay. I think. I haven't actually talked to her yet. She's in Utica with a cousin. Utica police talked with her. I talked with them."

"And learned something useful?"

"Can you come over to the North Station?"

"I guess so. That's where you are now?"

"And for the rest of my life is what it feels like."

The building that housed the police substation for Arbor Hill — like the building that housed the Community Development Agency — was part of the recent development promoted by the city to improve the appearance of Henry Johnson Boulevard. After finishing my coffee, I walked down Orange Street to Henry Johnson, then north the several blocks to the substation. I found Reilly behind a desk, looking as unrested as I felt. There appeared to be no one else in the building.

"I seem to see you a lot on Sunday mornings," I said.

"Homicide scenes and Sunday mornings," Reilly said. "It's time we had a serious talk."

"Why?"

"Bettleman says she was upstairs taking a nap. She woke up and started to come downstairs, and coming down she could hear voices in the dining room. McFadden's voice and two others — a man and a woman."

"Could she understand what they were saying?"

"She couldn't understand what McFadden was saying. She

says he was mostly making what she called a moaning sound. The other two were talking loud enough so she could hear — or the man was. Hard to understand, she says, but threatening. She couldn't figure out what it was about and she was too scared to stay on the stairs and listen. She went back upstairs and hid in a closet for some amount of time — she says hours — before she finally dared to sneak back down. It was quiet then and she looked into the dining room and saw what we found there after she called us."

"So she didn't actually hear anything that she understood?"

"Just one thing." Reilly stared grimly at me.

"What one thing?"

"Your name."

"My name?"

"Your name. Warren Crow."

"That was all? She didn't hear what was said about Warren Crow?"

"The Utica cop says she thought it sounded like 'Warren Crow *knows*.' She says it was the woman that said it and her voice wasn't real loud and was hard to hear. But she's sure it was your name."

"I don't know what to make of it," I said.

"I'll tell you what *I* make of it," Reilly said. "What I make of it is Warren Crow does in fact know stuff he hasn't been telling me about. And it's time he did."

I tried to remember exactly what I had and had not told Reilly. "It's got to be about the situation I filled you in on the other night," I said. "The properties that Eddie first optioned to Jonah's organization and then sold to this guy Breston's corporation Alton, Inc."

"Suppose you just fill me in some more."

"The only thing I know now that I didn't know then is that the options do actually exist and haven't yet expired. The originals turned up a couple of days ago."

Reilly stared at me. I felt slightly guilty. Once again I had passed up an opportunity to tell him everything I knew or had reason to suspect about the whole situation.

"Have you had any contact with this guy Breston since we talked?"

"I did meet with Breston on Friday, yes."

"And?"

I didn't like the feeling of being interrogated. I felt myself hardening against Reilly's questions, the guilty feeling evaporating. "And what?"

"What did you discuss?"

"We discussed the interests that Alton, Inc. and NHA have in various Sheridan Avenue properties. They're corporations with competing interests. One of them is going to have to give way and sell out to the other. We discussed prices."

Reilly picked up a coffee mug from his desk, peered into it, made a face and set it aside. "This was just you and Breston alone?"

"An attorney was present — a woman who is on the board of Alton, Inc. and represents people investing in Alton, Inc."

"Name?"

"Elizabeth Michaels. And that's about all I know about her."

"But you met her. What kind of woman is she?"

"What do you mean? She's an attorney."

"Very hard-nosed attorney, right?"

"You mean would she slit someone's throat in order to close a deal? I don't know what kind of woman would do that."

"Or what kind of man," Reilly said.

"Right. I can't begin to imagine anyone doing it. But the fact is, no one *needed* to slit Eddie McFadden's throat in order to close the deal. They might have needed to scare him, but that would have been easy. There was no reason to do anything like what they did once he had signed the documents."

"But apparently they did have some kind of reason," he said. "And I see just two possibilities. Either someone is flat-out psycho, or they went to some lengths to make an example of McFadden in order to influence someone else."

"Who do you think they were trying to influence?"

He stared at me. "I can't believe you asked that," he said. "Tell me — where are you at with your negotiations with Alton, Inc.?"

"I made an offer. They're supposed to call tomorrow."

"When tomorrow?"

"They didn't say."

"I want you to call as soon as you hear from them. Call me, and don't stop trying until you get me. I'm going to give you all my numbers."

He picked up, inspected and dropped several scraps of paper from among the piles on his desk. He picked up the coffee mug again, started to look into it, then turned in his chair and lobbed the cup into the waste basket against the wall six feet away. He opened the center drawer of his desk against his belly, took out a phone message pad, wrote on it briefly, tore off the sheet and handed it to me. "You're a pain in the ass," he said, "and I hope you live to regret it."

I tucked the paper into my pocket and stood up. "I'll be in touch," I said.

"By the way," he said, "it's starting to look like Loosh Burns might be in the clear. Charges haven't been dropped, but I'm looking elsewhere. I'm looking at this situation of yours."

I walked back down Henry Johnson Boulevard to Orange Street and up the two blocks to my house.

Back in my kitchen, I sat down at the table with the second cup of coffee that I'd wanted ever since I left to see Reilly. I needed to sort through what I'd just heard, and think about whether to give Reilly more information, and when.

Before I could get my mind around any of it, the phone rang. It was Breston.

"I need to talk to you," he said.

"Happy to talk."

"We need to talk without the others. Without Ms. Michaels."

"Okay."

"This evening?"

"Why don't we just talk now?"

"We need to have a serious face-to-face. I want to explain some stuff to you. I got a deal for you. It's kind of complicated but I think you and I can make this thing work for us."

"A deal without Elizabeth Michaels?"

"I'll explain when I see you."

"And without the investors she represents?"

"Whoa now, let's not get ahead of ourselves."

"Why don't you just tell me right now what you're proposing. So I can think about it. Then we can talk later."

"Can't do that. Not that simple of a deal to tell you about. We need a face-to-face and we need some time."

The man was sounding increasingly tense. I couldn't tell whether it was eagerness or fearfulness, or maybe desperation. I wished I could see him at this moment. "Where are you right now?" I asked.

"Doesn't matter where I am now. Where I'll be tonight at ten o'clock is Elk Street at the end of Swan. I'll be headed west in a white Explorer. Be there at ten sharp and I'll pick you up. Right by the top of those stairs. Be there and be alone. This is just about you and me."

"I don't see how it *can* be about just you and me," I said. I didn't know what to make of it. I didn't believe he would really try to cut out the investors that Elizabeth represented. Unless he was desperate enough to take a very big risk. If that was the case I definitely wanted to talk with him. I tried to think of a way to string him along until I could get a better idea of what he was up to. "How do I know you're really the person I should be dealing with?" I said.

"Be there," Breston said a final time, and hung up.

30

I was sitting in my pickup on Sheridan Avenue a block above the Gander Bay. The pickup was parked on the left side of the one-way street, so I was looking down the hill to the bar and then out across downtown rooftops to where the last rays of haze-filtered sunlight had faded, leaving the distant wooded crest above Rensselaer almost black. I had been here for more than an hour, slouched in the seat, with the windows open only an inch, and no air moving. It was hot and I was tired of holding still and sweating. I wanted to get out and walk around, but I'd set a timetable for myself and was determined to be methodical.

My first plan had been to drive over to Capitol Hill and park on Swan where I could stay in the pickup and watch the section of Elk at the top of the long stair until Breston arrived. I would get there at least a half hour early and keep an eye on the area to be sure no one else was hanging around, and I wouldn't get out of the pickup until the white Explorer showed up and actually stopped. If it hadn't showed up by ten after ten, or if it showed up but didn't stop, I would drive away and wait to hear again from Breston, or Elizabeth Michaels, or whoever it was going to be.

With this plan in mind, I had walked over to the corner of Elk and Swan, in the heat of mid-afternoon, to make sure I was remembering the place accurately. There were no surprises, but in looking at the top of the stairs I thought how easy it would be for someone — Bax or Bear or whoever — to come up the stairs, wait just down the slope until Breston arrived, then come up the final flight just as I was getting into Breston's vehicle. And do whatever.

I was beginning to feel foolish about the whole thing. If Breston was trying to set me up — or if someone like Elizabeth Michaels was using Breston to set me up — then there were plenty of ways it could be done. I was going to be hanging myself out there no matter what I did, but if there was some way I could have a better view of what I was getting into, that was the way I wanted to do it.

From one point of view, the only reasonable thing would have been to call Reilly, fill him in on everything, and then go to meet Breston with police backup. But that might mean losing the opportunity to make a deal for NHA. The organization would be left holding a couple of over-mortgaged Sheridan Avenue properties with no real use outside of the expensive multi-family project that never had made sense except as a way to block Breston's project.

So I hadn't gone to Reilly. I'd gone to Raymond.

My plan now was to hang out down here in the Hollow until it was time to meet Breston. I would keep an eye on who came and went along Sheridan, and when the time came, if the stairs looked clear, I would go up. The lights along the stairs would be on and I would have a fairly good view from the bottom to the top. If anyone was hanging out on the steps I would see them.

From where I sat, I could see that the door of the Gander Bay stood open to the street, as it normally did on warm evenings. An hour ago, I had seen Bear go in. He had not come out again. Only a few other people had passed in or out. It was a quiet Sunday evening. Quiet and hot, and getting darker.

At quarter of ten, I sat up behind the wheel, released the handbrake and disengaged the clutch. The pickup rolled quietly down the long incline of the street close to the curb. There was no traffic and I didn't turn my lights on. A half block down I stopped in front of Raymond's house and reset the brake.

I lifted the daypack from the floor of the cab and checked its contents. I had removed the laptop, but Lisa's thirty-eight was still there, and my audio recorder was tucked into the front pocket. It was a good recorder, one I'd purchased for the occasional interviews I did in the course of my work. It ran quietly and I didn't think the sound would be noticeable coming from the pack.

I got out with the pack and locked up the pickup. Raymond already had my spare set of keys. I walked back to the corner of Dove and headed up the steep slope northward toward Orange. I would have liked to just walk down Sheridan past the Gander Bay in the hope of getting a useful look inside, but I couldn't do that without making myself visible under the streetlight as I passed. So I had decided to go around — up Dove and over on Orange to Swan — which would also give me a view of the stairs from a safe distance.

When I reached Swan Street I could look out across Sheridan and see the full length of the stairs rising toward the wall of buildings along Elk. The lights were on along the stairway, and there were no people coming or going or sitting. So, with the daypack slung on one shoulder, I went on down Swan to the foot of the stairs and started up. On the first landing I swung the pack off my shoulder, reached into the front pocket and turned on the recorder before continuing upward.

The stairs themselves were well lighted, but on my right it was only a short distance to the ailanthus woods that covered the slope. They were not dense woods, but now at night they were thick with shadows, and the shadows were alive, sliding and weaving as I climbed from one light pole toward the next. I am not afraid of the dark — I normally enjoy being in the woods at night — but the moving shadows along the edge of these urban woods made me nervous. I wished I could see further into the shadows, but I had to keep one eye on the steps I was climbing, and my intermittent glances into the woods did more to stir my imagination than to reassure me that no one was lurking there.

But I was making progress. I crossed the third landing, then another dozen steps to the fourth landing. Then fifteen steps to the fifth landing. I was already sweating freely in the hot night air. The sixth landing was approximately halfway to the top. I paused and tilted my head back to look all the way to the top.

There was someone up there coming down. I stood still and watched the person coming toward me until I could make out that it was a small African American male, not very dark skinned. It could be Bax. I continued to watch and still was not sure but it looked very much like Bax. I turned and looked back down the stairs behind me and realized there was also someone coming up. A hulking white male with a big beard. It had to be Bear.

I couldn't just stand there and let them close in. I had to assume Bear would be slower coming up than Bax would be coming down. I charged down one flight of stairs, across the landing and started down the next flight. Bear had stopped in the middle of a flight and was staring up at me.

Without pausing I grabbed the railing on my left, vaulted over it and angled into the trees. As I entered the woods I could see Bear struggling to get himself up over the railing to come after me.

I ran as fast as I could along the side-hill on a long traverse through the trees. I had swung the daypack from my shoulder and now held it in front of me in both hands to shield myself from the branches. The slope was steep and it was hard to make much speed with one leg uphill and one leg downhill. It felt like a dream in which I was trying to run but couldn't seem to make myself go as fast as I should have been able to. But I charged ahead as best I could, hoping it would be even harder for Bear.

Though my eyes were adjusting to the dark, I could still see only a short way in front of me. Branches slapped at my arms and legs. I stepped in a hole and stumbled forward, almost going down before getting my feet back under me. Then a piece of the steep clay slope crumbled and slid beneath my right foot. I skidded and almost went down again. I needed to slow down a little, try to get my bearings, think ahead.

I didn't know where Bax was. It was possible that he would have gone back up the stairs and would loop around through the parking lot at the top, where the going was easier, in an effort to get ahead of me. I still didn't know what to expect of Bax. I would rather deal with Bear. Also Raymond was somewhere on the lower level. He had been positioned to watch the stairs. He should have seen me go into the woods with Bear after me. But what would he have done then? Where would he head for? Where would he expect me to come out of the woods? I adjusted my course a little more toward the bottom of the Hollow and scrambled onward.

I wasn't far now from the overgrown trash-filled alley that ran along the bottom of the slope. Further along the footpath ahead of me I knew there was a small playground, partly overgrown and little used — at least little used by the small children for whom it had been intended. The trees were thicker along the edge of the playground and it was very dark.

I could no longer tell where Bear was. I made myself stop and stand still until I could hear him coming, moving heavily, still trying to run — not far back but not visible in the dark. I could hear him panting, gasping for breath. If I was going to take on Bear directly, this would be the time.

A few yards ahead of me the dark shape of a large stump loomed near what I thought was the corner of the playground. I moved as quietly as possible to the stump and crouched behind it. I unzipped the daypack and took out the revolver and waited. Bear was maybe twenty yards away, still coming, panting like a steam engine. He would pass just uphill of the stump.

When the time came I launched myself out of my crouch, holding the revolver by the barrel and clubbing the butt hard into Bear's shins. Bear yelped and crashed forward, face-down, with me scrambling on all fours after him — and onto his back. Straddling him, I stuck the muzzle of the gun in his ear. "It's a thirty-eight," I hissed. "It's loaded. Lie quiet."

Bear didn't resist. He was gasping, face against the ground, struggling to catch his breath. His torso heaved under me. His shirt was soaked with sweat.

I heard myself say, "Bear, I want to know some things. You're going to tell me, and tell me quick, so I can let you go and won't have to shoot you in the ear." I hoped I sounded as though I knew what I was doing.

Bear's response was a wheezing grunt.

"First thing — who sent you after me?"

Bear gasped and wheezed, gasped and wheezed.

I screwed the gun tighter into his ear. "Who?"

He grunted. "Her."

"Elizabeth?"

"Yuh."

"Who else is after me right now?"

"Bax."

"Besides you and Bax."

Between wheezes Bear said something that sounded like "anthem."

"Who?"

"Anthony."

"And Breston?"

"Nuh."

"So Elizabeth set it up?"

"Yuh."

"All right. Who killed Eddie McFadden?"

Bear made a growling sound into the ground and his torso shifted under me.

I leaned on the gun, forcing it tighter into the ear. "Who? You were there. Who did it?"

"Not there, not me."

"Who was there?"

"Them."

"Elizabeth and Anthony?"

"Yuh."

"How do you know?"

"Drove 'em."

"You drove the car?"

"Yuh."

"So you were there."

"Jus' inacar."

"But you know what they did. Which one killed him?"

"Don' know, both of'm in 'ere."

I didn't know whether the tape recorder was picking up anything intelligible out of Bear's wheezing and mumbling. The daypack was five feet away, out of my reach. "So they were in there together," I said. "Did they come out together?"

"Yuh."

"Okay, and who killed Jonah?"

Bear made a sound that might have been a cough or might have been the name "Anthony."

I was going to ask if it was Anthony when I heard a sound behind me. I had started to turn my head when something crashed into it and drove me down into the darkness.

31

I thought I was still in the woods but couldn't remember how I got there. It seemed that I'd been doing some kind of physical work, and something had fallen on my head — maybe a dead limb out of a tree I was cutting, a widow-maker — and now I was pinned beneath its weight.

My head hurt where whatever it was had struck me. I wanted to reach up to see if there was blood, but I couldn't make my arms move.

I could hear voices nearby. At least two people — man and woman. I could hear fragments of what they were saying but couldn't put them together.

"...coming around..."

"...about time..."

"...not how it's supposed to..."

I needed to lift my head to see where the voices were coming from, but my head was very heavy. I was looking downward at the edge of a table — a curved edge with a metal molding around it — a kitchen table. I was in a chair at the table, slumped sideways.

"Could've finished already..." That was the man's voice, coming from behind me. He spoke in a rapid impatient mumble — hard to understand. Now he was saying something about "stop screwing around."

The woman was easier to understand. She spoke slowly and

clearly with a kind of forced patience, like a mother admonishing a child. "No," she said, "your way would not finish it. Any more than it did with Jonah Lee."

I managed to shift my position, straightening myself slightly, but there was something wrapped around my torso, holding me against the back of the chair. In fact I could see it — clothesline, several turns of it tight across my chest and binding me to the chair. My legs were tied also, to the front legs of the chair. Only my arms were free but they were very heavy and hard to move. I was extremely uncomfortable and I knew I was in a bad situation, but I still couldn't figure out what was going on.

Now the woman sat down at the end of the table to my left. She was that beautiful blond woman with the one eye that wasn't right. She said, "Good morning."

"What?" I was still confused. I knew it wasn't morning.

"How do you feel?" she asked.

I said I would feel better if I was untied.

She said not to worry about it. She reached toward me and touched my head near where it hurt and said, "Hmmm..." Like a nurse. I felt like a kid who's been banged up on the playground and sent to the school nurse, and is waiting to see what she's going to do about it.

Behind me the man mumbled something.

"My colleague doesn't understand that you and I have a lot to talk about," she said.

I raised my head and looked at her. She was looking past me, just as she had in the Alton, Inc. office. I couldn't see the bad eye, just the very beautiful right side of her face.

The man said something more. The part I understood was "...fucking signatures and go..."

The woman stood up. "Excuse us. We have to straighten something out." Turning to the man, she said, "In the other room."

She moved toward the doorway. She was wearing perfectly fitted jeans and a black tee-shirt. The blond hair fell smoothly to her shoulders. Her fingernails were glossy red.

The man came around the table and followed her. He carried a gun in his right hand. At the door he turned and raised his arm and pointed the gun at my chest and held it steady for a very long moment. There was a silencer on the muzzle. His lips shaped a silent word but I couldn't tell what it was. Then he lowered his arm and stepped through the door.

I was left alone in the room — an older working-class kitchen, not too different from my own, except that it smelled of mold and abandonment.

I reached my arms behind the back of the chair. I could feel the ropes back there, and knots — but no slack, no loose ends from which to approach the knots. My fingers couldn't find a starting place. I didn't even have the beginning of a strategy. So I gave up on the ropes. I decided the first thing I needed to do was to clear my head — try to get a clear idea of what was going on. What had happened in the dark woods?

I could put together parts of it. I remembered running from the stairs through the woods. I remembered straddling Bear's heaving sweat-soaked back, though I wasn't sure how I had managed to get there. I remembered questioning him, but I couldn't remember how it had ended. Something had gone wrong. It had been a mistake to do what I did with Bear. I should have kept going — out through the little playground. I could have got away. But now they had me. Not Bear or Bax, but the blond woman whose name I remembered now was Elizabeth, and this man with the gun, who was familiar in some way.

What had Bear said about this Elizabeth? I remembered asking Bear what happened with her at Eddie McFadden's. Then for the first time I connected my situation with the way McFadden was found tied to a chair with his throat slashed. I hadn't taken the threat seriously enough. I should have paid more attention to Lisa's fears — even my own fears. I'd been stupid.

It was probably a good thing the pain in my head bore down so relentlessly. It kept my thoughts from leaping into a panic. I could only drag my thinking slowly from one idea to the next.

I had no idea where I was. Where was this kitchen? How far from the place where I'd been with Bear? How long had I been unconscious and how far had they taken me? The window over the sink was dark. It was not yet morning. Other than that I had no idea how much time had passed.

If I was still in the neighborhood, Raymond could possibly have seen them bring me here.

On the far side of the table in front of me was a stack of paper. On top was a document with a title in type large enough so that I could read it. "ASSIGNMENT OF OPTION TO PURCHASE" was what it said.

I was just barely able to reach it with the finger tips of one hand and drag it toward me until I could pick it up. There were two pages stapled together. On the second page there were spaces for signatures. One was a space for my signature as Executive Director of the Neighborhood Housing Association. Then there was a space for a notary to sign.

The next document in the pile was also titled "ASSIGNMENT OF OPTION TO PURCHASE." I dragged it off the pile. Then one more with the same title. Then there was a document titled "DEED." And below it another "DEED."

So they were going to try to make me sign over the McFadden options and also sign over title to NHA's Duber properties.

On the table beyond the papers, and beyond my reach, was a black leather wallet. It looked like my wallet. I groped a hand toward the hip pocket where my wallet was supposed to be. The pocket was empty.

The pain in my head pulsed slowly, pulling slow waves of nausea up from the pit of my stomach. I tried to concentrate on the details of my surroundings, to steady myself and orient myself.

The door through which Elizabeth and the man had gone opened into a narrow hallway. They had turned right in the hall, which would mean toward the front of the building if the kitchen was in the rear of the building, as would be the usual situation if this was a typical Albany house squeezed into a linear arrangement of rooms by the narrow boundaries of a twenty-foot lot. I assumed that the window over the sink on my left looked to the rear. No street lights, no light of any kind, shone through it. I could see only reflections from within the kitchen, including the reflected frame of the door to the hall.

None of this told me where I was. I somehow felt I was still in Sheridan Hollow, but I couldn't be sure they hadn't got me into a car and taken me off to some distant place. I didn't even know what floor of the building I was on. It could be the ground floor or it could be a second or third floor apartment.

I tried listening hard, trying to catch any threads of sound that could be pulled out of the muffling late-night quiet. There were no nearby traffic sounds, but this told me nothing. I could be off in some quiet country place, or still in Sheridan Hollow where late-night traffic was rare. At certain times I did think I could hear traffic further away — the sounds of trucks on a highway somewhere, which could be I-787, relatively close by, or could be any highway anywhere. Also at certain times I could make out the voices of Elizabeth and the man with the gun somewhere off toward the front of the building. They were audible only in brief snatches, the way you hear the more emphatic moments in an otherwise hushed conversation. But most of the time I could hear only the murmuring undertone of deep night silence, barely distinguishable from the pain in my head.

Eventually I decided that what I really should be concentrating on was the pile of documents in front of me. What these people needed from me was my signature on those documents. How was I going to deal with that?

Did it matter now whether I signed or not? There was no NHA board resolution authorizing me to sign the deeds and option assignments, so my signature wouldn't be legally binding if I did sign. But who was going to argue this point for NHA if I wasn't there?

If I wasn't there. There wasn't a sliver of possibility that they would let me live, whether I signed or not. The one thing that they absolutely needed from me was for me to be absolutely gone. Getting my signatures would expedite their deal — allow them to treat the whole thing as a *done* deal, with any problems like the lack of a board resolution being merely technicalities to be cleaned up in due course by whatever means proved practical. They certainly couldn't let me report that I had been forced to sign the documents after being assaulted, kidnapped and tied to a kitchen chair. They couldn't let me report those circumstances whether I signed or not.

All I could do was try to stretch out the process, buy as much time as possible.

Part of me — the aching exhausted part — just wanted relief, wanted it to be over. But the stubborn part of me hated the idea of letting go and sinking into the darkness. The stubborn part of me wanted to see dawn come to the window above the sink. I would try to hold on that long — long enough to see the window brighten.

Elizabeth came back into the room alone. She came briskly to the table and this time she sat down directly facing me on the opposite side of the table. She no longer averted the damaged side of her face but looked straight at me. The damage, which I had only glimpsed before, was arresting though not extreme. The upper lid of her left eye drooped and appeared to have no mobility. A scar ran from the outer corner of that eye to her cheek bone, pulling the corner of the lower lid downward. The eye itself was as blue as the other one but seemed capable of looking only straight ahead, so the two eyes didn't move together. Not the worst sort of disfigurement, but the contrast between the flawless side of her face and the damaged side was strangely unnerving. I lowered my gaze.

"He'll be along in a minute," she said. "He wanted a cigarette and I made him go into the front room. I can't stand the smell."

I wanted to say something sarcastic but couldn't find words. This woman who objected to the smell of cigarette smoke had participated first-hand in the bloody murder of Eddie McFadden. She and the man that Bear had named, who I now assumed was the man with the gun who was having a cigarette. Who also had to be the man I had seen in the Alton, Inc. office, and maybe once before that.

"That would be your friend Anthony you're speaking of," I said.

"Not my friend."

"But you work closely with him."

"Only when I need someone to do the very specialized kind of work that he does."

"Such as now."

"Now he is on standby. I prefer to deal with you myself. You're an interesting man."

I had to push down the bit of hope that leapt up in me. *If she wants to deal with me alone and thinks I'm interesting...* But the only real hope was the hope of stretching out the process with her in order to see the light come beyond the window.

"And you're a very interesting woman," I said. "Beautiful and interesting and scary."

"Not beautiful," she said. "Deformed I think would be accurate, and I prefer accuracy. I am without illusions. I am a realist, and I think you too have a realistic view of things. I think we can discuss the present situation objectively."

"I'd be better able to discuss it objectively if I hadn't been hit over the head and tied to a chair."

"I'm sorry about that. I would enjoy this more if you weren't restrained, but it's after all necessary. I see you've looked at the documents."

"Only briefly. I'll need to read them more carefully, but I assume they're okay — if you've brought a check for the right amount."

"I don't know why you're bothering to bullshit me," she said. "You do understand the situation. Let's get on with it."

"If you've brought a check for the right amount," I persisted.

"I have brought not one but two checks, and that's not counting the one in your wallet." She picked up my wallet from the table. Sliding two fingers into it, she drew out the check I'd been carrying — from the page I had lifted from the Alton, Inc. office.

"This is another thing I don't understand," she said. "I didn't think stealing checks was your style."

"As you say, I'm a realist. Whatever works."

"But there was no way it could work."

Behind her, Anthony now stood in the doorway, staring at her back, the gun still in his right hand.

"It was just in case I found a way," I said.

"If I'm going to sign checks I'm going to do it properly, from the checkbook, with the check numbers in sequence."

"I'm sorry I offended your sense of order."

Anthony came into the room and stepped past the table. "Still screwing around," he said.

She looked up at him sharply. He shrugged and moved to the counter to the left of the sink, where he boosted himself up and settled himself on the counter top, the gun held in his lap.

"I'm not offended," she said. "But stealing the checks was more like stupid little grab-what-you-can McFadden than what I thought Warren Crow would do. Anyhow, we're not going to use your stolen check." She slid the blank check under the pile of documents, then flipped through the pile and extracted two fully made-out checks and dropped them on the table in front of me.

"Why two?" I asked.

"Look at them."

I picked them up. Both were signed by Elizabeth Michaels. One was made out to the Neighborhood Housing Association for five thousand dollars. The other was also made out for five thousand dollars but was payable to Warren Crow.

It took a little while to sink in. "I don't believe you really think you can buy me," I said finally.

"But other people may think so. When both checks come to the attention of your organization. The check to you will tend to explain why you agreed to sell out to Alton, Inc."

"It will also highlight the fact that there was not a legitimate sale to Alton, Inc. I'm sure you're aware of that."

"Of course." She sorted through the pile of papers again and pulled a sheet from near the bottom of the pile. It appeared to be one of my own invoices — the same type size and font and the same over-all format that I used for my invoices. It was dated the same as the checks and indicated that I was billing Alton, Inc. five thousand dollars for consulting services.

"You are a consultant," she said. "I am consulting with you right now, you might say. So if I need to explain the check..."

"Nonsense. The NHA board won't buy it. And even if they did, they know they didn't authorize these transactions. Where does that leave you?"

"It leaves Alton, Inc. perhaps having a talk with the NHA board, which is a struggling little community board badly in need of money."

"A deeply committed little community board that is determined not to betray the memory of Jonah Lee, whom they believe you killed."

"Because that's what you've told them."

"Yes."

"They may be less inclined to believe you when all of this is over."

"Don't count on it," I said. But I was wondering how the NHA board would in fact react. And how they should react. I didn't think they should do what I had done. They shouldn't get any more people killed. They should put the situation behind them. But that was not what I had prepared them for. I hated the feeling that I had let my own unresolved preoccupations get in the way of what was best for them.

"I'm not counting on anything," she said. "However this works out, I'm going to be holding all the cards. How I play them will depend on those people, and of course on you."

I tried a different angle. "And how are you going to deal with the bank that holds the mortgages on the Duber properties? There's twenty thousand dollars debt in each of those properties." I picked up the five thousand dollar check to NHA. "This doesn't cover it. The bank will have a problem with that, and the bank is not a struggling little community organization."

She stared at me, her good eye as unwavering and unreadable as the damaged eye that stared past me. Finally she nodded and said, "Okay, I know you're not as naïve as that sounded. You're just probing for details. Fine. The five thousand is for the options, which I've determined is what Jonah Lee paid Eddie McFadden for them. The price for the Duber properties is something else — it's the amount of the outstanding debt, which as you say is twenty thousand each. We will make the bank whole. We are also making the NHA whole. No one else would have paid what NHA owed on those buildings. So we are cleaning up the mess that Jonah Lee — and you — left behind. I think you should be grateful for the opportunity to help clean it up by signing these documents."

She leaned forward and once more sorted through the paper on the table. "To make sure it all works properly with no further mess, there is this, which you will also sign." She placed a single sheet of paper in front of me. A neatly printed letter. It was headed Sept Isles, Quebec, June 30, and was addressed to Harry Cooper, President, Neighborhood Housing Association. At the bottom was my name.

"We will make sure it's mailed from that place in Quebec on that date," she said. "It apologizes for your unavoidably early departure to Canada, and explains why this unavoidably rushed transaction is in the interest of the NHA. By signing it you will leave everything in order. No one else will be hurt."

The good eye gazed steadily at me. I was at a loss. I needed to do something to pull my thoughts together. I picked up the letter. "You're very thorough," I said. "Is there anything you don't know about me?"

"I know enough. I know some things about you that you yourself don't know yet."

"Such as?"

"That you are going to sign everything I'm asking you to sign — after you've thought about it for a little while. There *is* time for you to think about it."

Anthony stirred slightly on the countertop. "The fuck there is," he said.

She ignored him. To me she said, "I understand — you're not there yet."

"And I'm not going to get there as long as I'm tied to a chair with someone holding a gun on me."

"I agree the circumstances are unfortunate. I would much prefer that you could be untied and that I could send Anthony away. I would prefer that you be controlled entirely by my devices, not by a rope and a gun. But, again, I'm a realist."

"And again, I am too. Enough of a realist to understand that I have nothing to lose by resisting you."

"You would resist even though it means leaving a mess behind, leaving your friends in a messy, difficult situation — is that really what you want to do?"

"I trust them to deal with it. I don't trust you."

"I'm sorry you don't trust me. I'm being completely honest with you."

"I have no idea what the word honest means to you," I said. "I don't begin to understand you, or why you're in the kind of business you're in. You call yourself a realist, but I don't know what *that* means to you either. I would think a realistic attorney with your intelligence would be working for some Manhattan law firm or investment bank, making a lot of money, with a nice office, prestige, safety. Why would a realist choose to be sitting here in this moldy kitchen in the middle of the night pursuing a career that will sooner or later land her in jail?"

"Had the nice office with the Manhattan law firm been an option I would have chosen it," she said. "It was not an option."

"Why not? I'm sure you excelled as a law student."

"And you think that Manhattan firm is going to hire an attorney who cannot look a client in the eye?"

"You're looking me in the eye."

"And? What do you see?"

"A beautiful woman who was injured long ago."

She dropped her gaze momentarily, then looked back at me. Anthony shifted restlessly on the counter.

"But we're not talking about me," she said. "We're talking about you. We are exploring the truth about you, and we've only just begun."

"But for just a minute there," I said, "we were exploring the truth about you."

"Which is irrelevant. We have work to do here. We have to determine when you are going to sign these documents. I believe you saw what happened to Eddie McFadden."

"I saw what you did to him. And I noticed that it didn't do him much good to sign those deeds before you did it."

"Oh that didn't have much to do with his signing over those properties. I think you know that a pin prick would have made him sign, or the threat of a pin prick. The reason he had to go was that he had compromised himself, and therefore us, and in doing so learned more than was good for him to know."

"I understand you thought you needed to get rid of him — but why that way? Why the huge bloody mess? I thought you disapprove of messes."

"I disapprove of messy work. What was done to McFadden wasn't messy work. It was done exactly as we intended it — to send one message to the police and a different message to Warren Crow."

"Was it you who wrote the message in the blood?" I was looking at the hand with the scarlet nails resting on the table in front of me.

"Anthony's particular area of expertise doesn't include writing," she said.

"And what message are you going to write on this table in my blood?"

Asking the question, putting it into words, was a way to keep some slight distance from the idea.

"Oh it will be quite different in your case."

"No message?"

"The only message will be the letter from Canada. You yourself will simply disappear, leaving behind no mess at all. We are certainly not going to cut your throat."

"So kind of you."

"There are other parts of the body that bleed less but are far more sensitive."

"I'm not going to sign."

"The only question is whether you do it sooner, while you can still make a rational decision...or later, when you won't really have a choice at all."

"I won't choose to sign under any conditions."

She reached across the table and took my hands in both of hers. "Your hands are cold," she said.

I yanked both hands free and thrust them under the table. "Tell me how your eye was injured," I said.

She turned her face away so I could see only the unblemished side. After a moment she looked back at me and said, "All right, it doesn't matter. Officially it was an accident. I was three years old. The man who did it was my stepfather and he was drunk. I was crying and it annoyed him. He started toward me carrying his beer bottle and he fell and broke the bottle. I cried louder and he hit me with the broken bottle. I don't cry anymore."

I didn't know what to say. It felt like she had gained a point on me. What I finally did say was, "Cosmetic surgery could have made a difference."

"It was unsuccessful," she said. "Now please try to concentrate. You understand what will happen if you don't sign?"

"It would leave your situation a little less tidy."

"Not really. I would commission expert forgeries. No one would be able to tell the difference."

"Then why bother with all this?"

"Exactly. Why are you bothering to resist? It makes no difference what you do. Everything will flow along the same way after you're gone whether you put the mark on the paper or someone else does."

"Then why don't you just shoot me and get on with your plan?"

On my left Anthony said something half-under his breath that sounded like agreement.

"Because it matters to me that we do this the right way."

"So it's about you. You get off on this."

"It's a simple matter of control," she said.

"Control. You simply want to control me."

"Of course."

"And I simply want not to be controlled."

"The difference is that I will be alive and it will therefore matter to me. You will no longer be alive and it will therefore *not* matter to you. What you want now is meaningless."

I was looking at the window, wondering if the darkness beyond it was any less intense, but all I could make out still were the reflections. Then, as I gazed at the reflection of the door frame, I realized that there was the ghost of a person standing just around the corner.

I needed to keep the talk going. I said, "Do you think the whole meaning of a person's life just gets canceled out when the person dies?"

Raymond stepped into the kitchen with the shotgun on his hip, pointed at Anthony.

Anthony remained immobile except for the hand holding the gun, which sprang from his lap like a flushed bird.

Raymond fired. The blast from the shotgun was deafening in the small room. Anthony's body slammed backward and folded double under a set of overhead cupboards. One leg flopped over the edge of the counter and then kicked spasmodically.

Elizabeth sat as though frozen in place.

32

Raymond moved to where Anthony's gun had landed on the floor and kicked it in my direction. It slid to a stop against the leg of my chair. He then pointed the shotgun at Elizabeth. "Another one in the other barrel," he said. "Stand up."

She stood slowly, her arms falling slack at her sides, her face expressionless.

He moved around her, looking her up and down, then grasped the bottom of her tee shirt and twisted it tight around her slender waist. If she was concealing a weapon of any sort it couldn't have been anything bulkier that a nail file.

"Okay, sit down," he said.

She sat.

"And keep your hands on the table." He moved behind my chair, squatted, and untied the clothesline. Then he picked up Anthony's gun from the floor and handed it to me, and I took it from him mechanically and realized my fingers had gone numb. Standing up, he looked at Anthony and shuddered. "I think I need to sit," he said. He pulled a third chair to the table and sat down with the shotgun on his knees. "Are you okay?" he asked.

I nodded. I was numb but I was okay. I was going to be okay.

"Good. What the hell do we do now?"

I had to work at re-moistening the inside of my mouth before I could say anything. Finally I was able to ask, "Where are we?"

"Right here on Sheridan. One of the buildings they bought. I think Bear was living here, but I don't think he's going to need a place any more."

"Why, where is he?"

He glanced toward the crumpled body of Anthony. "Well, I saw you take off from the stairs with Bear after you. Bax went back up the stairs. I went up Sheridan and in by the playground. I was standing in the trees between the playground and the alley, trying to hear something but I couldn't hear a thing, until there was a shot, and I was afraid they must have got you. Then after a while Bax and this guy here came carrying a tall guy that had to be you out into the playground and I thought for sure they'd killed you. They came right down past where I was standing. Struggling along, two little guys having trouble carrying this big tall guy between them, and I wondered where Bear was. Then I realized they were arguing about something, and it sounded like this guy had done something to Bear, and I hoped maybe that was who was shot, not you. So I just stood there trying to figure out what to do. I had the shotgun, but it didn't seem like a good time for a shooting war with you in the middle, so I just stood and watched them take you down the alley and into the back door of this building."

"Did you call the police?"

"I had a hell of a time deciding. I started to go home to call but I got to thinking what could happen with three cop cars with flashing lights out front and you up there with them. So I waited and watched the building. A light went on downstairs in back when they went in. Then lights went on upstairs. A few minutes later Bax came out again and went up the alley and the light downstairs went off. So after a while I went and tried the back door and it wasn't locked. Then I spent just about forever, it seemed like, sneaking up here little by little." He shook his head as though trying to wake himself up. "I guess we should call the cops now though. There's a phone in the hall."

"Yes, but something else first — something here we have to finish. Elizabeth has to finish buying five properties from NHA. She has all the paper work right here, ready for me to sign."

No longer in control, Elizabeth had wilted like some frost-killed plant. She was sitting with her arms on the table in front of her, head hanging, hair spilled over her arms. I gathered the papers toward me and found the blank check at the bottom of the pile. "One more check for you to sign," I told her.

"I have no reason to do anything," she said tonelessly without lifting her head.

"That's not true. You can help yourself a lot here."

She looked up. "You mean you'd let me walk out of here?"

"You're going to walk out of here with the police. The question is what do we tell the police."

She looked briefly at the crumpled body of Anthony on the counter. "All right, what do you tell them?"

"That I was kidnapped by Bax and Anthony, and that you were connected with them and were present where I was being held. Beyond that I'm not sure yet." I put the check in front of her. "The check number is going to be out of sequence, but the amount this time will be correct — two hundred and ninety thousand. That's two fifty net for NHA, plus forty for the mortgage on the Duber properties."

"I want some assurance," she said.

"The only assurance you get is, if you don't sign the check I will report every last incriminating detail I know about you — and you've given me a lot of that to work with."

"But I don't know what you'll do if I do sign."

"No, you don't. And I really don't either. But if you sign the check I'll feel better about how things have turned out. And it's in your interest that I feel better."

She glanced again toward Anthony, as though to make sure he wasn't watching. Then she picked up the pen and quickly signed the check.

Raymond stood up and went out into the hall and I heard him pick up a phone. I began to yawn — the first of the yawning fits that were going to catch up with me periodically over the next several days.

33

"And it cleared," Lisa said. "The check actually cleared? The NHA got the two ninety, the quarter million to keep."

We we re celebrating, drinking martinis in Lisa's living room by the east windows. It was the first drink I'd had since being hit on the head, and I was beginning to feel like myself again.

"It cleared," I said. "Finally. I've been watching the NHA account online. Sometime during the afternoon two hundred ninety thousand came in."

"And the other check? The five thousand dollar one written to you that you also deposited."

"It cleared too."

"And you're going to give all of that to the NHA also? It seems to me you did earn at least a piece of it yourself."

"Not to the NHA. To the Zera Kay fund that Helen has organized. It's a year's rent for her while she finishes college. Raymond and I talked about it — because he earned that money if anyone did — and we both liked the idea of just putting it into the Zera fund. I wrote the check and dropped it off with Helen on my way over here. So now *I'm* cleared. Cleared to go north."

"Are you sure you're ready for that?"

"Absolutely. It's what I need."

"I suppose I understand — although it would be nice to think that *I'm* what you need."

"Oh you are — the other thing that I need."

"I guess I'll settle for that. You want another drink?"

"Yes. The one final other thing I need."

Retu rning from the kitchen with fresh drinks, she said, "And of course you're not exactly everything I need either."

"I should hope not."

She handed me the drink and sat down. "I'm curious about what's going to happen to Thomas Breston. Do you think he might actually get off?"

"I don't know. He's charged with conspiracy in connection with the murders of Jonah and McFadden, but I don't know that they'll have enough to make it stick."

"Elizabeth Michaels didn't incriminate him? I mean I can see her protecting the investors — because they'd probably have her killed if she didn't — but she doesn't have any reason to protect Breston, does she?"

"Her strategy has obviously been to say as little as possible about every thing. If the DA was as eager to get at Breston as he is to get at the investors, then I suppose she might have traded him for a lighter sentence. She *could* have traded the investors if she'd wanted to take that chance, but I don't think Breston had much trade value. So we may never know how much he really knew about what was going on."

"As long as he can't come back and restart the project. His corporation still exists, after all, and now that you've actually had the deeds recorded, it owns all the property that's needed to go ahead with the project."

"But that's all he's got. The project's dead. Too much has been dragged into the daylight for the city ever to want to have anything to do with it — or the investors either at this point."

"So there's really just the one problem," she said.

"What's that?"

"You lost my gun."

"I did lose your gun. It was Anthony's gun that killed Bear. Your gun just disappeared. I'm sure it had to be Bax that took it and hid it. The police found the backpack where I left it, just a couple of yards from Bear's body. But they didn't find the gun as far as I know, and I didn't tell them. So I'm going to have to buy you a new one."

"No, I'd rather you didn't. I'll get a new gun and you can just owe me, permanently. I want to be able to remind you from time to time."

"So I'll have to pay over and over again."

"Starting tonight."

* * *

I had got up at first light to go home and finish packing before heading for Saranac Lake to meet Dave Potter. But walking up Clinton Avenue, I had looked down Swan Street to where the long stair climbed the slope toward the Capitol, and had decided to make a short detour. Now I was sitting at the foot of the sixth landing, looking out over Sheridan Hollow. The sun was just rising over the Rensselaer Hills and was beginning to light the tops of the tall trees down in the Hollow, while the roofs of the buildings remained dark. It was the same mix of urban decay and resurgent greenery that I had become accustomed to. Nothing had changed. Nothing would change in the foreseeable future. There would be no new barrier between the Sheridan Hollow neighborhood and the New York State Capitol. Nor was anything going to happen to bring them closer together.

Afterword

When I wrote *The Long Stair*, between 1998 and 2000, there had been no discussion, at least publicly, of the construction of an actual, real-world parking garage on Albany's Sheridan Avenue. The parking garage project that is central to this novel is entirely fictional. More recently, however, an actual real-world parking garage *has* been planned and is now under construction in that location. Like the fictional garage it is being built into the steep slope between Sheridan Avenue and Elk Street, so that vehicles — 1,500 of them — will enter on the Sheridan Hollow level and people will exit to Elk Street on the upper level.

The striking similarity between the fictional and real projects — which has provided the occasion for publishing this novel — is *not* entirely coincidental. The description of Sheridan Hollow in this novel is realistic in most respects. The Gander Bay Bar is fictional, but Sheridan Hollow really is a deeply disinvested neighborhood immediately north of, and below, Capitol Hill. State workers really do park on the streets and walk up a very long stairway to Elk Street through a no-man's land between two very separate worlds. The idea that it might occur to someone to build a parking garage in that no-man's-land didn't require any great stretch of imagination on my part. Both the fictional garage and the real garage are outgrowths of real circumstances.

The real garage is of course not being developed by sinister, faceless investors as a way of laundering the proceeds of criminal activity. It is being built by the state itself to provide more parking for its employees — just as the steam plant on the other side of Sheridan was built by the state to heat state offices. Nor was the planning of the development done in secret. An environmental impact statement was developed as required. There was a certain amount of public discussion, sparking a limited amount of controversy. Some did argue that a neighborhood with very serious needs of its own was being asked to accommodate a project addressing not those needs but the needs of state government and its suburbanite employees and their cars. A few defenders of the plan, on the other hand, portrayed the garage as a neighborhood asset that would alleviate congestion on local streets. Perhaps so. Perhaps there will be a few car-owning Sheridan Hollow residents who will find it easier to park in front of their homes. But the project won't touch the more significant problems faced by residents of Sheridan Hollow and Arbor Hill.

In the introduction to her wonderful book *The Death and Life of Great American Cities*, Jane Jacobs observed, "The simple needs of automobiles are more easily understood and satisfied than the complex needs of cities...." The new parking garage will satisfy the needs of 1,500 automobiles and certain very specific needs of their drivers. It will not satisfy the city's complex need for interconnection, integration, integrity, civility. Warren Crow's next-to-last sentence — "There would be no new barrier between the Sheridan Hollow neighborhood and the New York State Capitol" — was apparently incorrect. But his final sentence remains true — "Nor was anything going to happen to bring them closer together."

—*Kirby White, summer 2005*

Construction of the real-world garage, summer 2005.
Photograph by El-Wise Noisette.